THE COPPER ISLE
GHOSTSLAYER

A THRILLER

TERRI GREENING

This is a work of fiction. Names, characters, places, and incidents are products of the author's imagination or are used fictitiously and are not to be construed as real. Any resemblance to actual events, locations, organizations, or persons, living or dead, is entirely coincidental.

World Castle Publishing, LLC
Pensacola, Florida
Copyright © 2024 Terri Greening
Paperback ISBN: 9798891261303
eBook ISBN: 9798891261310
First Edition World Castle Publishing, LLC, January 16, 2024
http://www.worldcastlepublishing.com
Licensing Notes
Cover: Cover Designs by Karen
https://www.cover-designs-by-karen.com
Editor: Karen Fuller

This novel is dedicated to all the readers who make thriller writing so rewarding. Thank you for reading.

The Ghostslayer

The rafters shake,
The thunder pounds.
He's rising from the underground.

He's come to take you where he goes
To depths of evil no one knows.

You're not alive
And yet, not dead.
Your soul knows not what lies ahead.

Run swift, young specter.
Scamper fast.
He knows the evil of your past.

This demon ghost with vengeful glee
Has slain the hearts of those like thee.

And when the Slayer slays your soul.
There is no heart that can console.

Beware the dark,
The midnight hue.
The Ghostslayer haunts and is coming for you.

A handwritten poem discovered in the historic logbook at Copper Isle Lighthouse.

CHAPTER 1

The coarse, gray walls of the prison sprang into view before me, framed in stark silhouette against the pure, azure blue of the sky. I caught my breath. I couldn't believe Tyler was trapped in there. My younger brother, who worked two jobs and struggled to finish high school after our mother died of cancer years ago and left us alone, was imprisoned for life for a murder he didn't commit. And I couldn't bear it. The only way I could make it through the long, lonely days of worrying about him was to come to see him as often as possible, and I was still trying to find a way to get him out.

I drove up the asphalt path through the rolling, spring-green hills with their portent of renewal, so opposite from the desolated aura of the prison, and stopped in front of the black iron bars of the gate. I shivered when an unfamiliar guard walked over and tapped on my window.

"Name," he said.

"Layla Devereaux. Here to see Tyler Lawrence," I said.

I hoped he couldn't see the drops of sweat beading on my forehead. Something was wrong with Tyler. I could feel it. But I didn't want to look nervous because the prison was on high alert after an escape attempt, and I didn't want my brother to be suspected of anything because of my demeanor. The last time I'd been here, he was bruised from a fight with his cellmate and had been threatened with isolation.

After the guard checked his roster and opened the gate, I hurried to park and meet Tyler in the visitors' room. I was so worried that I barely noticed the cement walls of the windowless hallways or the gruffness of the guard who took me to see him, although the first time I'd been here, I'd been a mess. The last time I'd seen my brother, he looked pale and tired, and his blue eyes had been milky under sleep-encrusted lashes, but it was nothing compared to how he looked now. The guard scowled and left. But he could still see us through a window in the door.

"Tyler," I said, trying to control the quiver in my voice when I saw his deathly pallor and stringy, blond hair. I didn't want him to realize how concerned I was and try to comfort me. I was there to comfort him. "I'm so glad to see you. How are you doing?"

He looked away and didn't answer at first. My chest tightened. There was definitely something awry.

"What is it? What's wrong?" I asked.

"How do you always know when there's something wrong?" he asked, turning back to look at me and sounding exasperated.

"I don't know. I just do," I answered. "What is it?"

"They're transferring me," he said, after a moment. "They're sending me to a maximum security prison down south before the end of the summer."

The words hit me like a sledgehammer, and I grabbed my head as it began to throb. "Tyler, no."

"Yeah, it sucks," he said, rubbing his hand over his face. "I'll never see the girl I was going to ask to marry me on the island again, either. She never even came to the trial."

"Girl? What girl?"

"It doesn't matter now. Nothing does."

"Yes, it does. You haven't done anything."

"That doesn't matter. They think I killed an old man for no reason, and they have it in for me here. The warden wants me gone for my own protection. You take what you get in life, that's all. Life isn't fair." He slumped back in his white, plastic chair.

"No, it isn't right," I said, determining that now was not the time to ask him more about his girlfriend.

"I know. Thanks. You're the only person that ever listens to me. You're the only person that believes anything I say. There's nothing anyone can do for me anymore. Not after all this time. Not after the jury found me guilty."

He sat up and leaned forward to rest his chin in his hands. His eyes were bloodshot and unfocused.

"Thanks for trying, sis. It means a lot," he said, quietly.

"I'm getting you out of here."

"How? How are you going to do that?" he asked.

"I don't know. But I'm not letting them take you away from me. I need you, and you need me. You're the only family I have left."

"You've got Damon, for what it's worth," he said.

I nipped my lip and tasted a salty drop of blood. "It's not worth much anymore. You know that. He yells at me and tells me I'm crazy all the time, and I'm starting to believe it myself. I will if I don't have you to talk to. I can't let you leave me."

"There's nothing you can do, Layla," he said.

"That's not true. I'm going to do something," I said, feeling my face get hot. "I think I'm going to go to Copper Isle myself to stay at the inn where you worked last summer and check out the lighthouse where you found Pappy, the tour guide, dead. They had no right to pin his murder on you. You told them about the gold coins Pappy found on the shipwreck. I don't know why they didn't believe you and follow a lead like that."

His eyes widened, and he sat straight up. He must have

seen in my gaze the desperate determination I felt.

"I know," he said. "The coins would have belonged to the island, too, because they were found within its boundary waters. I told Pappy that when he asked me to go diving with him and his friends to bring the gold up. I told the sheriff that, too. I don't know why the authorities couldn't find the gold later. It would have been worth a lot of money to the island."

His pale face accentuated the gray hollows in his cheeks. He was suffering. I could see it and feel it. I squeezed my eyes shut and drew on my investigative journalism training and increased perceptions to try to think of what to ask him next. There must be something the authorities had missed about what happened.

Something came to me, and I opened my eyes. "Who's the tour guide at the lighthouse now?" I asked.

Tyler frowned and hesitated before answering. "A man that Pappy knew who transferred to the island from a lighthouse on the mainland. My boss at the Copper Isle Inn gave me time off to fill in at the lighthouse, and I was there when he arrived. It was just before I was arrested. Why?"

"I'm going to go to the island and talk to him," I said.

"I don't think you should do that," he said gruffly.

"Why not?" I asked, unsure of what to think about his sudden shift in mood. He seemed wary and more than just protective of me as he'd always been despite being the younger sibling. "Is there something you're not telling me?"

He looked away for a moment, and when he looked back at me, his body was shaking. "Strange things happen on the island. I can't explain it right now. But the lighthouse is the last place you want to go right now, and you shouldn't stay at the inn overnight."

"What do you mean? What kind of strange things?" I asked.

"Nothing, okay. I just don't think you should go there,

that's all. Thanks anyway, sis," he said.

"Even if it means getting you out of prison?"

"I don't want to talk about it anymore," he said, forcefully, banging his fist on the table.

I was surprised, but not frightened, that he was so upset. He had always been a calm, peaceful person. But, given his hopelessness and his trapped situation, his reaction was understandable. Being imprisoned was doing this to him.

Three loud knocks interrupted our conversation. The guard stuck his head in the room. "Time's up. Let's go," he said, loudly.

We both stood. When Tyler came around the table, I grabbed him and hugged him. "Take care of yourself. I'll be back," I choked out.

He hugged me back, tightly. It was hard to let him go, but eventually, I did. He gazed at me for a long moment with tears in his eyes before walking past me out the door.

"I love you," I said, choking back a sob.

He stopped and turned. "I love you, too," he said, brushing away the tears with the back of his hand before the guard took his arm and led him away.

I swallowed hard as I watched him disappear down the hallway. Later, as I drove home, I tried to pinpoint what it was that bothered me so much about seeing Tyler this time. I had an extra sensitivity to people and happenings that I kept to myself because it was often misconstrued by others as peculiar. A friend in high school once asked me where I hid my crystal ball when I told her she was going to a dance with a boy who hadn't asked her yet, and he later asked her to go. I didn't know what to say. It was embarrassing to realize other people didn't know things in advance like I did.

Tyler knew about my sensitivities because I picked him up early after school one time on a sunny day when I had a strange feeling, and a gathering tornado stormed through town a half an hour later and blew down some trees. No one at the school was hurt because they sheltered in place, but Tyler never forgot about it. He told me I saved his life. He had gotten a pass to get out of gym class early that day because he wasn't feeling well. And if I hadn't picked him up, he would have been walking home by himself when the tornado hit.

I first noticed my heightened senses in eighth grade at Christmastime. Melancholy chimes rang quietly whenever my mother walked into a room, and I was the only one who heard them. Two days later, she told us she had lung cancer.

I turned the radio on low and listened to a light jazz station as I drove down the highway. The afternoon sun waned lower in the sky. I think it was Tyler's hopelessness that got to me. He seemed to have given up on life. I wondered what it must be like, to tell the truth over and over again and have no one believe you. I believed him. One time in third grade, he confessed to cheating on a test and spent all afternoon in detention until I stopped by to walk him home. He wasn't perfect, but he wasn't a liar, and he certainly wasn't a murderer. I had to prove that to the world.

Just after sunset, I typed in the code at the entrance to my gated community. I glanced behind me and noticed a car that I thought I'd seen at a stop light pass behind me and continue down the road. I wondered if I'd been followed. I often felt that way, and I couldn't help but think my husband had something to do with it. He could be keeping track of me. But I didn't have any concrete evidence of that.

I drove quickly through the gate and took the fork around the central garden toward the waterfront. When I pulled into the garage of the private lake house I lived in with my husband, I was surprised to see his car. The windows were dark, except for a small glow from the upstairs bedroom, and I hoped he was out walking on the beach. I didn't feel up to dealing with him after my day at the prison.

I walked into the house and tossed my purse on the counter island in the kitchen.

"Damon?" I called.

There was no answer, so I headed upstairs to change. He was probably on the beach, and I'd have to hurry to get dinner ready by the time he got back. When I reached the top of the stairs, I paused and looked around. Something wasn't right. I heard a sound.

"Damon?" I asked.

There was no answer.

"Who is it? Who's there?" I asked, feeling suddenly cautious.

After a moment, a soft voice said, "It's me, Layla. I'm sorry. I didn't know you'd be home."

"Buffy?" I asked, incredulously.

I walked into the room and was startled to see my next-door neighbor and newest best friend crawling around the white, plush carpeting in the bedroom and spreading her hands over the floor. There was a pillow on the floor, and the bedspread looked rumpled.

"What are you doing?" I asked.

"Oh, it's just the silliest thing," she said, standing slowly. "I lost my earring at the dinner party last night, and I thought maybe it was here. The coats were on the bed up here, you know."

"The coats were on the bed?" I asked, trying to remember which of our neighbors would have worn a coat in the warm weather.

"Yes. The door was open, so I thought I'd just run up and check, but it doesn't seem to be here." She turned her palms up in a gesture of defeat. "I guess I'll quit looking. If you see it, would you let me know? I'd better go now."

She brushed past me into the hall, and I turned and

followed her.

"Buffy. That doesn't make any sense. Why did you come in without asking?"

"I would have," she said, hurrying down the stairs, "but there wasn't anybody here. "I'll see you later."

I stood on the stairs with my mouth open until I heard the kitchen door slam. She lost an earring? I walked into the bedroom in a daze and changed before heading back downstairs to make dinner. The light was on in the family room when I got downstairs. Damon was sitting in the recliner with a drink. He blinked when he saw me and ran his fingers through his dark, wavy hair. He had on his usual casual attire of a button-down shirt, chinos, and dock shoes. His shirt was wrinkled, and a few of the buttons were undone. The overlook of the lake behind him looked black and smooth through the floor-to-ceiling windows.

"Where have you been this time? Sneaking out again?" he asked, piercing me with his black-eyed gaze.

"Where have you been?" I asked, shivering in spite of myself.

His eyes were deep and sharp. Their penetrating intelligence was what had attracted me to him in the first place, and he was still a handsome man. But now I was on the wrong side of their warmth or their wrath. He had shut me out long ago.

"And why didn't you lock the doors?" I continued, pushing aside the loss I felt over his emotional withdrawal from our relationship. I needed answers.

"Our neighbor was in our bedroom," I said, trying not to raise my voice.

"I never lock the doors when I go down the beach," he answered.

"Didn't you see her walking over here?"

"No, of course not. I didn't know she was here," he said, looking away.

"Why didn't you ask me who it was?" I asked.

"Who what was?"

"The neighbor," I replied, before clenching my teeth.

"Well, who was it?"

"Buffy. What about when she left? Did you see her then?"

"I told you. I didn't see anyone," he said. "What is this? An interrogation? Or maybe an interview from a has-been reporter?" he asked, laughing. "What's your angle, baby?"

"Is that really where you were?" I asked, shrugging off the insult and trying not to let it hurt.

"Don't be paranoid, babe. I told you I was on the beach, and that's where I was. Now I wanna know where you went. There was no one here to say 'hi' to me when I got home," he said, slurring his words.

My heart beat faster, and I struggled to take a breath. None of his answers made sense to me. He stood and gulped the last of his drink, which looked like his usual whiskey sour, before walking toward me. I took a step backward when I saw the sly glint in his black eyes. He looked like he was up to something again, and I was afraid to find out what it was. But I was more afraid of not answering him when he looked that way.

"If you must know, I went to see Tyler," I said, sucking in a shaky breath. "He's not doing well, and I'm worried about him."

"They're gonna put you away, too, if you keep worrying about that degenerate all the time. You're not his mother, you know, even if you did take care of him after she died. What's the matter with you?"

"I'm not discussing this. I'll make us some dinner," I said, moving toward the cupboards and hoping if I changed the subject, he would settle down.

I wished he hadn't mentioned my mother. I missed her so much, and Tyler did, too. We'd never known our father. I'd wanted to have children and create a family of my own, but Damon didn't want to. I swallowed hard. He brushed past me and walked around the kitchen island to dump his ice in the sink.

"That brother of yours is more trouble than he's worth. I don't want you going out there anymore. It takes time away from me, and you're always nuts when you get home."

"I'm not nuts, Damon. Leave me alone."

"You are nuts, baby. Anybody who sees ghosts in the boathouse is nuts. It's a good thing you got me to take care of you, or where would you be, huh? You better remember that."

"I'll remember," I said, turning away from him.

It upset me that he referred again to the ghosts I'd seen and disavowed their existence. I often strolled the beach at night when I couldn't sleep. One night, when I decided to take the rowboat out, I'd seen two young lovers dripping with seaweed floating in the rafters of the boathouse. I'd never seen ghosts before, despite my extra-sensitivities to things, but I knew that's what they were. They didn't say anything, and I didn't talk to them, although I hoped I might have the courage to do so at some point. Unfortunately, I had mentioned it to Damon, not realizing the downward spiral our marriage would take after that. My perceptions about people didn't work with him, perhaps because the love I had for him once blinded me to his true character. Anyway, he didn't believe in ghosts, and he didn't believe in people like me that did. He stopped listening to me, and he referred to the sighting often when he was upset. It was a convenient way for him to get me flustered and keep me from asking too many questions about his whereabouts.

"Good," he said. "Let's get some dinner going."

He filled a fresh glass with ice and whisky and walked back into the family room. Luckily, he turned on the big-screen TV and appeared to lose interest in the conversation. It was no use arguing with him. The only option I had was to agree with him. If I didn't, his behavior became unbearable, and I didn't know how to deal with it.

No one but me and Tyler, who had dealt with Damon's possessive rages over me when he tried to keep Tyler away from me, knew his other side. He told Tyler one time, even before all the happenings with the murder trial and the police, that if he came to the house again to see me when he wasn't there, he'd call the police on him. That scared me and Tyler. Damon always tried to cast Tyler in a bad light, and that wasn't the way my brother was at all. He was a caring, sensitive person. I'd had to meet Tyler privately elsewhere after that.

Damon acted like a completely different person around other people and charmed his way through life. In the exclusive social circles he ran in and at the formal business dinners we attended and hosted, I had no choice but to keep up appearances. I tried to do that by dressing well and keeping my dark-brown hair perfectly coiffed and my wide, hazel-green eyes mascaraed.

I'd overheard him talking on the phone once, telling someone he'd better watch his back and do what he was told. I didn't know what Damon was up to. I didn't want to know. I just wanted to get away from him and hide somewhere where he couldn't find me. Now, faced with the possibility that Tyler could disappear from my life, I had to find a way to escape and get to Copper Isle.

I pulled a copper skillet out of the cupboard and put it on the stainless-steel stove. All the appliances matched, and the stainless steel reflected the burnt-orange terracotta tiles of the floor and the amber oak of the island. The kitchen had a warm, homey feel that I loved to cook in. I would miss it.

"Can you hurry it up? I'm starving. If you hadn't been gone all day, dinner would be ready by now," Damon called out.

"It won't take long," I said.

I glanced at the May photograph I had taken for one

of the wall calendars I made as a hobby. I had started nature photography after I left my job as an investigative journalist and photographer at The City Chronicle to marry Damon. I was so happy then and excited to start my new life. But his demeanor changed drastically soon after we were married, and he became argumentative and aloof. He was often gone for days at a time, leaving me to wonder if he had another life of his own or if he was just neglectful.

"Do you want wine with dinner?" I asked. "We have a merlot."

"Yeah," he said, shortly, turning up the volume and kicking back in his chair.

A plump, red-breasted robin on the calendar stared back at me from its perch on a redbud branch amidst fluffy fuchsia blossoms. Its life looked so peaceful in comparison to the tumult of mine. I recalled snapping the photo in the woods nearby last spring before my world collapsed under the weight of Tyler's arrest and trial. I remembered sitting in the courtroom for hours on end, listening to what seemed like ridiculous evidence, and lying awake at night, hoping for some miracle to save him. But it never came. It seemed like years ago now. He had been as free as a bird one day and caged like one the next. I swallowed hard as I thought of the change. It was the same way I felt about myself.

I browned onions and garlic and threw together a marinara sauce, taking deep breaths and trying not to let Damon's mood bother me. Talking to him when he was in this state only made things worse. I had learned over time to control my emotions and not ask too many questions, although sometimes, like tonight, I couldn't help myself. I suppose that had to do with my journalism background and maybe the fact that, as his wife, I thought I deserved answers. But I didn't get them. I never did.

"Dinner's ready," I said.

"It's about time," he said, turning off the TV and heading

into the kitchen.

I served the marinara sauce atop buttered fettuccine and sat down to eat with him. He grunted his approval as he scarfed it down with the bottle of wine.

"Are you going to work in the morning?" I asked, casually.

"Yeah, why?" he asked.

"Just wondered," I said, looking away quickly and hoping that he wouldn't see my relief that he wouldn't be working from home tomorrow.

When I was done eating, I left him at the table and went to the master bedroom. I didn't believe Buffy's story about why she was in our bedroom, and I didn't believe Damon when he said he was on the beach. It wasn't the first time I had caught Damon with another woman. A few years ago, I'd caught him kissing my old roommate from college on the beach, but he had come up with a good story to make me think I was mistaken. It wasn't going to work this time.

I looked around the large, luxurious room and made plans to leave. I had decorated the bed and sofas with pale blue silks and silver satins with such love so long ago. A photo of us dancing at our wedding gazed at me from the rosewood nightstand. We looked so happy then. Was I ever that happy? I remembered Tyler walking me down the aisle that day. I'd missed my mother then, wishing she had been alive and there to share in my happiness. The photo blurred, and I rubbed my eyes, surprised that my cheeks felt wet.

My suitcase was stuffed in the walk-in closet behind my shoes, and I yanked it out, banging my head on the clothes rod as I did so. The last time I'd done that was five years ago when I was packing for my honeymoon in Bermuda. I remembered the coolness of the pink sand beaches we strolled together in the moonlight and the sounds of the tree frogs that sang in the evenings. He had kissed me with such passion then, and I had wanted him so much. I had loved him, and I thought he had loved me. He had treated me so well. We had traveled to exotic places together, and he had given me extravagant jewelry and gifts like an emerald and diamond ring for my twenty-fourth birthday. And he told me often that he loved me and that I was the only woman in the world for him.

How times had changed, I thought, rubbing my head as I pushed hangers aside, trying to decide what to take. I wasn't packing bikinis and resort wear this time. I wanted clothes that showed that I was a serious professional but still allowed me to blend in with the islanders. And also, the weather here on an island in May would be chillier than it had been in Bermuda. A light jacket would be appropriate, I thought, fingering a white cotton blazer. I was going to present myself as a freelance nature photographer working on a story in order to gain access to people and places that were relevant to last summer's murder. It would give me a reason to be there and to ask questions. When I heard a noise, I stopped sorting and turned. I gasped when I saw Damon standing right behind me. I had assumed he would watch TV until late into the night like he usually did.

"What are you doing?" he asked, kicking shoes out of the way.

"Nothing. I need to vacuum in here. Can you move?"

"It's time for bed. Do it in the morning. I'm going to take a shower."

"You're right, of course," I said.

I let out a slow breath once he'd left and shoved the suitcase back into the closet. The air conditioning was off, and the night was warm. To cool off, I opened the french doors and walked out onto the wide balcony that overlooked the gardens and the lake. A light breeze rustled the leaves of the silver birch trees, and currents rippled across the clear surface of the water. I stood for a while, taking in the scene. It would have been beautiful and relaxing in another lifetime. But that lifetime was over.

I felt the warmth of him before he lightly touched my arm. "Come to bed," he said, nuzzling my neck. "Be with me."

He reeked of a strongly-scented soap and wine.

"Not tonight. I need to be alone," I said, leaning away.

"Baby, I know what you need." He ran his fingers up my arm.

"I mean it, Damon."

He blew out a sharp breath. "You need a shrink."

"I know," I said, gritting my teeth. I'd had to say something to placate him. He didn't like being told "no."

He stomped away. I gazed out over the water, blinking away tears and making plans. I would pack the car and head for Copper Isle in the morning after he left for work. A simple note left on the counter, explaining that I needed to care for a sick friend and didn't know when I would return, would keep the police from looking for me when he found me gone.

When I heard him snoring, I tiptoed back into the room and got ready for bed. I padded to the kitchen in my slippers and robe to load the dishwasher and clean up. There was a crumpled cocktail napkin in Damon's whiskey glass, and I took it out to throw it away. But before I did, I noticed an unfamiliar imprint on it that read "The Copper Bar." I wondered what that could mean. Had Damon been there sometime, wherever it was? I threw the napkin away and turned off the lights before heading back to the bedroom. I hesitated before slipping under the covers and lying next to him. I laid there, staring at the ceiling. One last night, I would sleep in captivity. But tomorrow would mark the beginning of a new day and the freedom of a new way of life.

CHAPTER 2

I glimpsed the island through the mist of lake water spraying over the bow of the ferry. It shimmered like a shiny new penny in the sun, beckoning me to shore. It had taken most of the day to drive north along the two-lane highway near the lake to catch the ferry in the late afternoon. My escape from the house after Damon left in the morning had gone seamlessly, and I was relieved to be on board with my car stashed safely below deck. I tried not to wonder what he would do when he got home from work and found the note.

"Prepare to dock. Passengers get ready to disembark," the captain said over the loudspeaker. "We are approaching Copper Isle Harbor."

I gripped the railing, contentedly noticing my bare, recently emancipated wedding-ring finger, and gazed out over the water, excited to land. This could be the start of a new life for me, away from the confines of my home and failed marriage. I sighed, thinking momentarily of the past and wondering what I could have changed to make things work out. But I couldn't think of anything. I had done the best I could.

A silver-gray seagull caught my attention as it swooped and dived nearby, and I made a note to retrieve my camera from the trunk when I got to shore and photograph it.

I had begun my marriage with such hopes. Damon had asked me to stop working and stay home to focus on building our life together. His lifestyle had seemed exciting and sophisticated to me, and I had jumped at the chance to be part of it with him. I hadn't known what a mistake that was and how emotionally isolated and unhappy I would become. But that was in the past. I was free now. I impatiently brushed away the tears that the wind brought to my eyes and concentrated on our approach to the island.

A red-and-white lighthouse stood watch over the harbor on a far-off bluff, competing with fluffy puffs of clouds to reach for the azure blue sky. The lighthouse, along with the rolling blue waves of the harbor and the scenic landscape of the island, would make a lovely backdrop for a May calendar page.

As I made a mental note to plan another ferry ride soon, a sudden shift in the wind ruffled my hair and sent a dark cloud over the island. It shadowed the black rocks near the shore and obscured my view. Goosebumps prickled my arms, and I shivered. I squinted to look more closely. I had learned to trust my feelings and the reactions of my body to outside influences. It was the way I negotiated the world and kept myself safe and out of trouble. I perused the shoreline, trying to determine what it was that bothered me now. The island no longer appeared brilliant and welcoming but dark and threatening, as though overcome by something evil. I didn't see anything out of the ordinary, but I pulled my light sweater more closely around me.

"Docking off the port side," the captain said. "Steady as she goes."

The ferry slowed in the lightly rolling waves. I bit my lip and concentrated on keeping my footing as I followed the other passengers across the deck and down a metal staircase to the parking deck. My quest to free Tyler from prison and forge a new life for myself was soon to begin in earnest, and I wasn't going to let my growing sense of foreboding deter me.

As I neared my car, a signal horn blasted three times, and a frenzied dog overtook me.

"Excuse me. He doesn't like the noise," his owner said, apologetically over his shoulder as he followed the dog, which looked like a beautiful, silver-gray wolf, to a black pick-up truck parked next to my car. He opened the door and closed it after the dog leapt in. "I'm Colton," he said, turning to me. I live on the island. I haven't seen you before. Are you visiting?"

He was handsome, I saw now, with sandy brown hair, wearing hiking boots, a navy t-shirt and jeans.

"Yes, for a while," I said, evasively. I didn't want to disclose too much to a stranger, even a good-looking one. But then I noticed that he had a pale-blue aura about him that made him seem less threatening. I was pretty sure I was the only one who could see it, but I trusted my instincts. I let my guard down a bit.

"What breed of dog is that?" I asked.

The dog was photogenic, and I could picture him in a winter snow scene, though I didn't plan to stay on the island long enough to see snow.

"Husky. I'm watching him for the day for a friend of mine."

"Beautiful blue eyes."

"Yes. Not as lovely as your green ones, though," he said.

I felt my cheeks warm. It had been a long time since I'd been flirted with, and I wasn't sure how to react. But he seemed nice and not at all like Damon.

"Yes, well," I stammered.

The horn blasted again.

"I guess we better go. Maybe I'll see you around," he said, smiling and heading for the driver's side.

"Maybe," I said, getting in my car. I felt a little embarrassed that I didn't know what to say to him.

He waited for me to pull out and get in line. As I drove down the off-ramp and onto shore, I looked out over the white-capped waves for the seagull, but it was gone. I'd have to return to the shore another day. After all, I'd need to keep up the pretense that I was here for business. Besides, it wasn't the best idea anyway, given that a storm was probably moving in.

Colton pulled up next to me at a stop light and waved. I waved back and turned right down the road along the harbor. He turned left toward what looked to be the town. I had reserved a room at the Copper Isle Inn and was glad that the GPS on my phone worked this far from the mainland. A spritz of rain on the windshield below the darkening sky made me turn on my wipers and lights. As a gust blew the car sideways, I was reminded of how fast the weather could change near the water. I glanced in the rearview mirror as I struggled to stay in my lane. The headlights of a solitary car far behind me flickered through the growing drizzle, and I reflexively gripped the steering wheel, feeling a growing sense of apprehension. I was alone and far from home on a dark road in a strange place, and I shivered again, wondering if Damon had found the note yet. It didn't matter. I had made my decision. There was no going back now. I glanced in the mirror again. The car behind me seemed closer, but it was hard to tell through the sheets of rain that had started pounding the windows. I gripped the wheel more tightly and drove on.

A flash of light in the side-view mirror blinded me momentarily, and I gasped when my car jolted forward. The car behind me had somehow covered the distance between us in record time and had obviously just tapped my bumper. It seemed as though the headlight pointed directly into my eyes. I jammed my foot on the accelerator and bolted forward on the slippery pavement. Who would do such a thing? I raced down the winding road, peering through the rain and frantically checking the mirror as the wind buffeted the car. When I turned sharply to counter the force, the car slid sideways toward the steep drop to the harbor, and I screamed, twisting the wheel back toward land and darting ahead around another curve, hoping to lose my pursuer. A horn blasted behind me, and I braced for another impact while desperately looking for a safe place to turn off the road.

Suddenly, the sign for the inn appeared through tall grass next to a wooded drive. I almost missed it, but I yanked the wheel quickly, my tires skidding into the dirt and weeds before the car careened up the hill. When I reached the top, I stopped to look out the rear window and sighed, relieved to see no one behind me. Where had the driver been going in such a hurry and so carelessly on this winding road? I sat for a moment, patting my damp palms on my cotton skirt and listening to raindrops plink against the hood. This was not the warm island welcome I had hoped for. I took a deep breath to get my bearings and continued on.

The inn was set back in the trees on a bluff overlooking the lake. Its wide, white-railed porch sat dotted with rustic Adirondack chairs set on either side of a red door that shined faintly in the porch lights. Its white siding sported curtained windows glowing with a soft, golden light and flanked with dark, sea-blue shutters. An American flag flapped under the porch roof above potted red geraniums near the front door. Even in the rain, it appeared normal and comforting, especially compared to what I had just experienced. I hoped I had arrived in time for a late supper.

I drove around back and parked in a paved lot before grabbing my suitcase and scurrying through the cold rain. I ran up a wooden ramp to the side door. The rich aroma of simmering stew and baking bread wafted through the entryway, which jingled with a bell as I stepped inside. I closed the door on the gathering storm and was instantly engulfed in the warmth and coziness of another time. An antique desk sat next to a wall that was papered with large, dusky roses, and scrolled, mahogany chairs lined a small vestibule. As I stood and brushed the rain off my arms, a woman with puffed-up hair so white it appeared lavender in the soft light peeked around the corner and walked over to sit in the desk chair. She smoothed her flowered dress and plucked a pencil out of a mug, opening a leather folder as she did so, lifting reading glasses from a gold chain around her neck. I caught a light scent of lavender as she looked at a paper, then up at me over the top of her glasses.

"May I help you? Do you have a reservation? I hope so. Our last room was reserved this morning. It's the start of our busy season, you know, with the Memorial Day holiday coming up,"

"Yes. That was by me, I suppose," I said, hoping she couldn't see the near-panic I felt from my drive here.

"Oh, good. Let me see. Ms. Devereaux? And you're staying for the summer?"

"At least for the summer. I'm planning to take photographs of nature and wildlife in the area for a magazine article," I said.

I took a slow breath. I didn't mention anything about knowing Tyler or about why I was really there. I wanted to get an idea of what was happening on the island before revealing my true identity.

"How exciting. You've come to the right place. It's beautiful around here."

"Yes, so I've been told," I said.

"I'm Martha Harding, the manager here." She ran through the basics: here was the key to Room 12, and dinner was in the lounge until 9:00. "I'll have someone take your bag to your room if you'd like to eat first."

"Thank you. I'm sure I can manage if you point the way,"

I said.

I picked up my suitcase and followed her down a hallway to a carpeted staircase at the back.

"Top floor on the left," she said, smiling as she turned and headed back down the hall. "Oh, one more thing," she added, lavender hair bobbing as she glanced over her shoulder. "Sometimes the floors creak at night, especially during a storm like tonight's. Most people get used to it after a while and think it adds to the charm of the inn. Enjoy your stay."

As I walked up the stairs, I wondered what she meant about creaky floors adding to the charm of the inn. But I had other things to think about, like shaking off the adrenaline of the drive, and I was hungry. My room was the last door from the top of the staircase, and when I stepped inside, I was pleasantly surprised to find floral chintz chairs and a canopied double bed covered with a forest green damask spread and a folded, pieced quilt. I sighed as I dropped my bag on the floor and plopped down on the bed.

I willed my senses to let go of everything except the pale green, silk-curtained canopy and the quiet and the softness of the featherdown. For the first time in a long time, I felt free. It didn't matter if Damon tried to call me once he found the note. My phone was silenced, and his number was blocked. He had no power over me now. That was a comforting thought, but then I thought of something else. I might be free, but Tyler wasn't. I rummaged through my purse for my phone and found the number for the prison. He had looked so desolate when I visited. I had to make sure he was okay if I was going to continue my mission in peace. The phone rang a few times.

But when I told the prison operator who I was calling, she transferred me to a terse social worker, who wouldn't say anything more than that Tyler was on the no-communication list. She hung up promptly.

I stared at the phone, feeling dazed and trying desperately to remember what I'd learned during the prison orientation for family members. Was this simply a routine precursor to his transfer? Or did it mean something horrible, that he'd been injured or tried to injure himself? I clasped my head in my hands. How had things ever gotten to the point? My brother deserved so much out of life, and I would do whatever it took to get him out of there.

My stomach rumbled, reminding me that if I were going to help Tyler, I first needed to get something to eat.

It didn't take long to wash up and put on a light summer dress and sandals. I wandered down the stairs and entered the dimly lit restaurant in time to be seated at a two-person table with a view of the lake. Boat lights twinkled here and there through a drizzly fog.

When the waitress appeared, carrying yeast rolls and butter, I ordered baked cod and salad with the house wine and sat back to try to relax. The rolls were warm, and the butter melted on my tongue, but I didn't enjoy them as much as I thought I would. I couldn't help worrying about Tyler. The polished wood tables glowed in the soft light of candle centerpieces, and a few couples and families talked and ate nearby, and as I took another bite of my roll, I noticed a familiar face. Colton was sitting at a far table with a lovely young woman and two children. When the waitress, whose name was Rosie, returned with my wine and dinner, I asked her if she knew who he was after telling her that I was staying on the island for the summer and had met him briefly on the ferry ride over.

"That's Colton Harding. His family owns most of the island, including the inn. You'll probably see him again. He lives in town, but he comes here often for dinner."

I expressed my thanks as she left, somewhat disappointed that she'd been too discreet to explain who his dinner companions were. It clicked then that Martha, the manager, was also a Harding. They must be related. Maybe she'd tell me more.

I focused on savoring my dinner. The fish was flaky and flavorful, and the salad was crisp and fresh. It was obvious why the inn had a reputation as a premier place to stay. But I put my fork down after a few bites. Thoughts were whirling through my head, and I couldn't keep my mind on my food. I wondered what Tyler meant when he told me I shouldn't stay here overnight. I took a sip of wine and looked out over the murky harbor. It was the first time in a long time I'd had a nice dinner out without being overwhelmed with tension. Damon couldn't get to me now.

"Hello. I saw you sitting here, and I thought I'd come over and say 'hi.' I hope that's okay."

I turned when I heard Colton's voice. "Yes, of course. What a nice coincidence," I said, trying to make my voice sound light and carefree even though I didn't feel that way.

He looked even more handsome than he had on the ferry. His hair was casually combed back, and he wore a white shirt and khakis with leather dockers. And he wasn't wearing a wedding ring.

He chuckled. "I think you'll find that it's not such a coincidence after you've stayed here for a while. It's a small island, and you can't help but see the same people day to day."

"I suppose that's true. I hadn't thought of that."

"Are you staying here? My mother runs the place. Maybe you've met her."

"I think I did when I checked in. Yes, I'm planning to stay for the summer and take photographs for a nature magazine, specifically of birds."

"Great," Colton said. "I love birds. We have a lot of them here. I could show you around sometime if you'd like. I'll let you in on the local lore and show you some bird migration sites."

"That would be wonderful," I said, smiling.

"Good. Let's plan on it. I'll leave my number and any messages for you at the reception desk."

"I'd like that."

After he left, I wondered what it would be like to go out with someone who wanted to be with me and didn't tell me I was crazy all the time. It might be nice. I signaled for the check, and when it arrived, I gave Rosie a hefty tip and asked her if she could box up the leftover rolls for me to take to my room.

"I will, but you have to promise not to feed the ghosts," she said, smiling.

"What?" I asked, wondering if I'd heard her correctly.

"Didn't anyone tell you we have ghosts at the inn?" she asked.

"Well, no," I said, surprised that she seemed so nonchalant talking about them.

"You'll find out soon enough. They're a tourist attraction. They won't hurt you, but they might keep you awake at night. I'm only mentioning it because you're staying for the whole summer. If you stay around long enough, you'll encounter them. Some people, like Andy and Kirsten, our resident ghost hunters, come here every year just to see them. I'll tell you the whole story sometime, or maybe someone else will. Have a nice night," she said as she walked away, tossing her long, red hair behind her.

Creaky floors and ghosts? As I pulled on my pajamas and climbed into bed, I hoped I would be able to get a good night's sleep.

The banging woke me that night, and I stared into the blackness, wondering, for a moment, where I was. I bolted straight up in bed at the whooshing sound by the window. What was going on? Had the wind broken a pane? I suddenly felt wide awake, and I swung my legs off the mattress, gripping the quilt close around me. The banging started again as I padded toward the window, then stopped. Was it the door, the shutters, or both?

A chill iced my neck, and my body stiffened. Something was terribly wrong.

Go away. Rasped a whispery voice. It seemed to come from everywhere and nowhere. It filled the room with a resonant snarl, and I stood transfixed, unable to breathe.

You are not welcome here. Go away.

A cold breeze touched my cheek, and I jumped, catching my breath. It looked like the window was open, and I headed for it. When I reached it, I saw that it was, and I slammed it down the last half-inch to close it. I locked it tight, realizing as I did so that the shutters seemed secure. The banging must be coming from the hall. I turned just in time to see a crack of light from the hallway disappear from under the door.

Someone or something had been out there and had turned off the light. I shivered and looked around, hoping the incident had ended. After several minutes passed without a sound, I tiptoed back to bed and climbed under the covers, pulling the quilt over my head. I thought again about what Tyler had said about staying away from the island. Despite my desperate determination to free him, I couldn't help but wonder if, by coming here, I had made a terrible mistake.

CHAPTER 3

I awakened at first light and laid in bed, watching the pinks and oranges of a glorious sunrise fan out above the calm, glassy waters of the harbor. Memories of the storm and events of the night before filtered hazily back. Suddenly, a sharp pain punched me in the stomach. What had happened last night was obviously real and needed to be addressed. I rolled sideways and clutched my stomach as I thought about the strange incident. I was glad that Damon wasn't around to tell me it was all in my imagination. I had to keep my wits about me and analyze my situation to see if I was going to feel better and stay safe in my strange, new surroundings.

Although I didn't want to rule out the supernatural as the cause of my unease, I wasn't sure the voice sounded like that of a ghost, even though I didn't know what ghosts sounded like yet, anyway. It could have been that of a disgruntled person, someone who didn't like the inn or the people here. I still felt shaky when I thought about it. I wasn't sure what was making me feel this way, but I wondered if there were people on the island who didn't want mainlanders around. Were the islanders hiding something? A murderer, perhaps? Or something even more sinister? My stomach relaxed a bit, and I stood slowly to pad to the bathroom for water. I felt somewhat refreshed after a few sips and decided to get ready for the day.

After dressing and rummaging through my suitcase for my iPad, I headed downstairs to the restaurant. I was relieved to find a quiet table by the window where I accessed the WiFi. I scrolled through my nature photos to get ideas for new ones that I could take on the island. If I was going to leave Damon for good, I would need a way to support myself. Maybe I could turn my wall calendars into a profitable business by making more of them and selling them online. I could drive into town or out to the lighthouse for photo opportunities and see what I could find out, as well. My cameras were still in the trunk.

A different waitress brought my lemon tea, and as I thanked her, I noticed Martha Harding sitting with the young woman Colton had been having dinner with last night. They appeared to be in an animated conversation. The woman was stunning in the morning light with her long, blonde hair and delicate features. I sipped my tea and let the warm liquid soothe my aching stomach. The woman stood suddenly and left the table, and I was surprised to see Martha stand and walk toward me.

"Good morning. I hope you like your room," she said, when she reached me. "It's one of our nicer ones. The storm didn't keep you up, did it? Sometimes, the wind batters the shutters, and guests complain."

"It's a very lovely room, and I wasn't up for long," I replied. I didn't want to worry her by telling her what had happened when she seemed on edge already.

"Oh, good." Her hand shook as she patted a stray hair into place, and her face looked pale and wan, much different than her cool, business-like visage of the day before. "Be sure to let me know if there are any problems, any problems at all. I don't want a repeat of last summer where a number of guests left without telling me why."

"I'm sure that was very upsetting," I said. I took advantage of the opening to ask some questions. "Did their leaving have anything to do with the murder at the lighthouse?"

Martha stood still for a moment, and her eyes widened. "You've heard about that already?" she asked.

"Yes, I'm afraid so. It was in newspapers on the mainland."

"Oh, dear. That could be the reason, I suppose. It probably is. We try at the inn, not to mention the murder to tourists, and the island is usually insulated from the outside world, but I suppose word gets around. I hope it won't affect our current guest list. Perhaps the magazine article you're doing could portray the island in a more positive light that would be good for business?"

"Perhaps. It would help to know more about what happened," I said. "Won't you sit down?"

She sat across from me.

"There's not much I can tell you," she said, "other than that, we were all very surprised to find out that the nice young man who worked here as a server was responsible. He dated Melanie, the woman I was just talking to before she started dating my son. They were quite an item for a while, and she was extremely upset when he was convicted, although I think Colton helped her get through it. I'm not sure she's over it, though. It changed her personality. She's not happy anymore, and I don't think she's seeing Colton anymore, either. It's too bad."

She paused and looked down at the table before looking back up at me.

"The young man seemed so normal, but you never know, I guess. Sometimes, you think you know someone, but you really don't. But to find out he was a murderer?" She shuddered. "It's hard to believe. Anyway, all that is behind us now, and the perpetrator is behind bars. Maybe you could make it clear in your article that this is a great place to vacation and that there is nothing to worry about?"

"I'll see what I can do," I said, thinking it was sad that the murder had been committed and that it had affected everyone's lives in such a destructive way. From the way she spoke about Tyler, I knew it wouldn't be a good idea to reveal my connection to him anytime soon.

"Did the victim have any enemies?" I asked.

"Not that I know of. He was a tour guide who lived and worked at the lighthouse by himself. He never bothered anyone, and few people went out there other than tourists on and off. That's why they determined the murderer must have been his assistant, who was also a server here, because he was the only one who had been out at the lighthouse. The authorities have been all through this," she said, dismissively.

"I see," I said. I decided to wait to ask any more questions or give my opinion about the island authorities until she was more accommodating.

"Oh, by the way, a man called the desk last night and asked if you were staying here," she said. "I don't give out that information, but I thought you might want to know. He didn't leave his name, but he sounded rather curt."

My fingers stiffened around my tea mug as I struggled to choke out an answer.

"A man?" I asked. My voice sounded strangled, even to me.

"Yes. A very gruff man," she said.

"Oh, well, thanks for letting me know," I said, trying to look calm even though I wasn't. "I'll look into it."

"You're welcome. If you'll excuse me I have things to take care of. Please enjoy your stay," she said as she stood and left.

I sat back, gripping my mug and replaying the conversation. A man called the desk about me? It had to have been Damon. I cringed. He knew I'd been to see Tyler at the prison yesterday. It probably hadn't been hard for him to guess where I'd gone. I intended to keep my guard up. He might find a way to force me to go home, and I didn't want that. I had to stay and solve the murder.

I signed for the tea and headed out to my car. The air was fresh from the rain with a faint, fishy smell, and ash trees spilled droplets of water from their fluttering, silvery leaves. As I was getting in my car, Colton pulled into the parking lot and waved as he passed me. He parked and walked over.

"Looks like we survived the storm," he said, grinning. "They can get a lot worse around here."

He looked tan and casual in jeans and a forest-green pullover, with his sandy-brown hair ruffling in the light breeze. I wondered if Martha was correct and if he and Melanie had broken up.

"I would imagine," I replied. "There aren't any windbreaks around here for the island."

"That's true," he said. "By the way, I'm glad I ran into you. The town's having a Memorial Day parade and picnic this weekend, and I wondered if you might like to go with me. I helped plan it at the Chamber of Commerce that I chair. I could show you around and introduce you to people. It'll be fun."

I paused for only a moment. "I'd like that," I said, nodding. It would be a good way to get my mind off of things and meet people on the island.

"Good. Oh, and a few piping plovers are running around the beach on the way into town if you're looking for an interesting photo. They're on the endangered species list. They migrate and nest here in the spring. But you'll want to keep your distance to keep from scaring them away."

"Thanks," I said, surprised at his thoughtfulness. "I'll check it out."

"See you later, then," he said.

I smiled as he waved and walked away. It was nice to meet another nature lover, especially someone interested in birds. I was looking forward to spending more time with him. After driving down the hill to the harbor road, I turned left to head out to the lighthouse instead of right to go into town. The piping plovers could wait for now. It was more important to meet the current lighthouse tour guide and see what he could tell me about the previous one, Pappy Johnson. Maybe I could find out more about his murder.

I glimpsed sparkling, blue water through the trees lining the road as I turned on the radio and reflexively checked the side mirrors for last night's tailgater. There was no one there. I started to relax and enjoy the scenery, but then the local news came on. I caught my breath as I listened to the report.

"Several islanders have reported break-ins over the last several weeks and encounters with a darkly-cloaked, phantom-like figure threatening their lives if they don't leave the island," a reporter said. "Nothing was stolen, and no one was hurt, but residents are frightened. Police are looking for the culprit, but because no motive was apparent and the people were acquainted, investigators are looking into the possibility that the story was fabricated and the result of mass hysteria. Now, in other news…"

I turned the radio off. I didn't want to hear any more. I wondered why the police would have concluded that it was mass hysteria instead of believing the stories, but I didn't know all the details. The incident reminded me of what happened to me last night, although I hadn't seen anyone. I was frightened, too.

It didn't take long to find the turn-off to the lighthouse. A sign pointed to an isolated, gravel road winding uphill through the trees. I slowed to crunch through the loose stones that peppered the car and followed the path to the top of the bluff. The lighthouse overlooked the harbor with a spectacular view of the lake.

As I rolled to a stop near the entrance, a barely visible man waved from the balcony high above me and disappeared inside.

By the time I exited the car and shuffled through the hard-packed sand and scruffy grass, he was walking out the front door with a gray-and-white husky prancing beside him. He grabbed the dog's collar and held him still.

"Hello. Welcome. It's nice to see you. Would you like a tour?" he asked.

I was surprised at how genial he was, as I had been expecting someone who lived such a solitary life to be more withdrawn. It was hard to tell how old he was, but I guessed he was in his sixties. His face was pockmarked and craggy with a light scrape of whiskers, and his shoulder-length gray hair was wispy and windblown. I was surprised, also, to see another husky because the first time I'd ever seen one was yesterday, but Colton had said there were a lot of them on the island.

I held out my hand. "I'm Layla Devereaux. I'm a nature photographer looking for scenic pictures for an article I'm doing."

He shook my hand. "Name's Leif Drendahl. I give tours and maintain the grounds here. The lighthouse is automated now, but we keep it open for tourists as a historic site. Not too many people come out here, though. Milo and I have the place to ourselves most of the time," he said, petting the dog.

"Nice to meet you. The lighthouse and surrounding areas seem a natural choice for my subject matter. Would you mind if I took some photos sometime?"

"Go ahead. You can take some now if you want."

"Maybe I will." I paused for a moment, trying to decide how to ask about last summer without being obvious. "Have you been the tour guide here for a while? It seems like such an interesting job."

"It has its ups and downs. I took over last summer. I used to work in a lighthouse on the mainland, but they decided to close it down because there weren't many tourists, so they sent me here. It's a nice area," he said.

"Yes, it is. Did the previous tour guide have a dog, too?" I asked, trying to act casual as I patted Milo on the head.

Leif grinned. "No. I think I started a trend."

He paused when I nipped my lip and glanced behind me at my car. He stared at it for a moment, and when he looked back at me, his cheek twitched, and his eyes narrowed. I got the feeling that he was sizing me up. He suddenly seemed shrewder than I had thought, and I wondered if he was on to me.

He continued. "You probably haven't heard, but the previous tour guide passed away. He's buried in a cemetery up the road. Nice old guy."

"How sad," I said.

Leif nodded slowly. "Yes, it is," he said.

His words seemed careful and measured, and I wondered if he had told me about Pappy's death on purpose for some reason, perhaps to gauge my reaction.

"Was he sick?" I asked.

"No. He was murdered by his assistant."

I gasped at his sharp words in spite of myself.

"I know. It's awful. I met the guy. You'd never know it, although he came up with a heck of a crazy story about lost gold and shipwrecks to try to get out of it. But he's in prison now. Nothing to worry about."

I gritted my teeth as I felt my cheeks get warm. "If you say so," I said.

"I do," he said, holding my gaze.

"Okay, well then, I guess I'll just take some pictures and go," I said to fill the awkward silence.

"Sure. You do that. Take as many as you want. Come on, Milo."

He turned and went back inside, leaving me to wonder if he knew more than he was letting on. He could have told me what he did to fend off further questioning. He was obviously aware that I was searching for answers, and he had his guard up about something.

Despite my unease, I selected a camera from the trunk and took several photos from the bluff of seagulls and shorebirds and a sailboat far out in the harbor, but my heart wasn't in it. I glanced at the lighthouse on my way back to the car and saw something move near the top. Leif was staring at me from the balcony. I pretended not to see him as I jumped in my car and drove away, hoping I wouldn't have to come out here again. Something about him gave me chills.

As I drove by his car on the way out, I noticed a deep dent in the front grill that tilted the left headlight upwards. I sucked in a breath. A headlight angled in that way could blind someone coming from the other direction or someone glancing in a side view mirror as I had when I was hit from behind on my way to the inn the first night. I wondered if it had been him and why he would have done that. Maybe he already knew who I was and recognized my car, although I didn't see how that was possible, and he didn't want me here. I shivered and pressed my foot down hard on the accelerator, making a note not to come back to the lighthouse alone. I sped through the gravel down the driveway.

When I reached the harbor road, I stopped and took a deep breath. I wasn't sure which way to turn. Leif said Pappy was buried in the cemetery up the road, and I decided that would be my next destination. I quickly tapped the subject and my location into my GPS. As I waited for directions to possible endpoints, a text popped up from the inn saying there was a message at the desk for me. I ignored it. It was probably from Colton about plans for this weekend, and I could pick it up later. I hoped it wasn't from Damon telling me he knew I was here. It seemed like something he would do if he'd found me somehow. I brushed sweat from my brow and tried to relax. I had to if I was going to keep driving. My phone showed a funeral home five miles away, and I took another deep breath. I glanced in the rearview mirror to make sure Leif hadn't come up behind me before pulling out and heading down the road.

I passed a dog-breeding kennel that looked like an old, clapboard house surrounded by a fence about a mile up the road and wondered if that's where the huskies came from or if they were endemic to the island. It seemed like there were a lot of them, given that I'd already seen two in two days, and I wondered why. It didn't seem like an important detail, but I intended to find out. I always investigated things that made me feel curious, whether or not I understood the reason for my feelings. More often than not, it panned out with something.

The funeral home was set back from the road but not far. I followed the puddled, dirt driveway and parked next to the white picket fence, losing its peeling paint out front. It stood in concert with the weathered-gray siding of the home, and as I took in the closed shutters and scuffed-up door, I wondered if I was at the right place. It appeared abandoned, but the numbers on the mailbox by the road had matched the address, and there were several cracked tombstones, some with small American flags on them, behind a black iron gate in the backyard. I sat there, staring at the house and wondering what to do.

Before long, the door opened slowly, and a tiny lady with a leathery, wrinkled face and a long braid of wispy, silver hair hobbled onto the rickety porch. A black cat streaked past her, and I hopped out of the way as it ran down the stairs and around to the back of the house. Another one peeked through the door behind her. She stretched out her arm and pulled it back toward her, seeming to beckon me in. At that point, I wasn't sure if I wanted to go in, but I got out of the car anyway and walked up the sagging steps.

"It's okay, dear. Times like these are hard on everyone. Come in, and we'll make some plans. Were you thinking about a burial or a cremation?"

Her voice was as tiny as she was, but she seemed to be in charge. I wasn't sure how to answer.

"I'm not here for me or for anybody," I said after a moment. "Not about that, anyway. What I mean is I'd like to visit Pappy Johnson's grave. He was an old friend of the family."

"Pappy? I didn't think he had any friends. He lived by himself in the lighthouse for as long as I can remember."

"Well, it was a long time ago. Would you mind telling me where it is?" I asked.

She looked me up and down slowly, taking in my blue chambray skirt and white cotton blouse and sandals, and nodded. "I'll show you where he is."

I followed her as she shuffled around back through the thick, wet grass and opened the gate.

"He's by the back fence. Watch where you step," she said.

Mud splattered my sandals and made my toes wet and cold as I followed her down a dirt path to the far grave. The stone was fresh, with curly writing etched into its surface. Something about it seemed strange, and I looked more closely. As I did so, the hairs on my forearms stood up.

"His name was Eldrich Johnson?" I asked, reading the tombstone.

"Yes, but everyone called him Pappy.

"How old was he?"

"Sixty-seven," she said.

I looked again at the tombstone, wondering what affected me so much.

"Why does it only have his birth date on it? What about the date he died?"

"Oh, well, it was last year," she said.

"I know, but shouldn't that be on the tombstone?" I asked.

"Yes. And it will be. But the funeral happened so fast,

and there was some question about exactly what day he died. You know, of course, that there were unusual circumstances. We were waiting for confirmation and never got around to adding the final date."

"I see," I said. "Does that happen often?"

"No. It's never happened before, but there's a first time for everything. I'm sure they'll get back to me."

"Hmm. I suppose," I said. The next thing I was going to investigate was the exact date of death. It could be crucial to explaining what happened. I was sure it would be in the city records, and I decided to go into town soon to check on them.

"Shall we go back to the house?" she asked. "I could offer you something to drink."

"No, thank you," I said, standing for a moment in a reverent silence before following her back through the cemetery.

The other tombstones were crumbling and stained, with only a few flowers on the graves. The cemetery didn't appear to be well tended, and I wondered why. Something about it gave me goosebumps, and I stepped up my pace. I couldn't wait to get out of here. I glanced behind me and thought I saw a branch move in the woods behind the cemetery, but it wasn't windy. Could someone else be out here? I didn't know why that would be unless someone was following me. It was a feeling I'd had since arriving on the island that I couldn't shake. I caught up with Mrs. Pinley, when she opened the gate, I stepped quickly past her and through it and headed for my car.

"Thank you for your time. I need to be heading back," I said, briskly over my shoulder.

"Of course. It's nice to know Pappy had friends," she called after me.

I nearly ran to my car and jumped in, too frightened to wave to her. I drove away quickly, unsure of what to make of the funeral home and of Pappy's grave, but when I reached the bottom of the hill, I realized that the hairs on my forearms were still standing up.

CHAPTER 4

The drive back to the inn was uneventful, other than the fact my nerves were on edge. It made it difficult to concentrate on driving, but I did my best. It was hard to reconcile all the things that had happened to me in the last few days with the beauty of the island. It was as though the island had two sides to it: the evil, deathly side, and the beautiful, natural side. I had just escaped the first, and I turned my attention to the second to take my mind off of it.

Fascinating birds with rust-colored wings soared over the harbor, and I decided to return later to photograph them. I understood why the island was a bird sanctuary. It was a beautiful place, and it resonated with me that the birds that flew south for the winter came back year after year like the tourists, unable to stay away. I might join them in their annual return if things worked out the way I hoped they would and I was able to solve the mystery of the murder. I drove slowly down the harbor road with its border of green trees interspersed with views of the harbor and soaked in the peace of the natural scene as I tried to relax. I felt better by the time I reached the inn.

I checked for messages at the desk when I walked in because of the text I'd gotten from the inn when I was leaving the lighthouse. The young woman sitting behind it, who I recognized as Melanie, looked at me quizzically as she handed me a yellow slip.

"I don't know you, do I?" she asked. "I saw you talking with Martha this morning. Are you new to the island?"

"Yes. I'm here for the summer writing an article and taking nature photographs for a calendar that I plan to sell online," I replied.

"How nice. You've come to the right place. You'll find scenic views and wildlife everywhere around here, especially on the bluff outside the inn and near the harbor and the lighthouse," she said.

"Yes. It's very lovely around here," I said, glancing at the message.

"I've called twice now. Call me back," it said.

"I'm sorry. Who is this from?" I asked.

"That's the thing. He didn't say. I thought you'd know. He was very abrupt when he called this morning, and I didn't talk to him long, although his voice sounded familiar for some reason. I don't usually handle the desk, but the school where I teach is off today to start the long holiday weekend, and I'm filling in here. I wasn't sure what to do when he hung up," she said.

"Oh, well, I'm glad you gave me the message," I said, trying not to look flustered.

Another call from an unidentified man? Martha had alerted me to the one before. This one had to be from Damon, too, but I wasn't going to call him. Even if it was from him, I didn't want to talk to him.

"By the way," I said, changing the subject, "I was just at the lighthouse. I met Leif Drendahl, the tour guide."

"Did you?" Melanie asked. "I haven't met him yet. He took over last summer from a tour guide that my old boyfriend knew. But he stays to himself out there. I suppose I'll meet him sometime." Her lip trembled.

"Was your old boyfriend a tour guide, too?" I asked,

softly, remembering that Martha had told me that Melanie had
dated Tyler. It seemed as though she still cared for him.

She shook her head and looked away, and I decided not
to ask any more questions about him. It was odd that Tyler had
never mentioned her. Maybe he had been too hurt or embarrassed
to bring it up. I wondered how she felt about everything and if
she believed he was guilty, but I didn't want to alienate her by
appearing nosy. There would be time for questions later. I didn't
plan to leave the island for a while. I decided to ask her about her
job instead.

"So you teach at the school?" I asked.

"Yes, I'm a fifth-grade teacher at the elementary school on
the outskirts of town near the harbor. My children go there, too.
Susie is in my class, and Bobby is in second grade. We live here,
and in the summer, I guide island boat tours for the guests at the
inn. Tours start in a few weeks, and you can sign up for one if
you'd like."

"I would like that. Thank you," I said, making a note of it.

Touring the area in a boat seemed like a good way to find
out more about the island and bolster my investigation. I also
wondered how serious her relationship was with Colton, but
I didn't know how to ask without seeming rude. I thought of
another way to find out.

"Are there any other messages? Maybe one from Colton
Harding?" I asked.

"Colton? No. Were you expecting one?" she asked.

"Possibly," I said.

I watched her expression for any sign of jealousy or
resentment or even mild curiosity but found none. She was either
casually dating him or very secure in their relationship. I wasn't
sure which. Then I remembered Martha hadn't been sure they
were still together. Maybe they weren't, and that was why she
was so unemotional about it.

"He may come by later for dinner and to see Martha," she said. "She had another bad night last night. Nightmares, you know. And sometimes, she sees things that frighten her. But I shouldn't be telling you this. I hardly know you."

"That's all right. It was a stormy night. I'm sure she's not the only one who didn't sleep well," I said, thinking of my own experience with the frightening, disembodied voice that woke me up. I felt an empathetic connection with Martha.

"I suppose," she said, looking away as the telephone rang. "I have to answer this. Maybe I'll see you later."

"Yes," I said, nodding and walking past her to head up to my room.

The conversation bothered me for some reason. I wasn't sure that Melanie had Martha's best interests at heart. Maybe it was the way she said that Martha saw things that frightened her. It sounded as though she didn't believe her.

Melanie's children scooted past me in the hallway and disappeared into the reception room. They looked similar to each other with their dark, wavy hair and brown eyes, so different from their fair-haired mother, although they shared her delicate features. It seemed odd that neither one of them looked at me or acknowledged my presence in any way. I'd always thought I was good with children. But they were kids, and they probably had other things on their minds. Besides, I was a stranger, and they might not be allowed to talk to me.

I stood outside my room and looked both ways before entering, making sure no one was in the hallway waiting to scare me. When I was satisfied that there was no one there, I stepped inside and closed the door, sighing in the welcome silence. I was glad to be back and away from the funeral home, but I was still on edge about the missing date on the tombstone and the events of the night before.

I sat on the bed and shivered as I reread the phone message

from the desk. What if it was from Damon, and he made trouble? And if it wasn't from him, who else could it possibly be from? A private investigator, maybe? Would Damon really go that far to keep track of me?

I needed some air. The fresh breeze from the harbor revived me as I cracked open the window and enjoyed the calming view. For a moment, something in the parking lot distracted me, but I wasn't sure what it was. I looked around cautiously. In the far corner of the lot, a dark blue sports car glinted in the sun. Damon. I was sure of it. He was here, somewhere. I gritted my teeth and tried to decide what to do. I didn't see the car this morning when I left, so he probably arrived while I was at the funeral home. He must not have stopped at the desk to ask about me, or Melanie would have told me. He must be in the restaurant, and if he saw my car, he would know for sure that I was here. I had to leave now. I threw some things in a tote bag and hurried down the stairs to run out the back door, but I decided to alert Melanie first. She was still at the desk.

"Melanie, I have to leave. The man who probably called this morning is here in the inn somewhere. He's my husband, and I can't let him find me. Do you understand what I'm asking you?" I choked out the words as I sucked in short, shallow breaths.

Her face paled as she answered. "Yes, of course. You were never here. Go."

"Thank you." I scurried out the door, hoping I could escape before Damon saw me. But where could I run to? As I stumbled down the ramp, I glanced over at the car again and gasped. The license plate was the wrong color. It wasn't his car, after all. The plate was from another state. I put my hand to my heart as waves of relief washed over me. But I was upset with myself, too, for letting my fears overtake me. I needed to calm down if I was going to free Tyler. The events of the last few days had made me jumpy.

Melanie leapt up when I walked back into the inn. "Are you okay? Is he out there?" she asked. Her eyes widened, and her cheeks flushed.

"No, I'm sorry I frightened you. I thought I saw his car, but it wasn't his. He isn't here, after all," I said, trying to slow my breathing but not succeeding too well.

"Well, thank goodness for that," she said, sitting back down. "He must be quite a scary man to have you running out like that. At least we now know what you're dealing with. We'll keep your identity safe. This isn't the first time we've run into this type of thing. Our guests come here to get away from it all, and sometimes that includes other people."

"Thank you," I said, putting my hand to my chest. Her kind words relaxed me, although something about her made me want to keep my distance. I didn't know what it was.

"Do you have a picture of him so I'll know if he shows up?" she asked.

I took a deep breath and pulled my billfold out of my purse. I showed her our wedding photo from five years ago. Was it my imagination, or did she pull back and hesitate when she looked at it?

"Okay, I'll keep an eye out for him and let you know if I see him," she said, looking away.

She didn't say anything about the photo. It must have been my imagination. I still felt wary of her, though.

"Thanks. I really appreciate that," I said, starting to feel a little better. "I think I'll go back to my room and rest."

"Good idea," Melanie said. "I'll let you know if anyone asks for you."

"Thank you," I said as I left the reception area and headed into the hallway.

I changed my mind about resting when I caught a whiff of savory soup from the restaurant. I decided to stay for a late lunch and head into town afterwards. I had to quit letting my imagination run away with me and concentrate on solving the murder mystery. I had already accomplished quite a bit, but I wanted to go to the registrar's office and find the record of Pappy's death. A death certificate with the exact date and cause of death could go a long way toward explaining what had really happened to him. I sat at the same table by the window, and Rosie brought me the hot vegetable soup and baguette I ordered. I hoped she could give me more information about Pappy.

"I hope you don't mind my asking, but I went out to the lighthouse this morning to take photos, and the tour guide told me the previous tour guide had passed away. Do you know anything about that?" I asked.

"Oh, let me tell you," Rosie said, putting her hand to her chest before tucking a wavy strand of hair behind her ear and leaning toward me. "You don't want to know the details," she whispered, "but it was bad. Pappy was his name. Everyone was shocked when it happened, and most people don't want to talk about it. He took care of the grounds and gave tours at the lighthouse for as long as I can remember. He started there more than thirty years ago after the prison on the island closed, and he was released along with the few remaining inmates. I don't even know why he was in prison back then. All I know is that he was a good tour guide, and it's sad that things ended that way for him." She stood straight up again and glanced around before looking at me conspiratorially.

"That is sad," I said. "But you don't know what happened?"

"Only that one of the servers here found him and was blamed for his death," she said, softly.

"How awful."

"Yes, it was. But I'd rather not talk about it right now."

"I understand. But what happened to the other inmates in the prison?"

Rosie appeared taken aback that I asked. She paused before answering. "Some of them live and work around the island. A few of them work at the copper mine here on the island, which isn't the best place to work, from what I hear. They don't treat the miners very well. I'm not sure what happened to all of them. No one's ever asked me that before. Why?"

"Oh, no reason. It's just an interesting story, that's all."

"Yes, it is," she agreed. "It was a stone prison. It's still standing, but it's crumbling in the woods on the other side of the island. No one ever goes there. The last person who did said it was haunted and to stay away. I guess not all ghosts are harmless. There's one you probably haven't heard about yet, but I'm not going to be the one to tell you about him."

I shivered. "I see."

Rosie laughed, seeming to regain her amiable composure. "Sorry. Don't let it bother you. We've been living with ghosts on the island for a long time. You'll get used to it."

I gave her a half-smile. "If you say so," I said.

"I do. Well, enjoy your soup. I guess I better take care of my other customers," she said, as she turned to walk away. "Let me know if you need anything else."

After she left, I finished my lunch and walked out to my car. The sports car was gone, not that it really mattered. But it made me feel better. On my way into town, I thought about Damon and how his control over me had made my life miserable for so long. Maybe living on the island would allow me to finally break away from him and regain my freedom along with Tyler's.

The town was small and charming, as harbor towns tend to be, and I was immediately drawn to its old-fashioned atmosphere and welcoming appearance. Independent stores lined the Main Street, and American flags flapped in the breeze at their fronts. Colorful pansies lined the curbs, and the rich aroma of chocolate wafted by from a nearby fudge shop. A ship's horn honked in the harbor, and a seagull squawked nearby as I parked my car on the street. I looked up the address of the registrar's office on my phone and found that it was only a few blocks away. On my way there, I browsed through clothing stores, souvenir shops, and an art and photography studio that displayed works similar to my own. A beautiful photograph of a snowy owl gave me an idea for my calendar's month of January, and I exchanged phone numbers with the resident photographer, whose name was Stan, to keep in touch. He seemed like a nice man, but he kept looking past me over my shoulder instead of at me while I talked to him, even though when I checked behind me, there was no one there. It seemed like a strange thing to do, but I tried not to let it bother me. Everyone had their idiosyncrasies. I smiled and waved when I walked out. The bell over the door tinkled when I left. If someone had entered the shop behind me while I was there, I would have heard it. I don't know what Stan could have been looking at unless there was something outside, but I put it out of my mind. I had other things to do. When I finally reached the registrar's office, I found that it was closing early for the weekend.

     "Could you check something for me first?" I asked the young girl behind the counter, who tapped her pink-tipped fingernails briskly on the counter in a seemingly impatient way. "It won't take long. I only need to know the date of death for Pappy Johnson."

     "Are you a relative?" she asked.

     "Does it make a difference?"

     "I suppose not. Let me see."

     She clicked a few keys on her computer. "August 15th of last year," she said.

     "Really? Can I get a printout of that?" I asked.

     "No. I only told you because I need to lock up. Could you go now?"

I was surprised by her dismissive demeanor and wondered what the reason was. "Did you know Pappy?" I asked.

"It doesn't matter if I did or not. We're closed," she said.

"Well, could you at least tell me what the 'cause of death' was?"

"The coroner's office is two doors down. Now, do you mind?" she said, brusquely.

"Well, thank you for your time," I said, attempting to maintain my composure. It wouldn't be wise to insist and upset anyone on the island when I was trying to get valuable information. "Have a nice weekend," I said instead.

The lock clicked behind me after she nearly pushed me out the door, and I left, feeling bewildered by her attitude but relieved that I had at least found out Pappy's date of death. The coroner's office was open, and I tried not to look nervous when I walked in. I was still shaking from my encounter at the registrar's office. Something wasn't right. The woman behind the desk looked up when I walked in.

"May I help you?"

"I'm not sure. I was just at the registrar's office, and they sent me here. I need to find out the cause of Pappy Johnson's death last summer," I said.

"Pappy? I can tell you right now. It was in all the papers. He died of a broken neck," she said.

"Yes, they did say that, but I'm looking for the records."

"Oh, well, Dr. Pearson was the coroner on that case, and he left the island last summer. Are you from the sheriff's office?" she asked.

Her right eye twitched, and I wasn't sure if it was due to her heavily mascaraed lashes or something else.

"Well, no," I answered, wondering why she asked. "But surely the records remain here," I continued.

"Let me pull it up." She paused for a moment and looked

at her computer screen. "Broken neck, like I said."

"Does it show the date of death?" I asked to double-check what the registrar's office had told me.

"August 14th," she answered.

"August 14th? Are you sure?" I asked.

"That's what it says," she said, appearing to clench her teeth.

"Okay, thank you," I said, turning to go.

"You're from the sheriff's office, aren't you?" she asked.

I paused in mid-turn. "What? No," I said.

"Mr. Wellington warned me about this," she said. "The case is closed, and the perpetrator is in prison. There's no reason to harass the office about this."

"Harass? No, of course, I wouldn't do that. Who's Mr. Wellington? What are you referring to?" I asked.

"Never mind. I'm sick of you people. I'll tell you what I told everyone that called. Call Mrs. Pinley at the funeral home if you want more information. I think you'd better go now," she said, pursing her lips and brushing the air with the back of her hand.

I didn't move, in spite of her gesture. I put my hand on the counter and leaned toward her.

"All what people? Did other people ask you about Pappy's date of death?" I asked quietly.

She didn't respond and stared at her computer screen instead, with her lips pressed together in a thin line. I paused, perplexed. There could have been questions asked of her after Pappy's murder that bothered her. Whatever it was, it was obvious that I wasn't going to get any more answers from her.

"Yes. All right. Thank you for your time," I said, attempting to salvage some semblance of politeness in the conversation as I turned and walked toward the door. I pulled it open and left.

The shakiness in my arms radiated to my legs. August 14th

and August 15th? Two different dates of death? I needed to find out more about what was going on, but I was going to have to do it in a different way. No one with information about records was being helpful, and I was sure there was more to the discrepancy than a computer error. The attitudes of the office clerks I'd talked to were evidence of that. At least Damon wasn't around to tell me I was crazy again. I needed to trust myself and my instincts if I was going to make sense of things. The way everyone acted made me suspect that something nefarious was going on. Were they hiding the death certificate from me for some reason, or maybe something else? It had to do with Pappy and his unfortunate passing. That was clear. But there was more to it than that.

I walked back onto the street and headed for my car. It was a sunny afternoon with a clear blue sky, perfect for taking photographs of birds in the harbor. I grabbed a camera out of the trunk and walked to the beach. I needed to think. A piping plover popped back and forth in the sand, and I snapped a few photos of him. As I shifted my lens to capture a seagull, I noticed the lighthouse on the bluff far in the distance. Was Leif still there, looking out across the water in the same way Pappy had before him? Probably. I needed to find out if he also knew, in the same way that Pappy had, about the location of the sunken gold and the shipwreck. It wasn't just a story that Tyler made up. I was sure of it. It was true. And then it became clear to me what they were all hiding. The islanders, at least some of them, knew that Tyler's story was true, too.

CHAPTER 5

I tapped my foot in time to "This Land is Your Land" as the Copper Isle High School band marched down Main Street in front of me. It was a beautiful, sunny morning, and a fresh breeze blew in off the harbor. It ruffled my hair, but I didn't care. Being on the island relaxed me, and I wasn't as concerned about trying to look perfect as I'd been in my marriage. Colton looked very handsome in jeans and a navy sweater that accentuated the cornflower blue of his eyes. He'd picked me up at the inn after breakfast, and we'd driven into town together in his truck. His chiseled jaw and broad, muscular chest gave him the look of the rugged outdoorsman I imagined him to be when he wasn't running his island businesses, and I had trouble keeping my eyes off of him. It had been a while since I'd been so attracted to a man. Colton turned and waved to somebody in the parade.

"That's my history teacher from high school. He got me interested in the background of the island, and I'm kind of a history buff about it. I write a column for the Chamber of Commerce newsletter," he said.

I nodded, glad that Colton was opening up to me but wary of doing the same with him. It didn't seem right yet to tell him who I really was and that Tyler was my brother. First, I had to make sure that he was someone I could trust with my life and with Tyler's.

"Really? I'd love to find out more about the island's past for my article. Maybe we could talk about it sometime," I said.

"Sure. Anytime."

His smile made my heart flutter. Something about him touched a part of me I thought was lost forever, and I wanted to be near him. He was interesting and intelligent, too. In my soul, I was no longer married to Damon and hadn't been for a long time. I was ready to move on, and maybe Colton could be someone I moved on with. He could also be the key to finding the answers I was looking for, as he probably knew details about the murder last summer and about the island ghosts. I wondered if he believed Tyler's story about the shipwreck and the gold and if he could help me find it. That was next on my list of things to investigate.

Several pick-up trucks covered with decals and decorated with red, white and blue streamers drove by, following the veteran's group that everyone applauded, who marched behind the band.

"Those are the local guys advertising their businesses," Colton said. "That's Bob Littleton in the heating and cooling truck and Larry Portland in the plumbing truck. 'Harding Island Tours and Boat Rentals.' I guess that's us," he said, grinning, as a truck towing a speedboat drove by with Melanie waving from the side window. "My mom never passes up a chance for publicity."

"That's Melanie from the inn, isn't it? I met her last week," I said, hoping to find out how he felt about her.

"Yes. She leads the tours. She's a good friend of mine," he said, his cheek twitching slightly.

A good friend? Was that all? I hoped so. "How nice."

"Come on. Let's get some lunch. All that's left is the fire trucks bringing up the rear. We'll see those guys when they supervise the beach bonfire tonight. Have you ever had a corn dog?" He took my arm and led me toward the harbor, where concession stands were set up.

"A what?"

"A corn dog. It's a hot dog on a stick dipped in batter and fried," he said.

"I'll try it, but I usually eat soup or salad or yogurt for lunch."

"That's rabbit food. We'll get some real food."

"I don't think rabbits eat yogurt," I said.

He chuckled. "Maybe not. I have to confess, I don't know as much about animals and birds and nature as you do. I love birds, of course. How could I not? The whole island is a bird sanctuary, and we set aside money at the Chamber to support it. But I've been looking things up on the internet to have more to talk to you about. Is that wrong?"

He looked at me sheepishly, and I smiled at him. I was more than a little flattered that he had taken the time to do that. "No. I'm glad you told me. I'll tell you what. If you teach me about the history of the island, I'll teach you about birds and nature."

"It's a deal," he said, stopping in front of a concession stand. "Here we are. Would you like a coke, too?"

"Pop?"

"Yeah, you know, a coke. It has bubbles."

"Sure."

It had been a long time since I'd had such a casual date, and I was enjoying myself immensely. At the formal social occasions, I attended with Damon, the only drink with bubbles in it was champagne. We took our food to a picnic table under a nearby tree, where we watched boats dock in the harbor as the lake shimmered in the distance. The lake seemed so vast and endless, and I wondered what secrets it held. There was one secret about the sunken gold that I hoped to uncover, and I wanted Colton to help me with that.

"Do you know of any historic shipwrecks around here? That's another one of my interests," I said, hoping I could bluff my way through a conversation about history with him, although I was interested in shipwrecks.

He appeared lost in thought before he answered. "Yes, actually I do. A number of ships have sunk in the past, probably during storms, and are scattered around the bottom of the lake. Some of them brought supplies and payments to the islanders who worked at the copper mine that still operates here part-time more than a century ago.

"Really? Payments? Were they paid with coins or bills?" I asked.

"Good question. They were often paid with gold coins."

"Interesting." And it was interesting. Colton had just unwittingly told me that Tyler's story about the sunken treasure had a historical basis.

The breeze picked up, and I shook my flyaway hair back and tied it with the flowered silk scarf I wore around my neck. The last time I'd worn a ponytail, I had been a teenager. With Colton around, I felt young and free again in the same way I did then.

"So how did someone as lovely as you escape being married for this long?" Colton asked, smiling.

I wasn't sure how to answer. I didn't want to tell him I was married and possibly ruin my chances with him, but I didn't want to lie to him either. I was surprised Melanie hadn't already told him about my mistaking a car for my husband's at the inn and apprised him of my marital status. Maybe they weren't such close friends after all.

"Marriages don't always work out the way people want them to," I said, evasively. "What about you? How did you escape?"

He laughed. "It doesn't have so much to do with escaping

as it does with burying myself in my work. Several of the businesses I own on the island have had financial problems, and I'm working on digging them out. The inn is the only one that's been consistently profitable, and I'm hoping to keep it that way." He paused for a moment and frowned. "We've had run-ins with a night stalker scaring the guests. I call him a stalker because police reports describe him that way. Martha has had several encounters with him but has never been able to prove them to the police." He looked away, and when he turned back around, he lowered his head and murmured. "It's been difficult. Martha has had supernatural encounters before, but nothing like this. The police are disinclined to believe her because of her previous reports about ghosts at the inn scaring the guests. The ghosts have been tourist attractions for the island in the past, but now, I'm afraid, if the stalking doesn't end, the inn could go under like my other businesses."

"Have you thought about hiring security?" I asked.

"Yes, but I agree with Martha that it wouldn't do much good in protecting us from ghosts. We have alerted the resident ghost hunters, and they're on the lookout. So far, they haven't encountered him even after using all their instruments to search the inn." His eyes darkened. "It's almost as though someone wants us to leave," he said.

"Really?" I asked. It sounded that way to me, too, but I didn't tell him that, in case I was mistaken. "So you believe in ghosts?" I asked, hoping he didn't think I was being too forward but really wanting to know. It would be great to find in him a kindred spirit.

He pondered for a moment. "I believe there is something here and at other properties on the island that can't be explained," he answered. "I've come to believe over time that it is due to the supernatural, but as to what's happening lately, I don't know." He shook his head. "If the stalking doesn't stop, and the stalker continues to terrorize the islanders and drive tourism away, I don't know if the economy on the island will survive. I'm afraid of what that would mean for the inn and the island, in general."

I nodded. "That is frightening to think about. When did it start?" I asked.

"The stalking? Last summer." He paused. "I don't know if I should tell you this, but you'll probably find out eventually anyway. A man was found murdered at the lighthouse last year. The stalking started soon after that."

I looked down, unsure of what to say but happy that Colton trusted me enough to tell me these things. I wanted to trust him, too, and I was starting to. I was disappointed that he didn't see ghosts but glad that he didn't make fun of my question. When I looked back up, he was gazing at me intently.

"You won't leave because of this, will you? I was hoping to get to know you better," he said.

"No, I won't leave," I said, deciding to grasp the opportunity to talk about Tyler. I took a deep breath before continuing. "I want to know more about the murder. I want to find out what happened last summer."

"You do? Why? For your article?"

I paused, considering my answer before deciding to go ahead and tell him.

"No, because the man accused of the murder is my brother."

Colton's eyes widened. "Tyler Lawrence, is your brother? He was convicted," he said.

"Yes, but he didn't do it," I said, firmly.

"How do you know?"

"Because I know my brother."

Colton nodded slowly. "I see. So that's the real reason you've come to the island."

He leaned forward and seemed so interested in what I was

saying that I continued.

"That, among other things. But yes, that's the main reason. I want to get him out of prison."

Colton's kind expression touched my heart, and the feelings I had bottled up about Tyler suddenly welled up and poured out.

"I miss him so much. I miss his laugh. I miss having him to talk to. It was just the two of us after my mother died several years ago. I took care of him until he finished high school and went out on his own. We still talked after that and supported each other. Then, when he went to the island to work last summer, he didn't call as often. And, of course, after he was accused of the murder, everything changed. I miss the way it used to be. I miss him. I want him back."

"Of course you do," Colton said, touching my arm. "It must be very hard to have him away from you."

I saw in his eyes a depth of compassion that I hadn't expected. I sighed with relief that I had been able to unburden myself.

"Will you help me?" I asked. "Will you help me find out what really happened so I can free Tyler from prison? It's a terrible injustice that's been done to him." I gazed at him intently, feeling my eyes burn with tears.

Colton hesitated for a moment and then nodded. "I can see how passionate you are about this. I have to admit that Tyler's arrest and conviction were a great surprise to me. He was an upstanding, well-liked employee of the inn. It's possible that the verdict was a mistake. He was tried on the mainland, and maybe, because of the distance from here, there wasn't a thorough enough investigation of what actually happened on the island. I don't know if that's the case or what I can do, but I will help you in any way that I can."

"Thank you," I said, brushing the tears away. "You don't

know what it means to me to have someone on my side."

"I think I do," he said. "I've been in situations before where I was the only one promoting a cause, like when I'm trying to protect my mother from the night stalker. It's important to have support."

"Yes, it means a lot," I said. "I'll try to help with protecting your mother, too, in any way I can."

"Thank you," he said.

I was suddenly overwhelmed with gratitude. I hadn't realized how alone I felt. Having Colton as a friend made things seem less dire. It was all I could do to keep from throwing my arms around him and hugging him. But I didn't think that would be appropriate at this time in our relationship. I needed to get to know him better. I smiled instead.

We finished our lunch and took our drinks with us as we strolled through the picnic area to the beach. A man from the parade walked by, eating a snow cone and walking a beautiful black-and-white husky on a leash. Colton waved at him.

"Hi, Bob," he called out.

The man wiped his mouth on his red, rock 'n roll t-shirt shirt, leaving a dark stain, and smiled through his brown beard with blue lips. "Hi," he called back as he raised the cone in greeting. "Are you going to the Chamber of Commerce meeting next week?"

"Wouldn't miss it," Colton said.

"Good. We need to come up with a plan to deal with the decline in tourism and the resulting economic fall-out on the island," he said. "It's affecting my heating and cooling business big time."

"You got it," Colton said. "I couldn't agree more."

"Good. See you later, then," he said, nodding to Colton and me as he walked on.

I nodded back. He didn't look like a businessman to me,

but people on the island were much more casual in dress and attitude than those I'd known on the mainland. It would take some getting used to, but I was sure I would adjust. I enjoyed the freer atmosphere. It literally made me want to let my hair down and relax.

"Another husky? It seems like they're everywhere," I said, commenting on Bob's dog.

"Yes. There were a few large litters at a breeder on the island a few years ago, and people adopted them. That's probably why, although Bob got his full-grown last fall. They're great pets."

"I see. They're beautiful dogs. Maybe I could get them together in a group sometime and take photos."

"Maybe. I know people that own huskies are very proud of their dogs. They might like to have them photographed."

"How long have you known Bob?"

"I've known him since third grade, and Larry, who you saw in the parade, was on the swim team with me in high school. Larry's a lot taller and thinner than Bob, but that's because he still swims all the time. Bob would rather sit around with a beer, scratching his beard and shooting the breeze. They're both good friends."

"I'm glad."

We spent the afternoon walking along the beach and talking. Colton had grown up on the island and knew a lot about it. I was amazed that someone so down-to-earth and easy to talk to ran so many businesses and was obviously so well-connected socially. He was the complete opposite of Damon, who used his social connections to make himself seem important. Colton wasn't like that at all, and he wasn't pushy in the way that Damon was, either. He must have realized earlier that Tyler's last name was different from mine and that I was either married or divorced, but he didn't press me for more information or appear to be bothered by the discrepancy. He seemed only interested in me and in allowing our relationship to develop in its own time. Later, when he took my hand in his, a warmth radiated through me, and I sighed quietly.

"You're a very easy person to be with," I said, smiling up at him.

"Copy that," he said, smiling back. "You are, too."

We strolled up the beach to the road at sundown and had a nice dinner at the Schooner Restaurant and Bar that Colton mentioned he owned and toasted each other with glasses of Chardonnay as we gazed out over the harbor. I enjoyed the view and the company. As the evening sun waned lower in the sky and the clouds over the water turned shades of purple and pink, we left the restaurant and gathered with others on the beach around a tall, triangular stack of logs that suddenly burst into flames to a chorus of 'oohs' and 'ahhs.'

A few men hovered nearby, and Colton told me they were the firemen from the parade keeping a careful watch over the bonfire.

"That's quite a show," I said, feeling my cheeks heat up from the fire. The flames popped and crackled as they danced into life.

"Yeah, the kids from town like to set it up, and it's fun to crowd around. If you'd like, we can join the group in the lawn chairs set up over there on the sand. It might be more comfortable."

"Sure," I said, shuffling my sandals through the sand and smiling as the cool grit of it sifted between my toes.

We walked a little ways away and found some empty seats near a man strumming a guitar.

"That's Andy. He's one of the ghost hunters that comes to the island every year. He and his wife will probably tell ghost stories later. It's a big draw for the tourists."

"How fun."

"Yes, as long as you don't get scared."

"I won't as long as you're near me," I said, lightly.

His eyes glinted as he looked at me through the shadows flickering from the flames. "I'll be near you," he said, gruffly.

I shivered pleasantly, and it wasn't only due to the cool breeze that blew in from the harbor. "I'm glad," I said.

We listened to the music and chatted with a few people as the bonfire crackled nearby, surrounded by others who were laughing and talking and warming their hands. As I looked around at the convivial gathering I was a part of, I felt like an islander myself, and I sighed, contentedly.

As the evening darkened into night and the stars came out, the strumming stopped, and Andy stood to address the group, gesturing to a young woman nearby to join him. "I'm Andy. This is my wife, Kirsten. We're asked every year to tell the story of the Copper Rush shipwreck and of the sailors lost near Copper Isle in the terrible storm that claimed their lives more than a century ago. It has a particular meaning to us as we come to the island every summer to visit the ghosts of the shipwreck."

An almost imperceptible murmur hummed through the crowd as everyone gathered around, and Andy raised his palms in front of him and grinned. "Don't worry. The ghosts are real, but they won't hurt you. They've never hurt us. If you'll give me a chance and listen closely, I'll tell you how they came to be here," he said.

A ship's horn blasted mournfully in the harbor, and boat lights twinkled here and there above the smooth, black water behind him as he began to tell his story.

"Long ago, in the 1840s, copper was discovered on the island and on parts of the mainland by fur traders and others who frequented the area. Tinted, green rocks were unearthed, giving away the existence of copper deposits, and a Copper Rush, similar to the Gold Rush out west, ensued in the region. Many ships sailed here with men eager to work in the newly constructed copper mine, and other ships came loaded with supplies and support for the miners."

I glanced around at the silent crowd. Everyone seemed to be listening intently.

"One night, a ship carrying many men crashed near the lighthouse during a horrific gale, leaving the sailors on-board stranded and clinging to the rocks near shore. The islanders tried to rescue them, but the storm was unrelenting, and the men dropped off into the churning sea one by one until no one was left. The next morning, the rocks were clear as though no ship or unfortunate sailors had ever been there, but there were dozens of unexplained footprints in the wet sand on shore. In the coming weeks, the islanders were plagued by knocks on their doors and taps on their windows at night and low, moaning sounds that couldn't be explained by the wind. Some people heard muffled requests for food and shelter that could only be silenced by opening a door to the empty night."

I leaned forward in my chair to hear Andy better, entranced by the ghost story and its tragic history. He continued.

"Eventually, the sounds went away, but as time went on, the islanders realized that their homes were shared by other entities, ghosts, if you will, who had almost certainly entered through the opened doors. The ghosts of the drowned, shipwrecked sailors had come to live in their homes. Some say the ghosts will stay until they can find a way to return to the mainland and their families. For now, they still live on the island in any warm place that could give them shelter from the storm."

Andy finished his story to the collective sigh of the crowd. I reached for Colton's hand, and he grasped mine and squeezed it. His hand was warm and comforting. And far across the harbor, on a bluff high above the water, the lighthouse beacon flashed brightly in the hushed quiet of the night.

CHAPTER 6

The inn was quiet the next morning when I awoke late and went down to breakfast. Luckily, I'd slept deeply with no ghosts keeping me awake. I still hadn't seen them, even though I'd heard the stories, and I wondered if I would. Colton had dropped me off last night and asked to see me again today, which I had agreed to. He was an intriguing man even though he was occasionally lost in thought, leaving me to wonder what was bothering him.

Guests who had come for the long weekend had left, and as I saw no sign of Melanie or her children, I assumed the school was back in session. The school was another place I planned to visit, perhaps today on my way back from the abandoned prison. I'd seen a brochure that said the science department there took care of a bird sanctuary, and I hoped to find out more about it.

I was going to the prison because, although the ghosts in the story last evening had looked for warm places to stay, it appeared that they were found elsewhere, like the prison, as well. I wondered if other ghosts besides those of the shipwrecked sailors haunted the island. It seemed possible. Something felt amiss, and I wanted to find out what. Colton was talking to his mother by the doors to the kitchen, and he looked my way and smiled before turning and walking through them. Martha came over as I finished my breakfast.

"I'm so glad you two had a good time yesterday. Colton mentioned it. He drove out this morning to check on the inn and said you'd gone to the parade together and stayed late for the bonfire. Did you see our truck in the parade?"

"Yes, Melanie was in it, waving."

"Was she? Isn't that just like Colton not to relay that?" she murmured.

I didn't know but felt it best not to pursue the line of conversation. Although Colton hadn't told me much about his relationship with Melanie, he had said enough for me to deduce that it had ended, perhaps a short while ago. I had seen heartbreak before and experienced it myself with Damon, and I recognized it in Colton. I hoped he was ready to move on, as I was, but I didn't want to talk about it with Martha, who was looking out the window and patting her hair into place again.

"Is everything alright?" I asked. "Forgive me, but you seem a bit distracted."

"What? Oh, yes. It's only that yesterday, while you were in town, we had another incident at the inn. Nothing serious, but it frightened me."

"What happened?"

"Someone rifled through the front desk and took the guest roster and the preliminary budget sheets for this summer. As if that wasn't enough, they left a threatening note telling me and Colton to leave the inn and the island or suffer the consequences."

"What consequences?" I asked.

"It didn't say, but I'm afraid to find out. We're not leaving, of course, so we'll just have to wait and see."

"How awful."

"Yes. Again, please try not to let it bother you. Colton thinks the world of you, and so do I. I hope this won't affect your stay here."

"No, I'm staying for my article. Nothing's going to frighten me away," I said, trembling. I wasn't giving up on solving the mystery, and I wasn't leaving and running into possible danger from Damon. "Do you think it was the night stalker?"

"I don't know. I don't know what to think anymore. It doesn't seem like a ghost would rifle through a desk drawer," she said, "but I don't know who else to attribute it to." She put her hand on her heart. "He's very frightening. The last time I encountered him, I was sure he was the Ghostslayer himself. I'm sure you've heard about him by now. But it doesn't make sense that he would come here because the ghosts at the inn are good and not the evil ones he's looking for. I've never gotten a good look at his face under the cloak and hood he wears. Still, I and many other islanders can't help wondering if it is the Ghostslayer and worrying that he might mistake one of us for someone responsible for his death years ago and kill us in a horrible way."

"How awful for you," I said. "It must be extremely difficult to live with that kind of fear."

"It is," Martha said. "Thank you for understanding."

"What's going on?" Colton asked, walking up behind his mother.

"Oh, nothing. Layla and I were just having a little chat, weren't we, dear?"

I nodded, and Martha patted Colton on the arm and left.

"She told you about the note, didn't she?" he asked, sliding in next to me in the booth.

"Yes," I said, deciding not to discuss what Martha had told me about her fears. I was sure she shared them with him privately, as well.

He looked extremely handsome and well-rested, and I wondered how he did that, considering that I probably looked tired from being out late the night before. I nodded, and he grinned when he caught me staring.

"I'm sorry, it's just that it's nice to see you again," I said, feeling my cheeks get warm.

"You too," he said, holding my gaze for an instant before continuing. "Don't worry about the note."

"I'll try not to, but I'm concerned about the effect the harassment is having on your mother."

"Yes, it's obviously upsetting her, and it's kind of you to be concerned. I've made the staff aware of it, and they're looking out for her. We have things under control for the moment. If we had a more understanding sheriff, we wouldn't have to deal with this, but as it is, we have to take on most of the security ourselves. He doesn't believe in ghosts, and he doesn't believe Martha. But I do, and everyone here will watch out for her to the best of their abilities."

"I'm glad to hear you say that," I said.

He nodded. "Would you like to head out to take photos on the other side of the island now?" he asked, obviously referring to what I'd vaguely said yesterday about exploring the scenery around the prison. He had offered to come with me, and, being somewhat afraid of running into ghosts by myself, I had agreed.

"All right," I answered, taking his word for it that things were under control at the inn.

I picked up my camera and followed him to his truck. The morning was fresh and clear, and a robin chirped in a tree nearby, echoing the happy feeling I had at being with Colton again. As we drove down the harbor road together, it occurred to me that he probably knew about Tyler's relationship with Melanie and could enlighten me as to why my brother had never mentioned it. But I needed to be sensitive to his feelings if I asked him about it.

"I hope you don't mind the question, but was there anyone my brother could have talked to about the murder that wasn't at his trial?"

"Confided in, you mean?"

"Yes."

Colton was silent for a moment. "He may have talked to
Melanie about it," he said, stumbling over her name as he'd done
before when he talked about her. "They were quite an item for
a while, and she was deeply affected by all that happened last
summer. I was there for her through the rough times." He cleared
his throat. "She seems to have recovered, enough anyway, that
she doesn't need me anymore. I suppose you could ask her if
Tyler disclosed something to her, but you'd probably have to tell
her he's your brother."

"Thank you for telling me. I may talk to her," I said,
cringing at Colton's obvious distress.

Their break-up appeared to have hurt him deeply, and
I wasn't sure I trusted Melanie. She was very beautiful, and if
she knew her effect on men and used it, she could have casually
broken his heart. And she could have done the same thing with
Tyler, which would explain why he never mentioned her. It
could also explain why her children were so distant if people in
their lives came and went at her whim unless there was more to
it than that.

We continued down the road, driving through town on
our way to our destination. Store owners swept doorways and
sidewalks as they tidied up after the parade, and the street
bustled with people, probably on work breaks, waving and
greeting each other. I smiled at the pleasant scene, amazed that
something as dreadful as a murder could have happened in this
place. But it did, and the islanders were covering something up.
What I needed to do was find out what and why.

Sunlight peeked through the rustling trees and dappled
the harbor road as we drove to the far side of the island and up
a small hill to the prison. The woods were more dense here, and
even in the morning, shadows cast a pall over the crumbling
ruins of stone. I shivered. The island had changed from light to

dark so quickly again. Colton stopped the truck in an open glen, and I took a few photos after we got out and walked closer to the prison. Nature had crept in and filled the cracks and crevices with grasses and moss and a thick, black mold, and it had an unearthly appearance as though it had been abandoned suddenly. A cold chill hit me. It had housed evil and suffering. I felt it. But something even more evil had shut it down. Malevolent ghosts, perhaps, or something worse.

"Rosie at the inn told me Pappy was imprisoned here more than thirty years ago before he went to work at the lighthouse," I said, softly, hearing my voice shake.

"I didn't know that," Colton said. "No one knew much about Pappy. He stayed to himself out there in the same way that Leif does now. It's pretty isolated."

"Yes, it is, but even so, doesn't it seem strange that the prison was shut down, and he and the other prisoners were released, and no one knows why? Even if Pappy didn't say anything, it seems like someone would have."

Colton rubbed his chin. "Now that you mention it, it does seem odd that island history in relation to the prison is sketchy, at best. I'm going to check into that. I'd like to know more about that, too."

"Should we go in?" I asked.

He hesitated before answering. "I don't want to put you in danger. The doors and windows are boarded for a reason, and I don't think it's safe."

I agreed as I gazed at the towering rubble of stone. Even though I longed to know if there were ghosts inside, I didn't want to go in without Colton. I snapped a few more photos of the woods and the prison, and when I was satisfied, I turned to talk to him.

"Since we're talking about Pappy," I said, "maybe I should mention that I went to the cemetery where he was buried.

I talked to the woman in charge of the funeral home there, and she showed me Pappy's tombstone. It didn't have a date of death on it. Isn't that strange?"

"No date? That is strange. Did you ask her why?"

"Yes. She said she never received a definitive answer as to the day he died."

"What? That doesn't make sense," Colton said, furrowing his eyebrows.

"I don't think so, either, but I saw the marker, and the date was missing. Do you want to see it? We could go to the funeral home now, and I could visit the school on another day."

"Yes. Let's talk to Mrs. Pinley. I'm sure that's who you met. She's been there for years," he said, turning to go.

I took one last look at the prison and sucked in a breath. Did a board on the lower window shift to the left? I glanced over at Colton, who seemed unaware of anything wrong, before looking again more closely. Nothing moved. It must have been my imagination. I wrenched my gaze away and turned and followed Colton to the truck, where we got in and drove back through town and onto the cemetery.

The funeral home was as dreary looking as it had been last week, and, for a moment, I regretted returning. But Colton seemed determined when he pulled up and parked next to the fence, and I went with him up the sagging porch stairs to the door. He knocked gently, and the tiny lady I'd met before opened the door.

"Back so soon?" she asked when she saw me.

"Yes," I said.

"She's come back with me," Colton said. "Layla told me about Pappy's tombstone, and I'd like to talk to you about it."

"Of course, won't you come in?"

"Could I see the tombstone first?" he asked, abruptly.

"I suppose. Follow me."

The late morning was still cool, and a low, damp mist hovered over the cemetery and grounds as we walked around back and through the gate to Pappy's grave.

When we reached it, Colton stood in front of it, frowning. "This is extremely unusual. Why would you order a tombstone without the date of death on it?"

"I already told her. Layla, is it?" she asked, lifting her eyebrows and looking at me.

I nodded.

"We never received confirmation of the date, and leaving Pappy's grave unmarked would have been disrespectful. This was the only option," she continued.

"I see," Colton said, seeming unconvinced.

I stood next to Colton, watching Mrs. Pinley. Something about the way she talked struck me as odd. She didn't look at Colton when she answered him, and she didn't look at me either. I didn't trust her.

"Now, won't you come in and have a light brunch with me? I have tea and cucumber and cream cheese sandwiches. We always have appetizers on hand, you know, just in case," she said, tilting her head and looking at us as though we knew what she meant.

"That would be nice," I answered before realizing Colton was shaking his head.

"Well, maybe just for a little while," I said to placate him. I wanted to find out what was bothering me about Mrs. Pinley, and I was hungry after all of our running around.

We followed her back into the house and sat on faded, floral sofas in the living room while she fussed in the kitchen, telling us to wait and that she'd be out soon. Heavy, maroon drapes, tied back only slightly, smothered the small room and muted the natural light, making me feel entombed. I swallowed dryly, and when Mrs. Pinley returned with the refreshments, I gladly sipped the hot cup of tea she poured for me.

"I'm so glad you came. It gets lonely here, and it's always nice to have visitors," she said, maneuvering around a cat to sit on the sofa next to me.

"Thank you," I replied, watching Colton turn a finger sandwich around with his hand as though trying to decide what to do with it.

"How long have you lived here?" I asked, trying to make conversation. "I'm doing an article on the island, and I'm interested in its history."

"How nice," she answered. "I've lived here a long time. My husband and I raised our two daughters here, but they grew up and left the island several years ago after he passed away. His father owned the funeral home before he did and his grandfather before that."

"How interesting," I said.

"Yes, it is in a way," she answered, looking down. She picked up a black cat and sat back, frowning as she smoothed its fur.

"I'm sorry. Did I say something wrong?" I asked.

"No, not at all. There's no way you could have known what happened, although Colton probably does," she continued.

Not knowing what to make of such an enigmatic statement, I turned to Colton for answers, but he was concentrating on his sandwich.

"What do you mean?" I asked her.

"I'll tell you because the way you ask questions in such a non-intrusive way makes me feel as though I can trust you," she said, sitting up straight.

I nodded. "Please. You can," I said.

She looked at Colton and then back at me. "My husband was the only survivor of the mass murder of his family in this very home," she said.

I gasped and put my hand to my mouth.

"What do you mean?" I asked, unable to comprehend what she had said in such a normal manner.

"Let me tell you what happened," she continued. "When my husband was a child, his family ran the funeral home. One day, an inmate from the island prison, who was said to have died of accidental food poisoning, was brought here by the prison staff during a ferocious gale. Since the weather made it impossible to access a coroner at the time, he was given a short service and buried in the cemetery. Several weeks later, the incident was reported to authorities, and the coroner asked that the body be exhumed for examination, which it was. However, the next day, when authorities arrived to do the autopsy, my husband's family was found dead in the house."

"How awful," I said, trying to overcome my shock and listen to the story.

"Yes, it was gruesome," she said.

Another black cat padded into the room, and she picked it up and put it on the sofa next to the other one. Both cats had bright, green eyes, and they looked at me with the intentness of evil spirits. I shivered.

"But there's more. A ghastly discovery was made when the investigators opened the coffin, which was still resting next to the grave. Claw marks and gouges were found on the interior sides and top. The only explanation was that the man inside had been erroneously buried alive. He was not dead at the time he was laid to rest, as had been thought."

"Oh, no." I didn't know how to react to what she was telling me, so I just sat there, staring at her, along with Colton, who had put down his sandwich.

"Yes, it's horrible. My husband was visiting friends at the time, thankfully, but it was still a terrible trauma for him. The murderer was never found, but it's said by the islanders that the ghost of the man buried alive arose from the coffin when it was exhumed and murdered the family during another terrible storm that night in retribution for the terrible suffering he endured. It is surmised that the murders were so heinous they were deemed slayings and that his tortured soul was not allowed to stay and haunt the house but was taken underground by the forces of evil. It's said that the ghost of his dripping-wet, half-decayed body only rises again to find other evil ghosts and those, alive or dead, he thinks were responsible for his death and force them down below with him to the darkness of permanent torment. And because of that, he's known as The Ghostslayer."

I let out a deep breath and gripped the arm of the sofa to steady myself.

"Oh, no," I said. "What a ghoulish story."

The cats were staring at me, and I thought I would faint from the evil I felt in the room. There were spirits here. I could feel it. Perhaps they were embodied by the cats. I had to leave. I began to stand.

Mrs. Pinley continued. "People have disappeared from the island before with whereabouts unknown, and their absence has often been attributed to him."

"Layla, are you alright?" Colton asked, standing and walking over to me.

"Yes, I'm sorry. I'll be fine. It's just such a dreadful story," I said.

Colton touched my hand and looked at Mrs. Pinley. "I think it's time we left. Thank you for the tea. I'll get back to you about the actual date of Pappy's death," he said, taking my arm. "If you find out more about it before I do, I'd appreciate it if you'd let me know. You can leave a message at the inn. Goodbye now."

"Oh dear, I've upset you, and I only wanted to tell you about the island," she said.

She looked like she was smirking, and I wondered if she

had told me the story in such a cold way on purpose. But I didn't know why she would do that unless it was to drive me away, which was very possible. There could be an underlying reason she didn't want me or Colton there. I just needed to determine what it was, but not now. I was too upset.

"No. Thank you. I'll be okay. I appreciate your candor. Perhaps I'll talk with you another time," I said, wondering if I would.

The mist was gone by the time we left, but the wind had picked up, and it howled around the corners of the house as we hurried back to the truck. Colton held the door open and helped me in. I breathed a sigh of relief when he closed the door behind me, feeling safe in the silence of the cab. It was a welcome respite from the fear I'd felt at hearing Mrs. Pinley's story. Colton hopped in, himself, and patted me on the leg.

"I don't know why she went on like that. It's a horrific story, and there was no reason for her to tell you about it. It's almost as though she was trying to scare you away."

"No, I'm glad she told me. It gives me more perspective on the island," I said, taking a deep breath. "Maybe the tragedy has something to do with why the prison was shut down."

"Maybe. Let's go home," he said, putting the truck in gear.

We headed out to the harbor road and back to the inn.

CHAPTER 7

I pulled my light jacket closer around me the next day to protect my camera as we rounded a curve in the harbor and motored past the lighthouse on our way into the open lake. Our tour boat splashed through the wake of an early-summer jet skier, and water sprayed over the bow and through the railings, spritzing our small group and inducing a chorus of lighthearted shouts. I had signed up for the tour after lunch with Colton, who had offered to come with me, and I was looking forward to learning more about the island. Copper Isle glowed, lustrous and bright, in the golden rays of the sun, making it hard to remember its dark side. But I did. I remembered it all, especially the story about the Ghostslayer.

Melanie called out over the loudspeaker. "Please note the Copper Isle Lighthouse off the port side. It was built in the mid-1800s, and its beacon has guided sailors safely home since then. The light was automated in the 1950s and can be seen for miles across the lake."

The loudspeaker became silent as the group looked toward shore. The lighthouse stood tall and majestic on the bluff, and I gazed up at it, wondering if Leif was in the lantern room looking down on us. He had acted so strangely when I visited that it made me wonder if he had something to do with Pappy's death. It outwardly appeared that he had arrived at the island after the murder, but that didn't mean that that was the case or that he wasn't involved in some way. I decided to keep an eye out for him.

"Do you see that rocky reef off-shore near the lighthouse?" Colton asked, putting his arm around me and pointing toward the bluff. I caught the light, beachy scent of suntan lotion from him as he touched my shoulder with his deeply tanned arm, and I leaned into him. It gave me a heady, sensual feeling of well-being to be near him.

"Yes," I said, raising my voice to be heard over the motor as it chugged through the low-rolling, blue waves.

"That's where the shipwreck in the ghost story about the sailors supposedly happened."

"Supposedly?" I asked, grasping the railing.

"I say that because there is a wreck near there, but no gold was ever found on it," he said.

I glanced behind me to make sure no one was listening. "How do you know?"

Colton looked at me for a moment. "That's what I've heard."

"Maybe they didn't search hard enough," I said.

Colton chuckled. "I think divers would have been very careful to check everywhere, given the amount of money involved. It was said to be more than $30,000, and that was over a century ago. I'm sure it would be worth a lot more now."

"Well, maybe they were lying, or maybe it was a different shipwreck."

"Maybe," he said.

I thought for a moment and looked around to make sure Stan was gone and that no one was near us before continuing. "Isn't it possible that something missed in a dive could be discovered years later as a wreck settles and that the story about the gold being found last summer was true? You must have heard Tyler's account of Pappy saying he found gold in a shipwreck," I said.

"Yes, I have. Everyone on the island has. It's possible, I guess. I wish it were true. The Chamber of Commerce and the island could have certainly used the money from the sale of the gold to bolster businesses and get the island's economy moving again. But police divers checked on the shipwreck at the coordinates on record at the time, and nothing was found. If the story is true, then what happened to the gold?"

"Good question," I said.

I looked down, not wanting Colton to see me thinking. I was convinced that Pappy's discovery of the gold and his subsequent murder were related. If I could prove that Tyler's story was true and find out what happened to the gold, I could find out what really happened to Pappy and who the real murderer was. I was sure of it. I looked back up and raised my camera to snap a few photos of the reef and the lighthouse before taking photos of the island. We followed the shoreline as we headed into deeper water. Cottages and cabins looked out over the lake from their vantage points high in the dunes behind the beach. The waterfront filled in with trees as we continued on, and I noticed a small cabin tucked back in the woods near the shore fronted with a wooden dock that reached far out into the lake.

"That's a cozy spot. I wonder who lives there," I said, feeling my arms prickle with goosebumps. Something struck me as strange, but I didn't know what it was.

"That's a rental, I think. A lot of people buy lakeside properties and rent them out for the summer."

"Who lives in them in the winter?" I asked.

"Sometimes the owners. Sometimes, they remain vacant until the next summer when they're rented out again. Why?"

"Just interested," I said, releasing my camera and letting

it hang from the strap around my neck. I wasn't taking any more pictures for now. I had to think.

If divers had found gold in the shipwreck and decided to steal it instead of reporting it to authorities, they would have needed a place to hide it until they took it off the island. It seemed probable that a cottage or, especially, a secluded cabin nearby would have been a convenient place to offload the coins quickly for storage and avoid possible detection. If there was a lot of gold, as Colton had said, it could have taken more than one dive to retrieve it all, and it might have been quite heavy and difficult to transport very far.

"Is someone there now?" I asked.

"I don't know. I don't see a boat. The dock's set up for the summer, but I don't see anyone," he said.

As I gazed at the cabin, goosebumps prickled the back of my neck. It could be because of what I was thinking about or maybe because of something I saw. It looked like a sled, but it seemed odd that there would be a sled at a cabin.

"I wonder if kids go sledding down the dunes in the winter," I said.

"I suppose they could," he said.

I looked more closely. "Is there a shadow in the woods behind the cabin?" I asked.

Colton raised his hand to his forehead to shield his eyes as he looked toward shore. "I don't see anything," he said. "Is it a shadow from the trees or a rain cloud?"

"I don't know," I said, nipping my lip and leaning toward the railing. "I'm not sure what it is."

The shadow moved and hung for a moment over the cabin before disappearing into the woods. It didn't look like a cloud. It looked like an entity. I shivered.

"It's gone now," I said, leaning back. "I don't know what it was from."

"Well, that's good," Colton said, dropping his hand. "I wouldn't want it to rain on a beautiful day like this and interrupt the tour. It's too much fun being with you."

He smiled in such a charming way that I couldn't help but smile back.

"Thanks. It's fun to be with you, too," I said, amazed at the swirling realm of pleasurable emotions I felt. It would take me a while to sort them out, but I was looking forward to doing so.

A soft breeze blew in from across the lake and rippled the sapphire-blue water and the tiny waves. Seagulls squawked as they soared overhead, and I relented and took another quick photo.

"If you look off the starboard side, you can see the ferry in the distance heading for the island from the mainland. It's the main form of transportation to the island in the summer, serving tourists and residents alike. You can wave if you want to," Melanie said over the loudspeaker.

Our group waved, and the people on the ferry waved back. I saw Melanie's children waving near us by the bow and remembered that school had let out for the summer last week. Tyler was being transferred before it resumed again in the fall, and I intended to solve the mystery before then. I shook my head to clear it and tossed my hair back, enjoying the wind in my hair. It helped me stop worrying about Tyler and Damon and start to feel free again, a feeling I was getting used to after being on the island for a while. The sense of freedom made me want to let my hair down and run barefoot through the sand. I could picture myself doing that with Colton someday soon. He brought out the free spirit in me.

"I'm so glad you came with me," I said to Colton.

"I'm glad, too. It's been a while since I've gone on the tour. Being with a beautiful woman makes it more interesting," he said, holding my gaze.

"Thank you," I said, feeling a delicious shiver.

Damon hadn't said anything like that to me in a long time, and I reveled in the fact that Colton found me attractive. Other than a few suspiciously anonymous phone messages at the desk, I hadn't heard from Damon, and I hoped he had given up on finding me and would leave me alone. I wanted to explore my new relationship with Colton in peace.

As the ferry passed us in the distance, I thought about the day I came to the island on it. They had weighed the cars before boarding to make sure the weight limit wasn't exceeded. If the ferry was the only way to commute to and from the island, it would have taken a number of trips to transport a heavy stash of gold coins to keep from exceeding the limit. It would have been risky as well, given the possibility of discovery, and they may have had to lay low for a while because of the commotion surrounding Pappy's murder. That would have kept them from transporting the gold by motorboat or any other way, too, given that the sudden appearance of old gold coins for sale on the mainland would have focused a lot of attention on them at the time. It could have been done, but it was also possible that the gold was still here. And if it was, I needed to find it.

"If Pappy had wanted to take diving partners to the shipwreck, who would he have called?" I asked, moving nearer to Colton again so as not to be overheard. Colton didn't seem to mind. In fact, he moved in closer to me.

"Could have been anyone. A lot of people on the island are divers. There are beautiful reefs and rock formations all around here," he answered.

"Like who, exactly?" I asked.

"Well, Bob and Larry both dive. They're in the Chamber of Commerce with me. Larry's especially good at it because he's such a good swimmer. Other members of the Chamber dive, too. Stan Larson owns a photography studio in town, and he dives to take underwater pictures."

"I think I met him when I was browsing through the shops on my first day here," I said.

"Did you? He's a nice guy. He's taken some great photos of the lighthouse and the shipwreck. Maybe you could compare notes. I'm sure he'd be happy to show you his underwater photos," he said.

"Maybe I will," I said. "I might find a clue. Photos can sometimes harbor clues in plain sight that wouldn't otherwise be seen."

"I suppose that's true," Colton said. "And, let's see, Melanie dives."

"Melanie?" I asked, feeling my eyebrows move up.

"Yes, why? Does that surprise you? Would you like to go out diving sometime?" he asked.

"Yes, I would. I'd like to see the shipwreck. I guess I was just surprised that Melanie dives for some reason. Have you ever gone with her?"

"Now that you mention it, no. But there's a first time for everything. I could take you out to the reef. I don't know if you want to go down to the ship, but I could show you where it is," he said.

"I'd like that," I said, smiling.

Melanie spoke again. "Please note the chapel on the hill off the port side. Memorial Hill Chapel was built in the 1840s by miners who came to the island during the Copper Rush in the area. It's no longer used except by tourists for photo opportunities."

I took advantage of her suggestion to snap another picture. Her children stood near the railing talking to each other, and it seemed strange to me that they didn't come over to talk to Colton. I decided to try to find out why.

"I see Melanie's children over there, and I wonder if I could get a picture of you with them," I said.

Colton shook his head. "That's not a good idea. Melanie asked me to keep my distance after we broke up."

"Why does she want you to keep your distance?" I asked.

Colton frowned and looked down. "I guess it has something to do with her new boyfriend, who, as it turns out, she may have been seeing for longer than she let on."

"You mean she was seeing him while she was seeing you?"

"Looks that way."

"I'm sorry," I said.

"Yeah, well, that's the way it goes sometimes. Anyway, I respect her wishes."

I wished I could say something to bring a smile back to his face, but I couldn't think of anything. He looked so hurt that I didn't know how I would ever be able to tell him that I was seeing him while I was still married. I hoped that he would understand that it was different and that my marriage was over, emotionally, if not legally, and not hold it against me.

"It doesn't seem fair to the children or you," I said instead.

Colton looked back up. "Thanks. I agree."

We continued around the island as Melanie called out points of interest. She mentioned, as Colton had before, that the entire island was considered a bird sanctuary and that islanders helped maintain it. That boded well for more photo opportunities for my calendar.

As the sun waned lower in the sky and cast a golden hue across the water, we motored back into the harbor and tied up at the dock. Our group chatted pleasantly and disembarked after thanking Melanie for the tour.

I walked with Colton to his truck, and on the way home to the inn, he asked me to meet him in the restaurant for dinner, which I agreed to. The first thing I did when I got back to my room was to shower and blow-dry my hair into a long, smooth, underturned bob. When I was through, I pulled on a white cotton shift that I hoped would accentuate my lightly tanned arms. The few clothes in the closet reminded me that I needed to go into town and do some shopping soon. I slipped on some low-heeled, gold strappy sandals and headed downstairs.

Colton was waiting for me at a candlelit table near a window overlooking the harbor. Twilight had descended, and boat lights twinkled in the purple dusk.

"You look stunning," he said, standing and pulling my chair out for me.

"Thank you. You look very nice yourself," I said, admiring his pressed gray chinos and navy shirt.

"I asked Martha for a table overlooking the harbor, and she's having the chef make the inn specialty for us, pan-fried whitefish. I hope that's okay."

"Perfect," I said, as Colton sat down across from me.

"Are you a red wine or a white wine person?" he asked.

"Oh, white wine with the fish, I guess."

"Great. We have a house, Chardonnay, that gets rave reviews."

"That sounds nice," I said.

I relaxed and looked around as Colton ordered the wine. There were a few other couples at distant tables and a family in a booth. Other than that, we had the restaurant to ourselves. And the view of the harbor was very romantic. I smiled and leaned toward him, but before I could say anything, a man walked in, talking loudly to Rosie and asking to see Melanie. I gasped as I realized who it was. Damon. He was here.

"I'm sorry, Mr. Wellington. Melanie left a message saying she was staying in town tonight and that you could meet her there. She said you'd know where to go," Rosie said to him.

"Mr. Wellington? Wasn't that the same name the clerk in the coroner's office had mentioned when I asked her about the death certificate? Why would Rosie call Damon by that name?

I was glad we were sitting in a dark corner. I turned my head toward the window so he wouldn't see me and tried to control my trembling so Colton wouldn't notice.

"Yes, I do. Thank you," Damon said.

I waited a minute and mumbled an answer to a question Colton asked me until it seemed safe to turn around again. When I did, Damon was gone.

"Is everything okay?" Colton asked.

He didn't seem to have noticed or at least wasn't bothered by Damon's entrance or exit. But he did seem to notice my distress.

"Yes, of course. I was just thinking about something," I said, trying to regain my composure.

"I hope you'll think about me," he said in a deep voice.

I smiled, hoping I didn't look flustered. Now wasn't the time to tell Colton about Damon or that he was my husband. "Of course, I will," I said.

He smiled back.

Rosie brought our meals, and I tried to enjoy my time with Colton and not think about Damon. But it was impossible. My mind was racing. What was he doing here? Did he know I was here? And how did he know Melanie? Had she told him about me? I didn't know what to think.

Colton made small talk as we ate, and when we finished, we sipped wine in the glow of the candlelight. But I was too nervous to stay for long.

"It's been a wonderful day but a long one. I had such a good time with you, but I'm afraid it's time for me to turn in. I hope you understand," I said.

"Yes. It has been a long day," Colton said, standing as I stood up. "May I walk you back to your room?"

"Yes, please."

Colton walked with me up the stairs and waited for me to

unlock the door.

"I had a good time. Can I see you tomorrow?" he asked.

When I nodded, he leaned in to kiss me. His lips were warm and soft, and I melted into his arms. It had been so long since I'd felt such pleasure at a man's touch.

"Tomorrow then?" he asked, when I opened my eyes.

"Yes," I said, nodding.

He smiled and headed for the stairs, and I turned and walked into my room, breathing a sigh of relief that I didn't have to pretend to be okay anymore. I wasn't. I was terrified. Damon was on the island, and he knew Melanie. And Tyler had never mentioned seeing him here. As I plopped down on the bed, my cell phone rang. I didn't recognize the number and let it go to voicemail, but whoever it was didn't leave a message. I checked the number again. The area code was the same as the one at the prison, and I suddenly felt the need to check on Tyler again. The social worker there had my number, and I couldn't think of anyone else it could be at this time of night unless Damon had another phone, which I didn't think he did. I dialed the number.

"This is Layla Devereaux," I said, when a woman answered. "My brother, Tyler, is an inmate there. Did anyone try to call me?"

"Just a moment," the woman said.

The social worker, whose voice I remembered, answered after a moment.

"Miss Devereaux?"

"Yes," I replied.

"I didn't call you, but there is a message that was left here for you by your brother."

"What is it? Is he out of disciplinary restriction?" I asked, frantically.

"Yes, but he's being transferred in two weeks instead of at the end of the summer. The message says, "Thanks for trying, sis.

I love you. Tyler."

"Oh, no. Why so soon?" I heard my voice wavering, but I didn't want to cry on the phone.

"I don't know the reason. I'm sorry, Miss Devereaux."

I swallowed hard.

"Thank you," I said, before hanging up.

I sat on the bed, holding my head. It couldn't be true. I thought I had the whole summer to solve the mystery. Now I only had two weeks? And I was going to have to fight Damon off, too? And ghosts? What was I going to do? Poor Tyler. I rocked back and forth, trying to think. I needed to step up my pace. I needed answers, and I needed them now. I gritted my teeth and made a resolution. Starting tomorrow, I was going to get them.

CHAPTER 8

The silence woke me later that night. It was a silence of nothingness, no crickets, no splashing waves, no leaves rustling in the breeze. Just quiet. I slipped out of bed and walked to the open window where a gossamer sliver of moon silvered the white pine trees and the placid, indigo lake. Why was there no sound?

I used the soft light of the moon to find my slippers and tie a robe around my thin nightgown before padding down to the kitchen. Martha had said the chef left snacks in the refrigerator for guests who got hungry at night, and I hadn't eaten much at dinner after seeing Damon walk in. Rosie calling him by a different name had upset me more than I realized, and it had taken me a long time to fall asleep. I was surprised when I woke up to find that I had slept at all. I had been afraid that Damon would knock on my door at any moment, but it didn't seem that he had. I tiptoed down the stairs and through the dimly lit hallway to the restaurant, peering through the dark and hoping I didn't run into Damon or a ghostly night visitor on my way.

The restaurant was quiet and eerie, too, with its empty tables and booths and stools upended for the night on the bar. The tinseled night glimmered through the windows, and its beauty, or its ghostliness, took my breath away. I rubbed my arms and stood for a moment, gazing at the lake, before pressing through the vinyl doors and shuffling into the stainless steel surroundings of the kitchen. I didn't see a light switch, but the ice machine on the refrigerator glowed with a dim, blue light. I shuffled toward it but stopped and turned when I heard footsteps coming from the restaurant. Who else would be up at this hour? I moved back toward the doors and raised up on tiptoes to peek through a semi-frosted circle of glass on one. There was no one there. Or was there? A movement near the window caused me to blink and look more closely. I put my hand to my mouth to stifle a gasp.

The apparition of a man wavered in the shadows of the moon, fading in and out in a translucent whisper of light. He was peering through a telescope that wavered in the same way, looking at the stars above the dark harbor. I lowered my heels and inched the door open to see him better, being careful not to make any noise. He was dressed in a ship captain's uniform and wore a visored hat. And he had a full beard and mustache. I watched him scan the harbor, looking for something. I knew not what.

I don't know how long I stayed there, hunched over and shivering, before another apparition appeared. He was outside the window, screaming silently as he flailed in seemingly invisible water. He reached for the captain, who lowered his telescope and reached toward him before they both disappeared into the silent darkness of the night.

I let out a strangled breath and opened the door further to look around the restaurant and make sure they were gone. I jumped when I saw a shadow by the bar. It didn't look like an apparition. It looked like a person.

"Who is it? Who's there?" I called out.

I waited tensely for an answer. After a moment, a man responded.

"It's Andy. Who are you?"

"Layla," I answered tentatively. At least it wasn't Damon.

"I'm a guest here. I think I've seen you before telling ghost stories around the campfire."

"Oh, yes," he said, as he walked closer. "I remember. You're Colton's new girlfriend, aren't you? He told me you were a photographer doing an article on the island."

I was a little frightened to talk to a man in the dark restaurant but flattered that he thought I was Colton's girlfriend. And Martha had vouched for Andy and his wife when I first got here so I relaxed a little. Since I wasn't sure how to correct him about my being Colton's girlfriend, I didn't.

"Yes, that's right," I said.

He held a strange, black instrument in his palm that emitted a blue light from a small, square screen, and I was instantly intrigued. But before I asked about it, I wanted to know if he had seen what I saw.

"Did you see anything in the restaurant just now?" I asked, not wanting to let on that I'd seen something someone else might not have seen but taking a chance that, as a ghost hunter, he could validate my perceptions.

"You mean, like ghosts by the window?" He grinned, his face glowing eerily in the blue light.

"Well, yes," I said, pleasantly surprised to find a kindred spirit who noticed things outside of the normal realm of senses. That didn't happen often, if at all, as far as I could remember.

"That was the captain and one of the sailors. They're quite popular with the guests when they appear. They're usually inside, but sometimes not. I came down to look for them when my digital thermometer showed an excessive dip in air temperature, which signals paranormal activity. And there they were," he said.

"They're amazing," I said.

"Yes. That's why Kirsten and I come back every summer to see them and the other ghosts. They were very active late last summer, and we had quite a few sightings. It seems to have settled down a bit this year, but not much."

I pondered that for a moment. "Could paranormal activity increase if the site where it originated was disturbed?" I asked.

"It could," Andy said.

"That makes me wonder if the shipwreck near the rocky reef was disturbed last summer and agitated them."

"That's a thought. I'll have to think about that. I've seen the captain more lately than in any of the past summers that Kirsten and I have come here. He keeps watch for storms, and sometimes, he appears to warn the guests that a storm is coming. That doesn't seem to be the case tonight, though. The harbor and winds are calm. And he's said to warn other ghosts, as well, to watch for the Ghostslayer who comes for evil ghosts during thunderstorms."

"What does that mean?" I asked. I shivered despite the fact that the air had warmed slightly in the last few minutes. Seeing Damon and apparitions appear all in one night seemed to have affected me more than I realized.

"It's said that the Ghostslayer rises from the underground to slay evil ghosts and some evil people to take them down below with him."

"That's terrifying," I said.

"Yes," he agreed. "It is."

We stood in silence as I pondered what he'd told me.

"What brought you down here? Did you hear something?" Andy asked after a while.

He slipped his thermometer into the pocket of his cargo pants and looked at me.

"No, I was looking for something to eat. Would you care to join me?" I asked.

"Yes, now that you mention it. Chef Dillon made cherry tarts tonight that I don't think I can live without. I'm sure there are leftovers."

We found the tarts and some cold milk in the refrigerator, then sat at a small table in the kitchen alcove to eat. I waited for him to finish eating before asking him something I'd been wondering about.

"Have you ever seen the Ghostslayer?" I asked.

He looked at me over the top of his glass as he took a sip of milk.

"No, but I've heard about him from people who have. You don't want to be around when he shows up. I would because it's what I do, but it's not for a layperson to see."

"Why not?"

"Because he's from another world. And the stories of his returns to this world and captures of evil ghosts and some evil people are not speakable."

"I see," I said, trembling.

Knowing that a demon like the Ghostslayer haunted such a beautiful island was frightening. My feelings alternated between fear and curiosity about him. I wondered if I would see him sometime, and I didn't know if I wanted to.

I thought for a moment. "Have you seen the ghost that Martha talks about? The night stalker that scares her and the guests?"

Andy grimaced. "Oddly enough, I haven't. She reported the incidents to me afterwards, but I was never aware of a temperature drop or electromagnetic activity or anything that signaled paranormal activity during the times they happened."

"Hmm. So it couldn't have been a ghost," I said.

Andy shook his head. "Not according to my instruments. But she's seeing something or someone. There's no doubt about that."

I pondered his answer for a moment. "Could it be someone pretending to be an evil ghost to scare her and the guests and others on the island away?" I asked, thinking of what I had intuited on the morning after arriving on the island and hearing the disembodied voice.

"Could be," he said. "Although I don't know why someone would do that. Do you?"

"Maybe," I said. "But it's just a theory. I think the shipwreck and the story about gold being found last summer could have something to do with it, though. You did hear that gold coins were found, didn't you?"

"Yes, but as far as I know, it was just a story," he said.

"I think it's true," I said. "And I want to prove it. Would you be interested in taking a motorboat out to the reef with me in the morning? I'm taking nature photos for my article, and I plan to explore the dive site and maybe a cabin nearby, as well. I'm searching for something to prove my theory, and I'd love to have a paranormal expert come along. I'll try to get Colton to go, too."

"If it would help get rid of the night stalker Martha is dealing with, I'm up for it," he said. "Kirsten and I have been coming to the inn every summer for a long time, and it's sad to see Martha in such a state over this."

"Good," I said, breathing a sigh of relief that I had a plan and making a note to call Colton at dawn and ask him to go with me to the reef. Things were coming together to help me solve the mystery, and I hoped Tyler could hold on until I did.

"Well, shall we head back to our rooms? It looks like the captain's gone for the night," Andy said, taking his plate to the sink.

"Sure."

I set my plate next to his and followed him out of the kitchen. As we passed the reception area, the exterior door opened, and Melanie walked in, looking slightly disheveled. I stopped to talk to her, hoping to find out what was going on between her and Damon, and told Andy to go on up without me, which he did.

"Is everything alright?" I asked her as I walked into the reception area.

She tossed her purse on the desk, kicked off her high-heeled sandals, and plopped into the chair after turning on the lamp.

"I wouldn't say that, no," she said, leaning back and adjusting the strap on her light summer dress. "Is it cold in here?"

"It's warming up," I said. "What's wrong?"

She looked at me for a moment. "I'll tell you because, after hearing about your problems with your husband, who, from the picture you showed me, could almost be my boyfriend's younger brother with the same dark hair and good looks, I think you'll understand."

"Please, go ahead," I said, not sure what to make of her seemingly naive statement about Damon. The picture had been from five years ago, but he hadn't changed that much, although he did have shorter hair and a more weathered-looking face. I wondered if she really thought he was a different person than her boyfriend or if she just subconsciously made up a story for herself to believe, like I used to do when confronted with things about him that didn't make sense.

"Gregory, the man I'm seeing, has business dealings all over the world, including on the island, and it's hard for him to find time to see me. When he does, we usually argue, but he's such a handsome, exciting man that I don't want to give him up. I'm sure I can make it work, but sometimes, it gets me down."

I couldn't believe what I was hearing. "Your boyfriend's name is Gregory?" I asked, trying not to let my mouth drop open.

"Yes. Gregory Wellington. Do you know him?"

"No, I guess not," I said, letting out a breath. "I thought I did, but I don't know him at all."

"He stays on the island sometimes but usually at the Copper Isle Hotel in town near the harbor. That's where he is now, but he's leaving again tomorrow. At least I saw him for a little bit," she said, putting her elbows on the desk and resting her chin in her palms.

"Yes, of course. I'm sure that's very difficult for you. Long distance relationships are hard," I said, trying to sound understanding.

I heard myself speaking in echo as though I was floating outside of my body. Even though our marriage was emotionally over, the fact that Damon had obviously been cheating on me and had another name and another life was overwhelming. Despite my having had suspicions, I had loved him at one time. I wasn't sure I could handle Melanie telling me more, but I couldn't stop myself from asking.

"What does he do when he comes here?" I asked.

"I don't know exactly. Business of some sort. I think he owns the copper mine here on the island, among other things. He makes a lot of money, but he doesn't really tell me how," she said.

"Yeah, I know the type," I said. I paused. "Does he know anyone at the inn?" I asked, thinking of Tyler last summer.

"I don't think so. As I said, he stays in town. Why?"

"No reason. Just wondering if he does business at the inn," I said, taking a deep breath to calm myself.

It seemed that Melanie had been or was involved with three men in my life - Damon, Tyler, and Colton. I wasn't sure how to feel about that other than to be protective of Tyler and Colton. I wasn't sure why.

"Say, would I be able to rent a motorboat or something in the morning? I'd like to go out to the reef and take pictures," I said, changing the subject.

"What? Oh, yes. I can drive you, if you'd like. It looks like it's going to be a nice weekend, and I'm sure we could find others who'd like to go, too."

I wasn't sure I wanted her to after hearing about her and Damon, but I might be able to glean more information from her about him and about the police dive on the shipwreck last summer.

"That'd be great. Can we make it a diving trip?" I asked, putting a lilt in my voice.

"Only if you already dive. I don't train people," she said.

"I don't want to dive, but Colton might. He'll probably come with me," I said, watching her face for a reaction.

There wasn't one overall, although her eyes appeared to flicker.

"Maybe I'll dive, too," she said. "I haven't been to the reef in a while."

"Great. See you in the morning, then?" I said.

"Sure. Have a good night. I'm going to get something to eat and go up later."

"There are tarts in the refrigerator," I said.

"I know," she said. "That's what I'm after."

I smiled in what I hoped was an engaging manner and said goodnight before heading upstairs. When I got to my room, I locked the door and sat on the bed, thinking about the events of the evening. I wasn't scared, exactly. I was more bewildered than anything else. It seemed as though my sense of reality had been turned upside down. Not only were there ghosts on the island and people who saw them in the same way that I did, but there was a man who claimed to be my husband at home, staying here under a different identity. I didn't know what to think. And I didn't feel like sleeping. I felt like finding out why Damon was on the island.

Suddenly, I knew what I had to do. I had to drive into town and confront him. I leapt up and headed for the closet to dress just as someone knocked on the door. Who could it possibly be at this hour? The knocks came again, more frantically. When I opened the door, Martha nearly fell into the room.

"What is it? What happened?" I asked, taking her arm and leading her to the small sofa near the window.

She wore a lavender robe and slippers and had a grey-satin eye mask pushed up on her forehead. She sat down heavily and touched a tissue to her nose.

"Oh, my dear, I don't know what to do. He came after me again. He was moaning and yelling at me in a loud whisper to leave the island. Didn't you hear him?"

"Who? The night stalker?" I asked.

"Yes. Did you see him?"

"No. When did it happen?"

"An hour or so ago. He was outside my window. I waited to make sure he was gone before coming over. I'm still not sure it's safe," she said, glancing toward the door.

I walked over and locked it. I needed to protect Martha now. Confronting Damon could wait.

"Outside your window?" I asked.

"Yes, there's a small gable over the porch, and it looked like he was on the roof there. Didn't you hear him?" she asked again.

"No, I was downstairs having a late-night snack. I only got back to my room a little while ago. I'm surprised someone else didn't, though," I said.

"Maybe only I did because he was right outside my window. It was locked, and the curtains were pulled, so I peeked through them. I couldn't see him very well, but he sounded the same as always. I don't know what to do. It makes it worse that the police don't believe me, so I can't call them, and there's nothing else I can do. The last time I called and they came out, they looked like they wanted to put me in jail because they couldn't find him. But what could they really do about a ghost, anyway?" she asked.

She was trembling violently, and I pulled a quilt off the bed to tuck around her. "Here. This will keep you warm. Try to relax," I said.

"Thank you," she said, pulling it close and snuggling under it.

"I'm calling Colton," I said.

"No, don't bother him. I'll be okay," she said.

"I think it's important that he knows it happened again," I said, calling his number.

"Perhaps you're right."

Colton answered on the fourth ring. "Layla?" he asked, sounding concerned. I supposed that was because it was the middle of the night and because I didn't usually call him.

"Yes, it's me. Your mother is with me in my room. She just had another incident with the stalker, and she's not feeling well," I said.

"I'll be right over," he said. "Thanks for letting me know."

I hung up.

"He's coming right over," I told Martha, who appeared visibly relieved. "Would you like some tea while we're waiting?"

"Yes, please," she said.

I ran hot water through the coffee pot on the counter and dipped lemon tea bags in cups before turning to hand her one. She was curled up sound asleep with her eye mask pulled over her eyes and her head on a throw pillow. I set a cup on a table near her and took mine with me over to the window. I peeked out at the still night and scanned the porch roof and gables of the inn. To my relief, nothing was there. Whoever was out there was gone now. I went over and sat on the bed and made a few notes on my iPad about photos for calendars. As I finished my tea, there was another knock on the door. It was Colton this time.

"She's sleeping," I said, putting my finger to my lips as I let him in.

"How is she?" he asked, glancing at her as he moved toward the sofa.

"Pretty shaken up. Sleep is probably the best thing for her," I said.

"Yes. I'm sure you're right. What did she say?" he asked.

"That the night stalker was outside her window harassing her again."

"Outside her window?" he asked.

"Yes, on the roof."

"This is really getting bad. I'm going to call security companies in the morning. I don't know how to ask for protection from ghosts, but we have to do something," he said.

"Maybe it's not a ghost," I said, touching his arm. "Maybe it's a person."

He looked at me, and his eyes darkened. "You could be right. I'll check around outside and see if I can find anything. Try to get some sleep, won't you?" he said, heading for the door. He turned and glanced at Martha before glancing back at me as he put his hand on the doorknob. "Thanks for being there for her, for us. It's a great help, and I know Martha appreciates it."

"I'm glad to help," I said. "I'm glad your mother came to me, and I hope we can bring an end to whoever or whatever is behind this."

Colton nodded as he left. I closed the door behind him, turned off the light, and climbed into bed as I listened to Martha snore quietly on the sofa. I believed her. I knew what it was like to not be believed when something bad happened, and I didn't want that to happen to her. The fact that Colton believed her, too, filled me with a welcome sense of security that had always been missing in my life. Something about him made me feel safe. I pulled the covers around me and snuggled in. I needed to get some rest before the busy day I had planned, solving the mystery and searching for gold. I also needed to make sure that Damon was leaving the island, as Melanie had said. My emotions over finding out my suspicions of him were true had settled down, and I decided confronting him wasn't such a great idea, after all. At least, it wasn't now, especially if he didn't know I was here. I might be able to find out more about him if I kept my presence a secret. And I had to find a way to help Colton protect his mother.

"Good night, Martha. Sleep well," I whispered as I closed my eyes to sleep.

CHAPTER 9

Colton waved at me as he untied the diving boat from the harbor dock in the morning. I had just arrived to join the group he and Melanie must have put together for the dive on the shipwreck. I waved back and shouted 'hello' as I scurried down the dock toward them, knowing I was a little late. Martha seemed to have recovered after a good night's sleep and returned to her room, and Colton had called me soon afterwards, wondering about her. I told him that she seemed much better and mentioned the dive, and he agreed to meet me at the boat. It had taken me a while to arrange things with Melanie, call Andy and Colton with a cast-off time, and go down to the restaurant for breakfast, where I was relieved to see Martha taking charge of things in her usual way. I told her I was glad she was feeling better and drove to the harbor after that.

"Watch your step," Colton said, reaching for my hand.

I smiled as I hopped past him onto the deck, following the others. It was a beautiful day for a sail with a blue sky and moderate temperatures. I was excited to see what we found on the dive, too. Maybe the divers would uncover clues that had been missed last summer that would prove there had been gold on the shipwreck and provide leads as to what happened to it. Also, if we found something unusual or historic, it could make for a very interesting article. I was hoping to snap some good photos for my calendar, too.

Melanie was near the cabin, helping people stow their gear and guiding them to their seats. I was surprised to see Susie and Bobby there, too, having assumed that only adults would go on a diving excursion, but there they were. I'd found out from Colton that Susie was a precocious writer and had skipped a grade in school. She was writing something down in a flower-print journal, and Bobby was sitting next to her, snapping on a lifejacket. Susie glanced up, saw me, and said something to Bobby, who glanced up as well, but they both looked back down before I could acknowledge them. I got a strange feeling again.

I waved to Andy and to Kirsten, who had also wanted to come, and nodded at Bob and Larry, who I recognized as Colton's friends from the parade. They were putting on black wetsuits. Stan Larson, the photographer I'd met in town, was standing by the railing, holding a camera, and he waved when he saw me. I smiled back. His blond, curly hair whipped around his plump, sun-reddened face in the breeze, but he didn't seem to notice as he turned into the wind to snap some photos. I was pleasantly surprised that Melanie and, seemingly, Colton, as well, had been able to find three other divers to go with us on such short notice. We made a sizable group.

The morning was crisp and clear with a light breeze, and I breathed deeply of the fresh lake air and sighed. It was a perfect day for the first part of our treasure hunting expedition, whether Colton knew that's what it was about or not. I planned to tell him later and take photos along the way to disguise my true intention. Although Colton had said the police didn't find gold on their dive on the shipwreck last summer, I wanted to hear firsthand from him and the other divers what they found there today. Maybe there were clues the police missed as to where the gold was now. If the police didn't think Tyler's story was true and had only dived on the shipwreck to prove the gold didn't exist, they might not have been earnestly looking for answers as to where it was taken or by whom. That's what I was looking for.

I walked over to the railing and stood near Stan to snap photos of a pair of geese and some wood ducks floating near the dock. Colton finished casting off, and Melanie announced our departure. I looked up as the boat headed toward the open lake. The lighthouse shimmered majestically on the bluff in the late-morning sun, and I wondered if Leif was in the lantern room, watching us from afar.

"It's a beautiful day for this," Colton said, walking up beside me.

"Yes, I'm so glad you came with me," I said, tucking a recalcitrant strand of hair into my ponytail, which had become my new, casual, island hairstyle. That, along with a pair of white shorts and a dotted, light-blue windbreaker, completed my laid-back look. I was getting used to going casual, and I liked it. I think Colton did, too, given the way he had looked at me over the last few days.

He looked out over the lake and then leaned in nearer to me.

"I haven't had any luck yet finding security for the inn," he said, lowering his voice. "I may check into it again later, but I'm considering heading in a different direction."

"What do you mean?" I asked, unsure of what to make of his tone. He sounded very serious.

He hesitated. "I'll tell you after the dive. Let's just say I'm not going to wait for the sheriff to protect us anymore. I'm taking matters into my own hands."

"What do you mean?" I asked, worried about the serious look on his face.

"I'll tell you later," he said. "Let's try to enjoy the day."

"All right," I said, slowly, turning to gaze at the lake. I

wondered what he was referring to, but it was obvious I'd have to wait to find out.

The black rocks of the reef jutted out in the distance, and several seagulls swooped and dived around them. I rapidly snapped more photos as we drew nearer, exhilarated by the freedom of the open water. Colton dropped anchor while we were still a ways away, and I commented on the fact to Stan, who had positioned himself next to me and was taking photos of the reef.

"Shouldn't we be closer to the reef?" I asked. "Or is this where the shipwreck is?"

"We don't want to get too close and risk damaging the boat by running into underwater rocks from the reef," he said, answering my question. "This is a safe distance to roll backwards into the water from. That's how I usually get in. The shipwreck is right nearby. Are you diving?"

"No, but I'm interested to see what everyone finds in the shipwreck."

"There's not much to see. I dive to take photos of fish and underwater plant life. I took a beautiful shot of a colorful school of bluegills that sells quite well at my shop, and I have pictures of sub-surface sunlight and underwater shadows that sell well, too. I'm hoping to take more of those. I better get ready," he said, lifting his camera strap over his head and turning to go. "Nice talking to you."

"You, too, I'm sure," I replied.

It seemed odd that he turned the conversation away from the shipwreck in such a dismissive way after I'd expressed interest instead of mentioning the commercial photographs of it I'd seen in his shop or sharing his knowledge. I wondered if there was a reason he was so discreet. Maybe he had heard the story about the gold being found there and felt uncomfortable discussing it with a newcomer. Perhaps someone else would be more forthcoming. I followed him back to where Colton, Melanie, and the others were donning their fins and oxygen tanks.

"Keep an eye on the kids, won't you?" Melanie asked, addressing Andy, Kirsten, and me. "They'll be good. They've been out here before."

"Sure," I said.

"Looks like seagulls are nesting on the reef. Maybe you can get some good pictures while we're gone," she added.

"Thanks. I'll try," I said. "By the way, I heard rumors that gold was found on the shipwreck last summer. Any chance you know anything about that? It might make an interesting angle for a story. I was hoping you might check the cargo hold for disturbances while you're down there and look for anything that seems out of place." I was referring to clues to the whereabouts of the gold but also to paranormal activity.

There was a sudden silence on the boat, and I looked around to see Stan, Bob and Larry staring at me.

"Did I say something wrong?" I asked, seeing their stiff expressions.

"There was no gold," Melanie said after a moment. "There was never any gold. That was a rambling story told by a desperate murderer to save himself from justice."

I looked around again to see the others looking away and down before glancing at Colton, who must have seen the fear and insecurity I felt in my eyes. He jumped to my defense.

"She didn't ask for your opinion about Tyler. She only asked if you knew about the gold," he said to Melanie.

"Well, I don't. None of us do, do we?" she asked.

The others shook their heads, but I couldn't help but wonder why she was so adamant about her answer and why she had included them in it, as well.

"It's okay. You can answer. I won't put it in my article if you don't want me to," I said, attempting to assuage the situation.

Melanie's face turned a light shade of purple.

"There is no gold," she spat out. "There's nothing to put in your article."

"Melanie," Colton said, sharply.

"Colton, I can't believe you're siding with her and a convicted murderer," she said.

"Please, forget I asked," I said, frightened by the sudden difference in Melanie and surprised that she had referred to the gold in the present tense. "Go on your dive and have a good time."

"Yes, of course, that's what we'll do," Colton said, taking her arm and leading her toward the side of the boat.

She gave me a parting scowl before securing her face mask and striding into the water with Colton following her. After a moment, the others followed, doing backward rolls. I waited until the surface calmed down before turning and walking back to join Andy, Kirsten, and the children by the cabin.

"I hope they have a good dive. I didn't mean to say the wrong thing," I said to Kirsten, hoping for understanding but not knowing what her reaction would be. She had an aura of calm about her and looked like someone I could confide in. Her long, black hair was tied behind her ears with a navy bandana, and she wore several gold chains around her neck and gemstone rings on her long, slim fingers. For some reason, I felt a psychic connection to her.

"Of course you didn't," Kirsten said. "Everyone on the island is still on edge about the murder, and Melanie's no exception. I'm sure she'll be fine later."

"I hope you're right," I said, not feeling sure about that at all.

Melanie obviously still had strong feelings about Tyler. If she believed he killed someone, that was certainly understandable, but it seemed like there was more to it than that, like a sense of betrayal or something else. Whatever it was, I hoped she wouldn't take it out on Colton.

Kirsten moved toward the railing and paused as she looked toward the shore. Her eyebrows furrowed, and she appeared to be contemplating something.

"Do you see that?" she said, after a moment, pointing toward the cabin in the woods that I'd seen on the boat tour the other day.

"What?" I asked.

"The dark shadow there, hovering over the cabin."

I squinted to look more closely. I did see something. "Yes, what could that be? A storm cloud?" I asked. It seemed odd that a cloud would hang that low.

"No. Something else, I think." She closed her eyes. "I'm getting a strange feeling. Something's there, Andy. Something bad," she said, opening her eyes and looking toward the cabin again.

I followed her gaze. A cold chill hit me all of a sudden.

"There is something bad there," I said. "I feel it, too."

Kirsten looked at me and nodded. "Yes, I can feel that you have the sight, as I do. What could it be, Andy?" she asked.

"It's too far away to register on my instruments, but I'll make a note for us to check on it," Andy said. "I'd like to know what it is."

"Me, too," Kirsten said.

"Me, as well," I added.

Andy lowered his gaze and held another strange-looking instrument over the water.

"I'm registering something," he said. "It's an EMF 2, no, wait, it's an EMF 3. It appears there is paranormal activity in this area at this time."

"You mean there are ghosts on the shipwreck?" I asked, gasping.

"Could be. I'm going to check around the rest of the boat. Kirsten, what do you think?" he asked.

She paused and closed her eyes again. "Yes, I feel that there is something here. I don't know what it is, but it's not malevolent."

"That's good. Do you want to come with me?" he asked her.

"Sure. We'll be back in a little bit," she said, nodding toward me and following Andy.

I nodded back and watched them walk away. Kirsten seemed to be even more in touch with her psychic abilities than I was. Her work as a ghost hunter probably helped her develop them and connect with her intuitions. She seemed like an interesting person to know, and I hoped to find out more about what she knew about the supernatural. I turned and walked over to Susie, who was still writing something in her journal with Bobby sitting next to her.

"I've been meaning to introduce myself," I said when I reached them. "I'm Layla. I'm a writer, too," I said to Susie, "and a photographer."

"We know. My mom told us," Susie said, tersely.

"Oh, good," I replied, trying to think of something to say next, but Susie came up with something first.

"My mom liked Colton before you did, and I liked him better than her new boyfriend or her old boyfriend. I wish you'd go away so she can get him back," she said, peevishly.

"Yeah," Bobby said.

"Oh, well." Now, I really couldn't think of anything to say. I decided to try a different approach.

"I might not be here for that long. Colton's just being nice to me. Why don't you like her new boyfriend?" I asked, saving my curiosity about why she didn't like Tyler for another time. I was more interested in Damon right now.

"He said he was going to get us a husky puppy, and he never did. He's mean," she said.

"Yeah," Bobby agreed.

"That wasn't very nice of him," I said.

"And he gets in fights with my mom," Susie said.

"What do they fight about?" I couldn't help asking, even though I knew it was overstepping my bounds with Melanie to talk to her kids about Damon. But I had to find out what was going on.

"I don't know, but she always ends up doing what he tells her to. Yesterday, he told her she was going to end up at the lighthouse like the doctor if she didn't," she said.

"What doctor?" I asked. There wasn't a doctor at the lighthouse as far as I knew, and I wondered what Damon could have been referring to.

"I don't know. This is boring. I have to finish writing my detective story now," she said, looking down.

"Yeah," Bobby said.

"Okay. Well, I hope we can be friends."

She scribbled in her journal without answering while Bobby glared at me. I turned and walked away, making a note to talk to her again. She seemed very aware of what was going on around her, and that could be useful. Her eavesdropping and detecting abilities could come in handy, too. I went to find Andy and Kirsten, but before I did, the lake churned suddenly, and Bob surfaced near the boat. He yanked out his breathing apparatus and yelled to me.

"Colton's in trouble! We're bringing him up now. Come and help pull him onboard."

I ran to the side of the boat, hearing the kids running on deck close behind me and seeing Andy and Kirsten running from the other direction.

"What happened?" I yelled when Stan and Larry surfaced,

holding Colton under the arms.

"Get him onboard. He's turning blue!" Bob shouted.

We dragged him on deck and laid him prone after removing his oxygen tanks. Andy started mouth-to-mouth resuscitation, and I dropped to my knees beside him, compressing Colton's chest as the other divers, including Melanie, pulled themselves onboard.

"Please make it. Please make it," I murmured, coordinating Andy's breaths with my compressions. "Take his fins off," I shouted, wondering why no one else helped. "And his gloves."

After a moment, Stan did as I asked while we continued the rescue efforts.

"What happened?" I asked again.

"I don't know," Bob said, breathing heavily. He signaled that he saw something and swam around to the other side of the shipwreck. When he didn't return for a while, I swam around after him and found him lying on the bottom without his breathing apparatus. I started to shove it back in but stopped when I realized he was unconscious. I dragged him up through the water until Stan and Larry saw me and helped bring him to the surface. I don't know what could have happened."

I stopped compressing for a moment and waited for Andy to do breaths. Melanie was standing off to the side, hugging her children, who looked terrified.

"Where was Melanie?" I asked.

"Farther down the reef, I think. She didn't see him," Bob said.

"What did he find?" I asked.

"I have no idea. I didn't see anything," Bob said, brushing water out of his beard.

"Me either," Larry added.

I tried not to glare at him even though I didn't understand why they couldn't have gotten to Colton and brought him up sooner, especially since Colton had told me Larry was on the swim team in high school. It didn't make sense.

"He's coughing," Andy said, sitting back as Colton choked and spit out water.

He opened his eyes, turned on his side, and sat up slowly.

"What happened?" he asked, hoarsely.

"Are you okay?" I asked, touching his arm and fighting to hold back tears.

"I don't know. What happened?" he asked again.

We hoped you could tell us that," Stan said. "Glad you're okay, buddy. You gave us a scare."

I stared up at Stan, wondering how he could say that when he hadn't helped resuscitate him. Something seemed very wrong. They were all standing around looking at each other.

"The last thing I remember was hitting my head on something or something hitting me on the head. I don't know what it was," Colton said.

"I do," Larry said. "It was the damn ghosts. Everyone says they're down there, and they're right. Isn't that right, Andy?" he asked, giving me a sideways look. He must have seen my expression and realized how I felt about him.

Andy stood up quickly. "I wouldn't go so far as to say that. We don't know that the ghosts on the shipwreck are violent, and I don't think we should jump to conclusions. As far as I know, the ghosts here have always been a pretty nice group. Let's get Colton back to shore and discuss this another time, shall we?"

Larry nodded slowly as the others agreed. Melanie took off her wetsuit and headed for the cabin with the kids. Susie looked like she was going to go to Colton, but Melanie pulled her back with her and walked away. I stood next to Colton as he unzipped his wetsuit, trying not to make eye contact with anyone else. It occurred to me that people who didn't like someone could pretend to rescue him and bring him to safety if they had hurt him and thought he was already dead. And they might blame his misfortune on ghosts.

"I'm not sure you're safe with these people," I said quietly, glancing at their averted faces.

"What do you mean? They're my friends," he said, rubbing his head.

I didn't see disbelief in his eyes so much as bewilderment.

"I'm not so sure," I answered, thinking I should keep my thoughts to myself but unable to stop myself from warning Colton. My arms felt prickly, and I knew there was something wrong.

"Did you call them about the trip today, or did Melanie?" I asked.

"Melanie did, I guess. Why?"

"You didn't call any of them?" I asked.

"No. Is something the matter?" he asked.

"I'm not sure. I'll talk to you later. But I wish I'd known that before we went out. Take deep breaths, and try to relax. We'll be home before you know it," I said.

I stayed close to him as Melanie drove us toward the harbor. A drop of light bounced off the deck, and I looked up to see the lighthouse glinting in the sun. The reef would have been fully visible from there, and I wondered if Leif was watching us and had seen what happened. I glanced at the silent group one more time before leaning closer to Colton. It was time for us to both make it home together and safely, I hoped.

CHAPTER 10

After the diving incident, we made it back to the inn. Colton stayed in a room overnight at Martha's insistence. She had been horrified at what happened and wanted to keep an eye on him, not only to make sure he was okay, she said, but to keep him from any further harm. She seemed as worried about his overall safety as I was, although she didn't elaborate as to why. It took me until the next day to recover. I was shaking and nauseous all night. There was definitely an aura of iniquity surrounding the event, and it affected me badly.

I knocked on Colton's door in the afternoon. He opened it, looking better than he had yesterday but sporting a purple bruise on his temple that looked like it continued past his hairline.

"Oh my goodness, that looks sore," I said, walking past him as he gestured for me to come in. "Are you doing okay?"

He still had his robe on over his jeans, and it looked like he'd been resting in bed before I came over.

"Not too bad. I'll be all right. I hope you've recovered. You looked pretty scared on the boat," he said.

"I was," I said. "I was afraid we were going to lose you. But you pulled through. I'm so relieved."

"Thanks. It was due to you and Andy. I can't thank you enough," he said, earnestly.

"Of course. It's good to see you up and walking around today. I hope you're feeling better."

"I am. But let's talk about the dive," he said, sounding very serious. "I want to show you something."

"Sure," I said, following him to the nightstand, where he opened the drawer and pulled something out.

"I found this on the bottom of the lake and put it in my diving pouch right before I blacked out. I think you should look at it and tell me what you think," he said.

He handed me a blue, rubbery glove with a white outline of a lighthouse on it. It was puckered and torn and appeared unusable. It looked like someone had lost it."

"It's a diving glove," he said as I turned it over and inspected it.

"Is it? It has a lighthouse logo on it," I said.

"Yes. It could be a specialty item put out by the tour groups. Take a look at the tag inside."

I pinched the tag between my fingertips and looked closely.

"It has L. D. written in black Sharpie over the words," I said.

"Yeah. Anyone's initials you know?"

He looked at me a moment longer than usual, and I looked down at the tag again.

"Leif Drendahl? The lighthouse tour guide?" I asked, sucking in a breath.

"Could be. That's what I thought, too," he said.

"I wonder what he would have been doing diving on the shipwreck."

"Good question. Could be nothing, but on the other hand, he could be tied to the missing gold somehow."

"That's possible." I nipped my lip and concentrated. "Do you think someone saw you pick up the glove? Maybe it's significant, in some way, and incriminates somebody in the heist of the gold, and they knew that. They could have been trying to get rid of you to keep you from looking into it."

"Hard to say," Colton said, "but if someone did think that and wanted the glove, it seems like they would have taken it from me after hitting me on the head so that no one else would ever see it."

"Yes, you're right. There must have been another reason. Does someone have a grudge against you? It wasn't Melanie, was it?"

"No, of course not. I'm sure it wasn't. We broke up, but we're still friends. She doesn't hold anything against me because of it. She's the one that wanted to break up in the first place."

"Hmm," I said, considering his answer. I wasn't ready to rule out Melanie yet. "So you don't have any idea who it was?" I asked. "What about Bob? He's the one that said he found you."

"Bob would never do anything like that, and neither would Larry or Stan. There must have been someone else diving that we didn't know about. I didn't see another boat out there, but that doesn't mean someone wasn't down there. They could have swum out underwater from shore when they saw us diving."

"I suppose that's possible," I said, not really thinking that. It seemed to me that Colton wasn't willing to consider the possibility that one of his friends could have done something like that to him, even though it seemed clear to me that they had.

"I'm ruling out the possibility that I just hit my head," he said. "I think there's more to this than that. I think someone did it."

"Me, too," I said. "I think Martha thinks so, too."

"Now we have to figure out who and why," he said.

I nodded.

He winced and touched his head as he sat back on the bed.

"Would you like some ice?" I asked. "I could run down to

the kitchen and get some."

"Not right now. I may go down later," he said. "This leads me to something else I wanted to talk to you about. I'm more convinced than ever after the diving incident that this is the right course of action."

"What is?" I asked.

"I'm closing the inn for the summer," he said.

"What?" I asked. I couldn't believe I'd heard him correctly. The inn was so important to him.

"There's too much going on and too much danger here. I need to protect Martha, you, myself, and the guests, and I can't risk the liability that would come from having guests get hurt, either. I've considered it for a while, and it's time. With the bad publicity from the murder last summer, and the stalking and financial problems, and now this, it's become too much to keep it open. I'm sorry. I hope you understand and that you can find another place to stay," he said, choking on the last few words.

I sat on the bed next to him and touched his arm, saddened by how devastated he looked.

"Oh, no, Colton, are you sure?" I asked.

"I'm sure. I'll do what I can to help you free your brother from prison before we close down in the next few weeks, but I can't promise we'll find anything."

"I know. It means so much to me that you're on my side. I'm on your side, too," I said, caressing his cheek while being careful of his bruise.

"I am on your side," he said. "And to show you, I'm going to make a few calls, starting with a call to the coroner's office about the death certificate. Maybe they'll tell me more than they told you."

"Thanks," I said.

He picked up his phone, and I strolled to the window to gaze out at the lake while he murmured in the background. He hung up after a few minutes, and I turned to talk to him.

"Did you speak with the woman at Dr. Pearson's office?" I asked.

"Yes. She told me he left the island last summer, and no one's seen him since," Colton said.

"She told me something similar. What else did she say? Did anyone try to find out what happened to him?" I asked.

"A few people did, but he didn't leave much of a trail. His car was found in the ferry overflow parking lot, and it's assumed he left to go on an international trip. Travel brochures were on the passenger seat, and since he left without his car, it seemed probable that he was planning to take an airline flight somewhere where he wouldn't need to drive."

"But why wouldn't he take the car with him and drive to the airport to park?" I asked.

"Maybe to keep from paying airport parking fees. Extended parking at the ferry overflow lot is free."

"Hmm. Could be. Still, something doesn't feel right about it," I said.

"It does seem odd, now that you mention it," Colton said, rubbing his chin.

"What did she say about the death certificate?" I asked.

"She said he was unable to confirm the cause of Pappy's death, and that's why he wouldn't sign it," Colton said.

"That's strange. If he didn't sign it, then how could they go ahead with the burial?"

"Good question," he said. "There's obviously more to this than we know. There must be other people involved who know what is going on. We have to find them."

I nodded. "And we have to find Dr. Pearson," I said, pausing to think for a moment. "But what if he's dead?"

"The coroner? Why would you say that?" he asked.

"Because no one's seen him since last summer, and no

one knows where he is. Maybe he knew something other people didn't want him to know about what happened, and that's why he didn't sign the death certificate. It's possible, isn't it?"

"I suppose."

"Then it follows that someone might have wanted him dead," I said, suddenly thinking of something. "I think we need to check the trunk of his car for his body," I said.

"What? A body couldn't be in there for that long. There would have been an odor," he said.

"Maybe. Maybe not. I think we need to check. There might be something in there that's important to the investigation."

Colton paused. "I'll talk to my friend at the sheriff's office and see if we can get a warrant," he said, after a moment, pressing numbers on his phone.

This time, when he hung up, he grabbed his wallet and keys and stuffed them in his jeans pocket, and tossed his robe on the bed.

"Let's go," he said, grabbing a cotton shirt off a nearby chair and buttoning it quickly. "My friend says the judge is a friend of the sheriff's, and he got approval right away. He said the authorities were never alerted that the coroner was missing for this long. And since there aren't many people on the island in the winter, the fact that he wasn't here wasn't deemed unusual and was never formally investigated. We need to meet the sheriff and a locksmith at the car."

"I'm with you," I said, grabbing my purse.

We headed down to his truck together and drove into town. We arrived at the parking lot just as the ferry was pulling away from the dock and drove to the overflow lot behind it. Several cars dotted the area, but a blue Audi in a far corner stood out because of its dusty appearance. It looked like it sat low to the ground in the back. Colton pulled up next to it and parked, and we got out and walked over to the car. White splats that were probably from the seagulls that squawked and strutted nearby speckled the windshield and roof.

"It's obviously been here for a long time," Colton said, peering in a side window.

"Yes," I agreed. "This must be it."

"Yes, it is," the locksmith said as he walked up behind us. "Sheriff's on his way."

He checked a paper he pulled out of his pocket. "Yep. That's the license plate number I have. Let me get to work."

He set a toolkit on the ground and knelt next to the driver's side door. I cupped my face with my hands and peered in the passenger window. There were brochures on the seat, and I squinted to see what they said. I sucked in a breath when I realized one of them included a picture of the cabin in the woods we'd seen from the boat on the tour. I wondered why he would have had that.

After a while, the sheriff walked up behind us, and we waited together for the locksmith to open the door. When he did, the sheriff leaned in and pressed the button to open the trunk. I took a deep breath before following him and Colton to the back of the car. This is what I'd been waiting for. All my deductions led to this point, and I was afraid of what we were going to find. Even though I was sure we would find the body of the coroner in the trunk, I wasn't sure I could handle seeing it.

I gasped when I looked inside. The body wasn't there, but there was a suitcase and a carry-on bag.

"Why would he leave his luggage here?" I asked. "That doesn't make sense."

"You're right," Colton said. "This doesn't bode well for him. You could be right that he's dead, or he could be in danger somewhere."

"Stand back. I want to check this out myself," the sheriff said, reaching into the trunk. He pulled on the carry-on bag, but it didn't move. "What the...?" the sheriff said, pulling on it again to no avail. He unzipped the top. "Holy Hannah," he said, looking inside. "It looks like we struck gold." He reached in and pulled out a handful of coins. "If I didn't see it with my own eyes, I wouldn't have believed it." The gold coins glinted in the sun as the sheriff looked at them closely. "Looks like they're dated in the 1800s," he said.

"Could I see one of those?" Colton asked.

The sheriff gave him one.

"Yes, these are gold dollars," Colton said, inspecting it. "If this is from the shipwreck, the bag of coins here could represent only a small portion of what was actually found. Historically, the amount of money said to be on the ship was quite substantial. There could be a lot more somewhere else, perhaps still on the island."

"I don't understand," I said. "Why would he bring a heavy bag like this on a trip? His car would have weighed too much to transport by ferry."

"Maybe he didn't know that. He's a doctor, not a ferryman. He could have been on the run and realized at the last minute that he couldn't bring it with him," Colton said.

"But, still, it doesn't make sense that he would leave a stash like this behind," I said.

"You're right," the sheriff said, taking the coin back from Colton and returning it with the others to the bag. I'm confiscating the car and its contents. This is now an official missing person's investigation. And we're going to find out where the gold came from and why it was left here. You can both go now. I appreciate the report."

His words left me momentarily relieved that, at last, someone in authority was taking charge. But then I wondered if we could trust the sheriff with the gold. I glanced at Colton to see if he shared my concern, but he nodded and agreed with the sheriff. I hoped my concerns weren't justified. We had to trust somebody.

The sheriff closed the trunk and walked back to his car while talking on his phone. He walked back over to us after a moment.

"Tell me again how you knew the coroner was missing," he said, looking at Colton suspiciously.

"I didn't," Colton said. "It was just a hunch."

I was going to tell the sheriff I was the one who suspected it, but Colton shook his head, and I stayed quiet.

"Hmm," the sheriff said, sounding unconvinced. "That's quite a hunch. We'll be in touch," he added as he walked away.

"What do you think he meant?" I asked Colton, getting a funny feeling in the pit of my stomach.

"I'm not sure, but I didn't want him suspecting you of something. Let's just leave it at that."

"Thank you for protecting me," I said. It gave me a warm feeling to think that he would do that for me.

"No problem," he answered. "Stick with me, and I'll take care of you."

We headed back to his truck.

"Would you like to grab something to eat in town before we head back to the inn?" he asked.

"Could we go to the hotel restaurant?" I asked, thinking I could see if Damon's car was still in the parking lot.

"Sure," he answered.

We drove into town, parked at a meter, and walked across the street to the hotel. I gasped when I saw Damon's car parked out front. He hadn't left the island, after all, as I had suspected.

"Do you know Gregory Wellington?" I asked as we walked past the car.

"As a matter of fact, I do know of him, although I haven't met him. He's Melanie's new boyfriend. I guess he's quite well-connected on the mainland and does business with people in town. Why do you ask?"

"No reason. I heard the name from someone and thought I'd check it out. That's all," I said.

As we waited in line to be seated in the hotel restaurant, I saw Damon sitting at a booth near the window, talking with the young woman I recognized from the coroner's office. I put my hand over my eyes and ducked my head as a rivulet of sweat slid down my back. I hoped he hadn't seen me. Something wasn't right, and it hit me right in my gut.

"You know what? I'm not hungry after all," I said, turning to leave.

As I turned my head, I noticed that the name inscribed above the door to the restaurant was "The Copper Bar." I sucked in a breath. It was the same name I had seen on the cocktail napkin wadded up in Damon's whiskey glass at home before I came to the island. He had obviously been here before. It was all I could do to keep from running out the door.

"Can we go back to the inn and see how Martha's doing? With everything that's been going on and finding the gold, I'm feeling a little on edge. I hope you understand," I said.

"Of course," Colton said.

"Thank you," I said, breathing a sigh of relief and trying not to let my panic show as I walked with him out to the truck.

I had to think about what all this meant before discussing it with Colton. It was so nice to be with someone who listened to and respected my feelings instead of telling me there was something wrong with me. Having Colton on my side with Martha, Rosie, and hopefully, the sheriff, as well, was a good feeling. Maybe there was hope for Tyler after all.

"There's one other thing I want to check," I said, as we drove home. "Remember the cabin we saw on the boat tour? There was a brochure about it in the coroner's car. I think we should check it out, given its proximity to the shipwreck. It could be connected to the missing gold. Is there a way we could do that?"

"It's probably one of my rental properties. I'll check with the real estate office and see if anyone is renting it this week. If there isn't, we can go over there tomorrow," he said.

"If you feel up to it," I said, noticing that he was sweating.

I wondered if the events of the day affected him as much as they affected me. And I hoped the bruise on his head wasn't bothering him too much.

"I'll be fine. After another good night's sleep at the inn, I'll be as good as new."

"Okay, if you're sure," I said.

"I am," he said.

We drove in silence for a while.

"I just want to say a few more things," I said, thinking of something. "It seems possible that the night stalking is targeting people who knew about the gold being found. And I think it was stolen by someone who didn't want to give it to the island but wanted to keep it for themselves. Tyler wouldn't have gone along with that. He knew that the location of the gold made it the property of the island, and he told Pappy that when he asked him to go on the dive with him. Pappy could have told others what Tyler said. I think someone framed Tyler for the murder to cast doubt on his story and make him seem like a desperate liar instead of a believable whistleblower. I'm more convinced than ever that that's the case now that we know the gold exists and that there is probably more stashed somewhere on the island."

"Who do you think it was?" Colton said in a low voice. "Who do you think is behind the night stalking and the coroner's disappearance? I've come to believe more and more in your instincts. You've been right on the money so far, so to speak."

I wasn't sure how to answer. I had a big picture of what

was going on, but it seemed so far-fetched that I didn't want to disclose it too soon and risk not being believed, even by Colton. If my deductions were right, it could be too much for him to handle. It seemed better to lead him in the direction I was going and let him figure things out for himself. Then maybe we could compare notes and meet in the middle.

I glanced over at him. His eyebrows furrowed as he concentrated on the road.

"I think it's Leif," I said. "I think he knows a lot more about what's going on than anyone imagines. He could be the key to this whole thing."

"But he didn't come to the island until after the murder," Colton said.

"Not that we know of, but that could be only the way it appears. He could have been here and taken part in retrieving the gold. And if Pappy refused to give him any, Leif could have killed him. That would make him a prime suspect in the murder."

Colton let out a breath as he turned onto the drive to the inn.

"It's possible," he said. "Let's keep this between ourselves for now and see how things play out with the formal investigation of the coroner's disappearance. I don't want you to reveal too much about your deductions and risk putting your life in immediate danger."

"Okay," I said.

I sat for a moment, staring out the window at the peaceful woods surrounding us. It seemed so calm in comparison to the turmoil my life had become. I hoped Colton and I could find a way to bring an end to the mystery and restore peace to the island and to Tyler.

CHAPTER 11

Slate-gray storm clouds rolled in over the lake and sent sailboats and jet skiers racing for cover as I stood and bent over to roll up our beach blanket a few days later.

"Hey, we better find a place to stay dry," I called to Colton, who was wading in the shallow waves in front of me.

I slogged through the sand toward him, taking in his broad, tan back and muscular shoulders. He really was a rugged, handsome man and surprisingly sensitive and intelligent, as well. I could fall for him. Maybe I already had. I missed him when he wasn't around. We'd walked down to the beach from the inn after lunch to enjoy the beautiful afternoon and find respite from our recent excursions and investigations. We hadn't been here long before the sky changed from azure to gray.

"Here, this is for you," he said, handing me a colorful, banded stone when I reached him.

"What for?" I asked, taking it and turning it over in my hand.

"For skipping. It's an agate. There are lots of them underwater near the shore."

I threw it and watched it skip twice before disappearing into the lake.

"Not bad," he said, smiling and handing me another one.

"Here, try again."

"Thanks, but we better get going. It looks like rain is almost here," I said.

He looked up at the sky. "You're right. Why don't you keep that one? They're said to make people calm and improve analytical ability."

"Oh," I said, looking it over and thinking about the gold we found in the trunk yesterday and where it could lead. "I could certainly use that right now."

"We both could," Colton said.

We hurried to grab the blanket and small cooler as plump drops of rain pummeled the sand and matted our hair. The wind picked up swiftly and blew sand into my mouth as we ran down the beach. I crunched on the gritty grains of it as I held the blanket over my head and tried to keep up with Colton.

"There's a shelter at the map-viewing area up ahead. Let's run for it," Colton said.

"Okay," I said.

I dashed with him across the sand to a roofed, open, wooden shelter partway up a dune and climbed the steps to a platform.

"Looks like we're the only ones who thought of this," Colton said, dropping onto a weathered, gray bench attached to a railing.

Cold droplets of rain lashed sideways into the shelter as I sat down next to him and unfurled the beach blanket to cover our legs.

"This will keep us warm and dry," I said. "I hope."

"Good idea," he said, helping me arrange it around our legs.

We sat huddled together, watching the storm whip the once-calm waves into a frenzy as the wind picked up over the lake. Colton had told me storms came up fast on the island, but it was awe-inspiring to see it happen. The horizon disappeared behind an unrelenting sheet of silver rain as whitecapped waves crashed to shore. A black shelf of thunderclouds rolled in the distance and cloaked the gray sky like the cape of a phantom. I leaned my head on Colton's shoulder and snuggled against him for warmth. It seemed that we were still going to get wet, but at least we had a roof over our heads, and we were far enough back in the shelter to avoid the worst of rain.

"You know," he said, putting his arm around me. "I'm glad you came to the island. I've never met a woman as interesting and intuitive as you are. It's nice to meet someone who's finally figuring out what's been going on around here. Maybe, with your help, I can find a way to save the inn and the island from permanent financial ruin. I'd sure like to think so."

"You're helping me, too," I said, taking my head off his shoulder and looking up at him. His bruise was fading, and I was glad that he seemed to be returning to his old self.

"Your knowledge of the island and its history gives me a lot to go on in determining what happened to Tyler. It gives me hope of freeing him," I said.

"I'm glad," he said.

Suddenly, lightning cracked in a bright, jagged streak through the sky, followed by a loud boom of thunder, and I jumped. Colton pulled me closer to him and tucked the blanket in around us. We sat, watching, as the bolts of lightning lit up the sky and sliced through the thick blanket of dark clouds, leaving momentary flashes of light in the distance over the vast lake.

"It's beautiful in an indescribable way. I've never seen anything like this," I said.

"Yes, it is," Colton replied. "It's the power and the beauty of nature. It's everywhere on and around the island. That's why I love it here so much."

"I know you do," I said. "It's obvious. It must be nice to

love a place so much and know that it's your home."

"Yes," Colton said. "It is. I'm grateful for it."

"Have you always lived here?" I asked.

"Yes, except for going to college on the mainland. I was gone for a few years for that, but I couldn't stay away. I missed it too much. The island is a part of me. It always will be. I'll live here for the rest of my life."

"It is an exceptional place," I said. "I can see why someone would never want to leave," I said.

I was referring to myself, but I was also thinking of the ghosts that stayed on the island and never returned to their families in their countries or on the mainland. Something about this place drew a lonely spirit, such as mine, in and made it want to stay. I laid my head on Colton's shoulder, glad that he wanted me to stay but conscious of the fact that he was still hurting over his break-up with Melanie. I didn't want to push a new relationship on him until he was ready, even though it was something I wanted. I decided to stick with talking about the island instead. But I wanted to talk about the dark side of it.

"Andy says the Ghostslayer comes back during storms. Have you ever seen him?" I asked, when the thunder rolled again.

"No, but I've heard from others who have. You don't want to be around when he shows up," he said.

"So I hear. Has Martha seen him?" I asked.

"No, but she's seen other ghosts. I, on the other hand, have not, but I believe the stories. There's something of the paranormal here," he said.

The wind blew the blanket off, and Colton grabbed it and tucked it around us again.

"Would you believe me if I told you I saw the ghosts of the captain and a sailor at the inn?" I said when we were covered and shielded from the rain again.

"Did you? When?" he asked.

"One night, when I went down to the kitchen for a snack," I answered.

"Well, you're in good company. Martha, Andy and Kirsten, and other guests have reported seeing them, too. They're a tourist attraction," he said.

"Yes, Andy was there at the time, recording them with his instruments. They're quite something."

"So I hear," Colton said.

"It seems strange that some ghosts bring people in and some scare them away," I said.

"That's the way it is on the island. That's what makes it so unique. That's why I want you to stay. You fit in. You see things that I can't see, and your insights are a big help to me."

"I'm glad. No one's ever said that to me before," I said.

In fact, it was quite the opposite. Damon had always told me my feelings and observations were inappropriate. I reveled in this new feeling of belonging.

"Really? That's too bad," he said. "Maybe that's why it seems like you hide your true self. You don't need to. You're a wonderful, caring, sensitive woman with extraordinary gifts of insight. If you'd let others see that, I think you'd be surprised at how they listen to you and follow you."

I sat for a moment in stunned silence.

"Wow. I can't believe you just said that. Can you say that again?"

"Which part?"

"The whole thing."

He chuckled. "Believe in yourself, Layla. I do."

"Thank you," I said, snuggling closer to him. It was nice to have someone believe what I said and want to hear what I had to say. I found myself opening up to Colton and telling him things I would never have told anyone before. I was starting to feel like my feelings counted and my intuitions were important. I didn't have to hide from him like I did from Damon.

The wind picked up again, and Colton drew the blanket over our heads. We huddled together in the dim warmth of our homemade cocoon. I tilted my head up to say something more, but before I did, he pressed his lips to mine and kissed me. I kissed him back, releasing the pent-up emotions I felt for him and feeling the power of the pleasure that surged through me. I didn't care if it was right or not. It felt right, and I would make things right. Somehow, I would get out of my marriage. I needed Colton, and I wanted our relationship to last. We kissed until the wind quieted down. He released me and touched my cheek, pulling the blanket off our heads with his other hand. The storm had ended, although the sky was still gray. The waves had smoothed into low rolls.

"I hope it's not too forward to ask," he said, looking deep into my eyes, but I'd hate to see you leave when the inn closes. Martha's moving in with me at my house in town, and there's room for you, too, if you'd like."

"Are you asking me to move in with you?" I asked, lightly. His eyes were soft and clear.

"If you want to," he said, quietly. "I want you to stay."

I smiled. "I'll think about it," I said.

The wind quieted and softened the buffeting of the rain. The faint booms of thunder echoed in the distance.

"It looks like the rain let up," I said.

"You're right," Colton said, standing and walking over to a viewing scope mounted on a railing. "Do you want a close-up view of the lighthouse? Look through this. You can see it in detail from here," he said, bending and trying it himself.

"Sure," I said.

I took his place at the scope and adjusted it to gaze out over the lake and up at the lighthouse. The detail was amazing, even though the lens was wet. Someone stepped out onto the lighthouse balcony, but I couldn't see who it was. I shook out my ponytail and used my damp bandana to polish the lens before trying again. It was still filmy, but the view was better. I looked more closely and gasped. It was Damon. He was talking to Leif, who stepped out on the balcony with Melanie behind him. But it couldn't be. I squinted. It was him. He pointed to the reef and seemed to be shouting as he waved his arms. Leif did the same and gestured toward a freighter floating far out in the lake. For a moment, I was scared for Melanie. But then Leif abruptly turned and walked back inside. Melanie followed him with Damon close behind her. I let out a breath. I wasn't sure what their relationships were with each other, but something bothered me about seeing them all together. It probably had to do with the gold or Pappy's death or both. More and more, I was beginning to think that Leif was intricately involved in Pappy's murder. For now, I decided to keep my musings to myself until I could come up with a more concrete reason for my feelings, even though I knew Colton would listen to me.

"Here. You can look again, if you'd like," I said, moving aside to give him another chance.

"No, I'm good. I've seen it before. Would you like to head back? Looks like there's a break in the rain. It'll probably start up again later."

"Okay," I said, folding the blanket and following him out of the shelter and down the wooden stairs to step onto the beach. The sand was wet and gritty between my toes.

"Maybe this would be a good day to check out the cabin," I said.

Colton nodded and softly snapped his fingers. "Right. I've been meaning to tell you. The records at the real estate office showed that the coroner rented the cabin for a month at the end of last summer. After that, it was rented out for the fall and winter, but there's no one there now. I picked up the keys this morning, and we can head over there now if you want."

"Great. Maybe we can get Andy and Kirsten to go with us. He said on the boat tour that his instruments showed paranormal activity in the area. We might as well check that out, too," I said.

"Okay," he said.

We made it back to the inn before it started raining again and separated to freshen up in our rooms before heading for the cabin. Andy and Kirsten had passed us in the parking lot and agreed to meet us at the cabin later.

As I unlocked the door to my room, Martha called to me from down the hall.

"I'm so glad you're back, dear. Did you get caught in the rain? Colton told me you were going to the beach together," she said.

"Yes, I'm afraid so, but we're none the worse for wear."

She walked up to me and continued talking.

"Good. I wanted to tell you how sorry I am that the inn is closing. It's been so nice having you here. I hope you'll find another place to stay on the island and continue taking your photographs and writing your article. You will be kind in what you write about the inn, though, won't you? We're hoping things could turn around, and we can open again next summer."

"Yes, of course," I answered. "It's a beautiful place to stay, and you've made me feel quite welcome. I'm so sorry it's come to this. Maybe things will change, and the stalker will be apprehended."

I didn't want to mention that Colton asked me to stay at his house in order to give him a chance to tell her first, especially since she would be living there, too. I also wasn't sure yet what my answer would be.

"Thank you. I hope things will change. It's been so dreadful dealing with these frightening incidents and so unfair to us and the other businesses on the island who may have to close because of them," she said.

I nodded. It occurred to me that the other island businesses, such as those owned by Stan, Bob, and Larry, could take a hit from the reduced tourism and loss of money caused by a stalker scaring tourists away. But maybe they wouldn't mind if the final result was keeping the gold and becoming owners of the island. But I didn't mention that, either.

"Well, we'll talk later," she said. "I have to taste a new dish Chef Dillon put on the menu for tonight and give my approval."

"Okay."

After she left, I changed and met Colton in his room to go to the cabin. By the time we arrived there, it had started raining again, but not hard, so I didn't mind getting out of the truck and splashing through puddles to get to the back door. Colton followed me, but before we went in, something I'd seen while I was running piqued my interest. I held my hands over my head as a rain shield and led Colton to the side of the cabin that overlooked the lake.

"What's this?" I asked. "I saw it from the boat when we were on the tour. It looked like a kid's sled from there, but now I'm not so sure."

I pointed at a long, curved sled with a wide, tall handle and curled metal runners.

"That's a dogsled," Colton said. "People use them in the winter to pull supplies and things across the ice on the lake."

"How?" I asked.

"Four to six dogs, sometimes more, wear harnesses attached to the sled and pull it while the owner stands on the back of the sled and guides them along," he said.

"That's amazing."

"Yes. The town sponsors races sometimes. It's fun."

"Sounds like it," I said.

The feeling of unease I had when I saw the dogsled from

the boat came back, but I didn't know what was causing it yet.

"I wonder why there's a dogsled here if this is a rental property," I said.

Colton paused for a moment.

"I don't know. That does seem strange," he said. "Let's go in before we get soaked."

"Okay." I followed him around back again.

"What's this?" I asked, clutching his elbow when I almost tripped over something obscured by the rain.

"A generator," he answered, as I used his arm to steady myself. "It's battery operated and kicks in to keep the power on if a storm knocks it out. We keep them at rental properties such as fishing cabins, where we have large storage freezers for fish and food supplies. It keeps it from thawing and spoiling if the power goes out."

"Good idea," I said, releasing his arm.

He unlocked the door, and I stepped through into a cool, dark room that smelled of mothballs and dampened wood. Windows overlooked the lake, and a small sofa and chairs sat under them, cornered with driftwood end tables. A rustic wooden coffee table was strewn with magazines and a few old-looking books which I supposed were for the entertainment of the renters. Something peeked out from under a book, and I walked over and bent down to look more closely. I picked up the book and gasped. It was another glove. And it looked like the match for the one Colton found on the dive.

"Look at this," I said, unable to contain my excitement. "It's Leif's other glove. That proves that he was here or that another diver on the shipwreck found it and brought it here. Either way, it lends credibility to my theory that the robbers used the cabin to stash the gold after their dive. I wonder if there's more of it here."

We checked around the cabin, looking for clues, as we waited for Andy and Kirsten to arrive. It didn't look like it had been rented for the whole winter, as Colton had mentioned. Blankets were only on one bed, and there were folded beach towels in the bathroom. Maybe someone had stayed here for a short time.

I walked down the narrow hall in the back while Colton went into the kitchen. The second bedroom was cramped and packed with fishing paraphernalia and camping supplies. And it smelled funny, like wet fur. What looked like a snowmobile outfit and boots were stuffed in the corner. The closet door was open, and I walked over to look inside. Diving equipment and luggage spilled from makeshift shelves, and I pulled the chain on the bare bulb hanging overhead to get a better look. Something glinted in the corner, and I bent to look at it. It was a coin.

"Colton," I shouted. "In here."

He ran in from the other room.

"What is it?" he asked.

"A coin. The same kind that was in the trunk, I think," I said, handing it to him.

He took it and examined it.

"You're right. It's a gold dollar from the 1800s. Whoever took the gold was here, and it seems like it must have been the coroner."

"And Leif was here, too," I said. "We found his glove."

"Two people, then," Colton said. "This is getting serious."

"Yes," I said, thinking it was at least two people.

"Let's check the rest of the closet," he said, just as someone knocked on the door.

I sifted through more things on the shelves as he went to answer it. He came back with Andy and Kirsten as a crash of thunder shook the cabin.

"Oh, my gosh," I said, bolting straight up and feeling the hairs on the backs of my arms stand up. "The storm's back in full force."

I wasn't sure if the prickles on my arms were due to fear, static from lightning, or something else.

"Yes, it was building on our drive over here," Kirsten said. "I'm glad we made it here before it hit. Andy, let's scan the cabin. Use your EMF meter."

"Good idea," he said, pulling the black instrument I'd seen before out of his pocket.

He turned it on, and we all jumped when it emitted a high-pitched screech.

"It's red," Andy said, looking frightened. "That's EMF5. The only time that's ever happened before was in the woods near the prison. We better get out of here."

"Why? What does that mean?" I asked, watching everyone's faces pale.

"It's the highest level register of ghost activity. That means a dangerous ghost is nearby or with us right now. It could be the Ghostslayer, and I don't want you guys to see that. We have to leave," Andy said.

"No, it can't be," I said, feeling my heart race.

"Yes, it can. I don't know why he's here or who or what he's after, but we need to go."

"But what about the storm?" I asked.

"We'll have to risk it and drive on through," Andy said.

"Okay. Colton, maybe we can come back another time," I said, trusting Andy.

"Sure," he replied. "Let's get out of here."

We ran to our cars as cracks of lightning split the sky between deafening rumbles of thunder. I looked around for a sign of what we were running from, but all I saw was a dim red glow in the woods behind the cabin.

"Floor it!" Andy shouted as he slammed the passenger door of his car and took off down the road with Kirsten.

Colton jumped into the driver's side of his truck as I

climbed in and locked the passenger side door behind me. He jammed it into drive and raced down the road after Andy and Kirsten. And we didn't stop until we made it back to the inn.

CHAPTER 12

After the harrowing experience at the cabin, I laid low for a few days, staying in my room at the inn and working on my article while the rain pattered against the windows. The discoveries Colton and I had made led my mind in different directions as I continued to wriggle together the pieces of last summer's puzzle.

My brother hadn't killed Pappy. I was certain of that. But it was becoming more and more difficult for me to determine who had, and why they would have done it and pinned it on Tyler. It had to be someone who knew the island and islanders well, or they wouldn't have gotten away with it. There were too many things that didn't fit, like the two different dates of death and the missing date on the tombstone, that were obviously covered up when outsiders came asking. Islanders would only do that for one of their own or someone they trusted implicitly. I considered myself lucky to have found out what I did. And it had to be someone who would profit from Pappy's death or Tyler being framed for it, or both. It didn't make sense to me yet, although, after finding the diving gloves, I had my suspicions about Leif, but I was working on it. Someone knocked on the door, and I put my iPad down and went to answer it. Susie stood in the hallway with a plate of cookies.

"Mrs. Harding said to bring you these," she said, handing

them over. "Chef Dillon made them special today for all the guests that had to stay inside because of the rain. They're still warm."

"Thank you," I said, taking them from her. "Would you like one?"

"Maybe. I think they're chocolate chip," she said, following me into the room.

I handed her one and sat down on the bed.

"How's the detective story you're writing going?" I asked.

"All right," she said, shortly before taking a bite of her cookie. "They found out who the murderer was," she added with her mouth full.

"Really? Who was it?"

"It was the last person you would have suspected, but the first person I suspected. No one else suspected him, either, not even the police."

"Not even the police?" I asked.

"Nope. They thought he was somebody else."

"Well, who did they think he was?"

"I'm not telling," she said.

"Hmm. Do you ever base your stories on real life?" I asked.

She paused and looked at me through the big-framed, round glasses that she occasionally wore. They made her look wise, which seemed appropriate given the insights she often had.

"Sometimes," she said.

She took another bite, and while she was chewing, I thought of another question.

"Do any of the kids ever ride on a dogsled in the winter?" I asked, thinking of the one we found at the cabin.

"No. My mom wouldn't let me. Only adults do," she answered.

"Where do they go?" I asked.

"On races over the ice and sometimes to the mainland in

the winter."

"To the mainland?"

"Yes, when the ice freezes over enough, there's an ice road between the island and the mainland, and people walk over it or take a dogsled over it," she said.

"That's amazing."

"Not really. People do it all the time. I have to go now. Bobby wants to play checkers."

"Okay. Nice talking to you. Let me know if I can read your story sometime," I said.

"Nope," she said. "I only write them, and I don't let anyone read them. Unless they're smart enough."

"Okay. I won't read it then," I said, grinning, as I closed the door behind her.

She was an interesting girl and very aware. She was a fountain of information about the island, and she had good insights into people, as well. I hoped to talk to her more, even though she didn't have the best manners and didn't seem to care too much for me. It was worth it to deal with those things as long as I could talk to her. I thought she could help me solve the mystery of what happened last summer because she'd been here then, and she probably had her own ideas as to what went on, especially if her mother was involved.

I laid down on the bed and closed my eyes to think about what she'd said. The fact that there was an ice road to the mainland in the winter was fascinating, and I wondered if the dogsled at the cabin had been used to travel on it. The gold would have been too heavy to transport over the ice or to be pulled by dogs, but it seemed like something illicit was transported that way. I felt it in my bones, but I didn't know what it was. I was sure the dogsled was a clue and that the ice road fit in somewhere. I just didn't know where yet.

Later, when the rain let up a bit, I took the cookie plate

back to the kitchen and walked to the outdoor deck of the restaurant. The table umbrellas were still dripping, and the cushioned, wrought iron chairs were wet, but I wiped a seat with the napkin that I had stuffed in my pocket and sat down. The harbor was hazy with drizzle, and I strained to see if the ferry was coming in, but it wasn't. I remembered coming to the island on it, hoping to escape my old life and start a new one, only to find that Damon was here, too. It was disheartening at best and more than a coincidence at worst. I hoped he had left and gone back to the mainland by now. I was thinking of him because a man who looked like him was opening an umbrella at a table under an awning nearby. He sat down and took off his sunglasses, which seemed like strange apparel for a rainy day, and turned to look at me. I gasped. It was Damon. He grinned and lifted his drink toward me.

"How you doing, babe?" he asked. "Thought you might like some company."

"How did you know I was here?" I choked out.

"Magic, baby. Magic. He sees all, and he knows all," he said, smirking as he obviously referred to himself. "You believe in magic, don't you, baby?"

I shook my head.

"Sure you do," he said. "Ghosts and magic."

"What do you want, Damon?" I asked, not even trying to disguise my irritation. I couldn't believe he had followed me here and was playing this ridiculous game, or whatever it was, on the island.

"You. I want you to come home. It's where you belong. You should never have left. You know that."

"You don't own me," I said.

"Really? We'll see." He smiled and sipped his drink.

I looked around to see if anyone could help me, but we were alone.

"I'm not going home. I'm staying here. And I want to know why you're using a different name. Who are you, really?" I asked.

He paused before piercing me with his shrewd, black eyes. "I'm your worst nightmare, Layla. You should never have taken me on. No one leaves me and gets away with it. You'll come home. You'll see."

He stood and sauntered closer, gulping the last of what looked to be a whiskey sour.

"Stay back, Damon," I said, trembling. "You have no power over me here, and you didn't have the right to follow me here."

"Wanna bet?" he asked, moving closer.

"What do you mean?" I asked, leaning away.

"I have more right to be here than you do," he said. "And you better not talk to anybody here if you know what's good for you. Take my advice, and go home."

"I'm not leaving, Damon. You are," I said, forcefully. "I have friends here now." I clenched my hands and tried not to let him see me shaking.

"Sure you do," he said, sarcastically. "Don't kid yourself, Layla. No one wants to be friends with someone who sees things that aren't there and says things that aren't true. You're nuts. You belong at home."

"Go away," I said. "You're the one that says things that aren't true. Leave me alone." I sat, trembling and hoping he would leave.

"Whatever you say, babe. But I'm not leaving the island until you do. So you better decide what you're going to do with me around. I'll make it really interesting for you."

He grinned as he pressed two fingers to his forehead in a mock salute and walked past me and down the outside steps. A car screeched out of the parking lot moments later, and I sat still, gritting my teeth. I hadn't realized how tense I was. He had threatened me, and I didn't know what to think. I didn't know what to do. My legs felt wobbly as I got up and walked through the restaurant to go back to my room. Martha came out of the kitchen and called to me.

"Have you seen Colton today? I haven't seen him since this morning at breakfast," she said.

"No, but I'm on my way upstairs now if you want me to give him a message," I said, still on edge from my encounter with Damon. I didn't want to tell her about it because she already had her own problems with the night stalker and the imminent closing of the inn. And I wasn't sure I wanted to tell anyone who he really was until I could determine why he had been using a different name on the island. I took a deep breath to calm myself instead.

Martha put her hand on her cheek and appeared to contemplate her options.

"Well, okay," she said. "I only wanted to tell him that Andy and Kirsten told me that tonight would be a prime night for paranormal activity. It usually starts around midnight when the moon is high, and the lake is calm, if it happens at all. They didn't specify if it would be the night stalker, the ghosts at the inn, or something else. But since he's staying over again, I thought he'd want to know. I hope it's the good ghosts and not the bad ones. I can't take much more of the bad ones like the night stalker."

I patted her arm. "You've been very brave. I'm glad you told me. I'll tell him," I said.

"Good," she said. "Oh, and also tell him I need to move some things into his house in town, and I need a key made."

"Okay," I said.

I left as she walked back to the kitchen and headed up to Colton's room. He opened the door right away.

"Were you on your way out?" I asked, surprised.

"No. I thought I heard someone in the hall just before you knocked, and I was checking to see who was there," he said.

"Oh," I said, looking down the hallway, "I don't see anyone."

"Yeah," he said, peeking out the door. "That's strange. Anyway, do you want to come in? I think we should discuss what happened at the cabin yesterday."

"Sure," I said.

I glanced around again before following him into his room and closing the door. I gave him Martha's messages and agreed to meet him downstairs tonight to see if ghosts showed up again before sitting down with him to talk about our near encounter with the Ghostslayer yesterday. We had both been extremely scared, but the more I thought about it, the more I wondered why the Ghostslayer kept coming back.

"So, in a way, the Ghostslayer is protecting the island, is that right?" I asked, after we had talked for a while.

"No, I wouldn't say that," Colton said, frowning.

"Well, if evil ghosts and evil people disappear because of him, isn't that protection?" I asked.

"I suppose, but in an odd way. The Ghostslayer of the story isn't doing it for that reason. He's doing it for revenge. He's not a hero, if that's what you mean."

"But the effect is the same. He saves the island ghosts and islanders from evil," I said.

"What are you getting at?" he asked.

"That the ghosts that remain on the island may feel some loyalty to the Ghostslayer for keeping them safe and therefore don't interfere with him or his mission when he returns. That's why he keeps coming back. That's why the other ghosts are still here and haven't returned to the mainland or the countries they came from to find their families. They feel safe here, and because of that, they will always remain on the island," I said.

"But he's terrorizing people and scaring them away," Colton said.

"Is he? Or is it someone pretending to be him or an evil ghost? If the night stalker was a real, evil ghost and not a person, wouldn't the real Ghostslayer have taken him away by now?"

Colton sat back and appeared to be deep in thought.

"Good point. But why would someone do that?" he asked, after a moment. "Money? That doesn't make sense. The island is going under financially because of this. There won't be any money left."

"No. Gold. Someone wants anyone who believes the story about the gold being found to leave the island. And that could include a lot of people. The story is well known. Also, whoever has the gold in their possession could sell it and finance a takeover of the island when everyone else leaves. He or she will then be very rich and very powerful, and that could be the goal."

"Who do you think is?" Colton asked.

"The clues point to Leif. He conveniently arrived on the island almost immediately after Pappy's suspicious death and took over his duties. We found his gloves at the site of the shipwreck and the cabin. He spread rumors that the coroner had left the island last summer when it now appears that he didn't. And, he could certainly benefit from having a treasure of gold fall into his possession. One more thing. The condition of his car when I visited the lighthouse leads me to believe he may have purposely tried to drive me off the road when I first arrived on the island," I said.

"What?" Colton said, looking appalled.

"Someone with a damaged headlight rear-ended my car, and it may have been him," I said.

"That's it. I'm going to the sheriff with this," Colton said.

"No. I want to find out more information first, and I don't want Leif to know we suspect him," I said.

"But you may be in danger," he said.

"Everyone on the island could be in danger. It's up to us to figure out what's going on and change that," I said.

Colton stood and rubbed his chin as he paced the room.

"All right. I see your point. We'll keep it between us for now, but I want you to promise me that you'll be careful."

"I will be," I said. "You, too."

Colton nodded and paused in mid-stride. "Do you hear something?" he asked.

"Yes. It sounds like scratching," I said, springing to alert.

I didn't want a repeat of what had happened to me in my room on my first night here. If the night stalker was in the hallway, I didn't want him to know I'd heard him. Two could play this game. I raised my fingers to my lips to signal Colton to be quiet and tiptoed to the door. I took a deep breath and yanked it open. Susie almost fell into the room.

"What are you doing here?" I asked, reaching down to help her up.

"Nothing. I have to go now," she said, shaking off my hand and running away down the hall.

"Does she listen at doors?" I asked Colton while peering after her down the hallway.

"Apparently so," he said.

"Hmm. I hope she didn't hear too much, especially what I said about Leif and the gold. I wouldn't want that to get back to Melanie, although I'm not sure she tells her mother everything. We'll have to keep an eye out for her and keep her from eavesdropping in the future."

"You're right," Colton said. "Melanie could use that type of information to turn things against us if she knows where the gold is, much as I hate to think that. Sometimes, I wonder how I could have fallen for her. I guess I got so caught up in helping her get over Tyler that I didn't see the big picture and realize that she may have been playing me for a fool."

"I'm sorry, Colton. I hope that isn't the case," I said. "You deserve so much better."

I patted him on the arm and left to go back to my room to dress for dinner. I wondered if Susie eavesdropped to get ideas for her detective novels or if she was just nosy. I hoped she didn't tell anyone what I said.

I met Colton later at the restaurant for dinner with Andy and Kirsten. He had invited me and asked them to join us to discuss their predictions of a paranormal event this evening. We sat in a booth by the window and watched the sun set brilliantly on the horizon. Melanie was sitting at a table with her children, but she didn't look our way or come over to say 'hi.' Susie didn't either, and they left soon after we ordered. That was fine with me. I didn't know what to say to them anyway, and I didn't want anything I said to inadvertently get back to Damon through Melanie. Besides, Colton had told me Melanie didn't think much of Andy and Kirsten because they were ghost hunters, and she didn't believe in ghosts. I didn't want her to come over and be rude to them. Rosie brought our food out, and Andy asked her if she wanted to stay after dinner and wait to see the ghosts with us.

"Are they coming again tonight? I haven't seen them in a while. The last time I did was last summer after Pappy disappeared. They were all over the place for a few nights there, and they'd been coming around for weeks before that, too. Then, when things slowed down at the inn for the winter, the sightings slowed down, as well. I don't know why," she said, seeming perplexed.

"I have a theory about that," I said, when she placed my plate in front of me. "I think the shipwreck at the reef was disturbed and agitated the ghosts. That's probably why they showed up."

"I agree with that possibility," Andy said.

"Really?" Rosie said. "Maybe that's why there were so many of them. There was one that I remember I hadn't seen before. He had a pickaxe in his belt, and he looked like a miner."

"That's interesting," Colton said. "I haven't seen the ghosts myself, but historically speaking, many of the sailors that went down on that shipwreck were coming to the island to work in the copper mine. That lends credence to the sighting."

"Oh, well, good," Rosie said. "Maybe I will be there tonight. I haven't seen them in a long time, and I kind of miss them."

"Good. We'll look for you," Andy said.

I was amazed again at how many people on the island spoke of ghosts so freely and seemed interested in my observances instead of flippant and dismissive about them as Damon and others had been at home. I was feeling more and more at home here and less like I had a home on the mainland to ever return to. That was a past life, and one I hoped I could forget and move on from. I could be myself on the island, and I wanted to stay here with people who let me be that way. And it didn't matter to me that Colton couldn't see ghosts. He accepted the fact that I could and welcomed my insights, and that's all I cared about.

Rosie finished handing out our dinners and left to go back to the kitchen, passing Martha, who came through the doors in the other direction and headed for our table with a pitcher of water. When she reached us, she refilled our glasses and smiled.

"Nice to see you all tonight. I hoped you'd have dinner here. I feel more comfortable having people around when I know the ghosts are going to appear. I never know if they'll be good ones or bad ones," she said, shaking her head.

"They'll be good ones, Mom," Colton said. "Don't worry. If they aren't, there's safety in numbers, and there are a lot of us here tonight."

"That's what I was thinking," Martha said. "They usually appear after midnight. I thought we could wait for them together in the restaurant. Kirsten, what do you think?"

"Definitely. The EMF meter shows imminent activity, and it's centered right around here."

"Okay. That's what we'll do then," Martha said. "Enjoy your dinners. I'll be back out later."

We ate in silence for a while, and as I contemplated what we might see tonight, I felt glad that Colton was near me to share it with. We'd almost encountered a bad ghost at the cabin in the Ghostslayer, and I was looking forward to seeing good ghosts and telling Colton what I saw. I gazed out the window at the calm harbor and at the night sky twinkling with the sparkles of a thousand diamonds, and I wondered what the future held for us.

CHAPTER 13

The lighting in the restaurant at midnight was as translucent and ghostly as it had been the last time I'd encountered apparitions here after dark. The moon cast eerie shadows on the floor near the windows that looked out over the still harbor. We gathered behind the bar, away from the windows but with a respectable view of the room. Rosie crouched next to me, and Martha knelt halfway down on my other side. Andy, Kirsten, and Colton were bolder and stood, leaning against the counter. Andy consulted his instruments while his wife looked on. But I didn't need to do that to know there was paranormal activity around. I felt the chill creep in, slowly, silently. Suddenly, something shattered at a nearby table.

"What was that?" Rosie asked.

"Shh," Andy said. "We're at EF 3, no EF 4. There's a ghost in the room, and he must have knocked over a centerpiece."

It seemed as though we all held our breath forever, waiting for another sound. There wasn't one. A shadow in the corner caught my eye, but it seemed to be only the outline of a branch waving in the wind outside the window.

"Where is he?" Martha asked after a while.

"I'm not sure," Andy whispered, "but it looks like something's about to happen. The readings show more ghosts here now."

I waited with bated breath, wondering if the captain or some other ghost would appear soon. As long as it wasn't the night stalker or the Ghostslayer, I would be happy. I'd had enough of them.

The first apparition faded in near the window. It was the sailor I'd seen last time, silently screaming and reaching for help, but he faded away quickly. Another appeared in his stead. It was a young man wearing a sailor cap squashed down over his long, wavy hair with a washed-out bandana tied around his neck. He grinned and appeared to whistle a tune as he grew more visible.

"That's Sailor Joe," Andy whispered. "He's popular with the ladies."

"What does that mean?" I asked.

Rosie stood and inched around the counter closer to him. "I've seen him before. I think he's the same one, but I want to make sure," she said.

She tiptoed toward the window until she paused, backlit by the light of the moon, and peered at Sailor Joe.

"What is she doing?" Kirsten whispered, seemingly unaware until that moment that Rosie had moved. "She could scare them away."

Kirsten's black hair and red lips stood out in the dim, blue glow of the EMF meter, and for a moment, she looked like a strange apparition herself. I stifled a scream and turned to watch Rosie. The apparition tipped his cap at her and smiled.

"Rosie, come back," Kirsten whispered loudly.

Rosie turned to look at us and then turned back to Sailor Joe. She gasped and stepped back as she looked our way again.

"He winked at me," she said. "Did you see that? He tipped his cap and winked at me."

"Come back here," Kirsten said again, not bothering to whisper this time. "What are you doing?"

I moved away from Kirsten and closer to where Rosie had been. Rosie scooted across the floor and back behind the counter.

"I didn't know ghosts could do that," she said, ducking down next to us.

"Sailor Joe does," Andy said. "I guess he doesn't know he's not supposed to."

"Stay here now," Kirsten said. "We want more ghosts to feel free to appear."

"Yes, that's true," I added, averting my gaze away from Kirsten. I hoped she would look better again when the lights came back on.

As Sailor Joe hovered near the window, another apparition showed up. This one was older and wore a tool belt.

"That's Casey, the miner," Andy said. "Lore has it that he was sailing to the island to work in the copper mine when the storm wrecked the ship. His family was inconsolable."

"I remember that," Colton said. "It's in the history books about the island. What does he look like? I've always wanted to know."

I remembered that Colton had told me he couldn't see ghosts but still believed in the supernatural and thought it existed on the island. I'd never been in a situation before where other people saw ghosts, along with me, and explained them to someone who couldn't. I'd always been the only one in a group who saw things others couldn't and had to keep my feelings to myself. It gave me a warm feeling of belonging that I'd never experienced before, and I was thrilled to share what the ghosts looked like with Colton.

"He's not much more than five feet tall," I said. "And he has long, curly hair and a mustache."

"Thanks for telling me," he said.

"Quiet," Andy said under his breath. "More ghosts are arriving."

The light from his meter tinted his face a deathly blue. Given the way he looked and the way Kirsten looked, I wasn't sure what to think anymore. I was pretty sure they weren't ghosts themselves, but you never knew. I tried to think about something else.

"Andy and I saw the captain the first time I saw the ghosts," I whispered, leaning toward Colton. "He wears a uniform and has a telescope."

"Yes. And that's his first mate over there," Andy said quietly. "You can tell by the insignia on his cap. The first time I saw him was last summer. I think he also has something to do with keeping the gold safe, or did, anyway. He carries a leather book that looks like an accounting ledger."

"Interesting," Colton said.

More apparitions appeared, hovering near the windows and chatting with each other. Most of them wore cobbled-together work clothes that didn't look like sailor outfits but seemed appropriate for a sailing crew. One of them appeared to tell a joke, and the others laughed heartily.

"It looks like most of the crew of the shipwreck showed up tonight. Why do you suppose they're all here?" I asked.

"Good question," Andy said. "It could have something to do with the Ghostslayer being around again. I'm pretty sure we almost ran into him at the cabin. They could wonder who he's after. Or, maybe something life-changing is happening soon that affects the spirit world, and they're agitated because of it."

"Life changing? You mean someone could die?" I asked.

"Maybe. Or, someone is already dead, and their ghost is making trouble. It could be that they just want to get together, but my inkling, given the size of the gathering, is that something life-threatening is about to happen on the island," he continued. "They could be gathering to cement their friendships so that they stick together during the difficult times to come. It's hard to say what the reason is or what's going to happen."

I shivered as I tried to think of what that could be. The only thing I came up with was the recent news reports that said the night stalker had been terrorizing even more people over the last few weeks and causing many to leave or contemplate leaving the island. Many of them had given statements that included saying they knew about the gold being found on the shipwreck and believed the story that had been circulating about it being stolen. It seemed to me that there was a concentrated effort to change people's beliefs about that or get them to leave, although the authorities still didn't appear to take it seriously for some reason. I wondered if a resident or even the night stalker himself would be killed tonight.

An apparition with a large belly suddenly appeared, sitting on a barrel. He laughed and passed out mugs of a brown liquid. The other ghosts accepted them, threw back their heads, and chugged it down.

"That's Whisky Will," Andy said.

His voice startled me out of my reverie, and I strained to hear what he had to say.

"The ship carried dozens of barrels of whisky when it went down, and he often appears to pass out liquor. Unfortunately, the whisky has no substance, so the only ones drinking it are the ghosts," he said.

"Well, they look like they're having a good time," Rosie said, standing up again to peer at them.

"Probably," Andy said, chuckling.

"I wonder if they're celebrating something," I said.

"Could be. But it's not unusual to see them drinking. There were evidently many barrels of whiskey aboard the ship, and the sailors probably took full advantage of it like they're doing now," Andy said.

I stood, transfixed. It was as though we were witness to

another world inhabited only by ghosts, and I marveled at their antics. I knew ghosts existed, but this was the first time I'd seen so many of them in one place. I felt like I was experiencing something phenomenal and unique to the island, and I was honored to be a part of it. Suddenly, a hush fell over the room, and a ghostly ball of light appeared near the window.

"What is that?" I asked.

Andy put his fingers to his lips.

The light intensified until it wavered and turned into an apparition. It was the captain in his captain's uniform, standing tall and leveling his gaze on the sailors in the room. He looked like a man in authority with his shining white hair and beard. At first, it seemed that the other ghosts were frightened of him, but then Whiskey Will handed him a mug of whiskey. He grinned, raised it, and threw it back while the others cheered before holding it out for a refill. The party continued as the captain stood by the window with his telescope, appearing to search the harbor for something.

"What's he looking for?" I asked.

"He keeps watch for storms and for the Ghostslayer," Andy said. "Usually, he only looks for him when a storm is coming, but I don't see anything out there. I don't know what he's looking for now."

I shivered.

"Sailor Joe just winked at me again," Rosie said, huffing and ducking down below the counter again to peek over the top.

The blue glow from Andy's meter tinted her red hair green, giving her an unusual neon glow, and I was momentarily taken aback when I looked over at her. But maybe a ghost would find that attractive.

"Maybe you should say 'hi,'" I said, smiling.

"Don't be silly," Rosie said. "What would I have in common with a ghost?"

"You never know," I said.

The ghosts appeared to dance to a ditty they were singing, and Sailor Joe extended his hand toward Rosie as he shuffled transparently toward her. He could apparently still see where she was.

"This is getting ridiculous," she said. "Would someone please tell him to leave me alone?"

"Maybe you should dance with him. He seems to like you," I said.

"Oh, don't be silly," Rosie said. "Dance with a ghost? I wouldn't even know who would lead."

I laughed, and she grinned.

A cool draft suddenly blew in over the counter, and we all stopped talking. Sailor Joe turned and headed in the other direction.

"What's going on? Is it another ghost?" Colton asked, rubbing his arms.

"If it is, it's not registering," Andy answered. "Maybe someone opened an outside door. It's cooling off out there."

The ghosts stopped moving all of a sudden. They set down their mugs and looked around. The captain faded away, and soon, the others began to disappear. Eventually, Sailor Joe was gone, too, not bothering to wave 'goodbye' to Rosie, although she didn't seem to mind. The moon disappeared and left the restaurant dark and quiet.

"What's happening?" I asked.

"I don't know," Andy said, looking around.

Suddenly, a door banged shut, and a dark figure ran through the restaurant with another one chasing him. They didn't talk, but one seemed intent on pursuing the other. I thought for a moment that I recognized them, but it was hard to tell without the moon to light their faces. They looked like people and not apparitions.

"Stay down," Colton said, patting my arm and Martha's.

"Why?" I asked.

"One of them's got a gun," he said.

We ducked lower behind the counter, and Martha slapped her hand over her mouth before removing it to say something.

"It's the night stalker, isn't it?" she asked. "He's come back to frighten me again." Her breaths came in short bursts.

"No, Mom. It's someone else. Just stay put. They'll be gone soon," Colton whispered.

We heard more scuffling and running before the back door slammed shut, leaving the restaurant quiet again. I didn't hear a car speed away, and I wondered if they had run down the beach. I couldn't get it out of my thoughts that the man with the gun was the same height as Damon, and the man he was chasing had the same lanky build as Leif. I wondered what could be going on. I didn't understand why Damon showed up every time I was close to figuring things out and ruined everything. It was almost as though he had a sixth sense, like me. But, it seemed more likely that he was getting information about me from spies like Melanie and a private detective and using it to thwart my investigation, although I didn't know why.

"I don't know what that was all about, but they've left. And it appears the ghost sighting is over for tonight," Colton said. "Somebody turn on the lights. We need to get back to our rooms and safety as soon as possible."

Before anyone moved, the lights flickered on. I turned to see Melanie, dressed in a blue robe and slippers, standing near the switches with her hands on her hips.

"What's all the commotion?" she asked. "I can hear you guys all the way upstairs. What are you doing behind the bar?"

"We had a ghost sighting," Andy said. "We saw apparitions from the shipwreck."

"Ghosts again? And nobody told me?" she said, icily. "I'm

the one that drove you guys out to the reef, remember? I should think you'd keep me informed, although frankly, I'm surprised you don't have better things to do besides look for things that aren't there. I'm going back to bed, and I think everyone else should, too. It's late."

I was still scared of her and tried to blend into the background. It seemed strange that she didn't appear to have seen the men running through the restaurant unless she had seen them and knew what they were doing there. Either way, she didn't mention them. And she obviously didn't believe in ghosts or think much of people who did. That, in itself, wouldn't have bothered me so much if she hadn't seemed so aggressive about it.

"Stay away from her," I whispered to Colton. "I think she's dangerous."

"Okay," he whispered back.

"I'll make sure to tell you next time," Andy said, walking over to her and seemingly trying to smooth things over. "I didn't know you'd want to be here."

"I didn't want to be here. I just wanted to know about it," she said. "I don't like people keeping things from me. Now. Everybody go back to bed," she said. "I need to get some sleep, and I can't have all this noise going on."

Everyone shuffled toward the hallway.

"We should call the police about the man with the gun," Martha whispered.

"No. They're long gone, and we didn't get a good look at them anyway," Colton said. "The police could say they were more ghosts, and we don't want them not believing you, or the rest of us, again. Especially since we're closing the inn, anyway."

Martha nodded, and we all agreed and headed for our rooms. Melanie turned the light off behind us. More and more, I was beginning to think she was involved in the disappearance of the gold, and it seemed as though Damon was behind her every step of the way. I wasn't sure why I thought that, but it was a strong feeling. I added her to my list of suspects in the heist of the gold.

It would be so nice not to have to worry about the mystery and Tyler, but even though I had more suspects, I felt further away from finding out what happened to the gold than I ever had before. If the men running through the restaurant just now were Damon and Leif, that could add credence to the possibility that Leif was involved in something shady, and Damon, as well. But I didn't know what it was. And the fact that it happened when the ghosts from the shipwreck appeared, signaling a change in the spirit world, made me afraid someone would die before the night was over. And I didn't know why. I trembled and reached for Colton. He took my arm and led me down the hallway toward the stairs, calling 'goodnight' to everyone as we left.

"It's been a long, strange night," Colton said. "But, I'm glad I had you to share it with. Can I walk you to your room?"

"Sure," I answered.

We walked upstairs together, and he stopped outside my room and waited for me to unlock the door. Someone scurried down the hall in the shadows, sounding like a lost little mouse. I turned to see who it was but missed them. It occurred to me that someone could be watching us. It might be Susie or Melanie or even the night stalker. I told Colton and asked him to lower his voice. We leaned closer together, and then he followed me into the room. I closed the door behind him.

"Thanks for telling me what the ghosts looked like," he said quietly. "I have a much better picture of them now, and it's nice to get it from such an intelligent source."

"Thank you," I said.

"You're a very beautiful woman," he said, "inside and out. And very perceptive."

He paused and leaned toward me, and for a moment, I

thought he was going to kiss me. But then he looked away.

"Beautiful women tend to break my heart," he murmured.

I didn't know what to say. I felt so close to him after sharing the ghost encounters with him, and I was happy that he was opening up to me. I think he felt close to me, too. I wanted him to stay with me, but I was sad that he still seemed so hurt by Melanie's betrayal. Seeing her tonight may have brought those feelings up in him again.

I touched his arm. "I know what it's like to have your heart broken," I said. "My heart was broken, too. I wouldn't wish it on anyone. But I wouldn't have met you otherwise, so I don't think it was such a bad thing anymore. Maybe it happened so that we could be together."

"I'm sorry that happened to you," he said. "Was it recent?"

"You could say that," I said, putting my hand down. "I left my husband and came to the island to get away from him."

"Your husband?"

"Yes. I'm sorry I didn't tell you. He and I are not emotionally connected anymore. It's been over for a long time."

"You're still married?"

"Legally," I said, worried about the look in his eyes.

"Why didn't you tell me?" he asked.

"I was afraid you wouldn't want to see me anymore," I said, suddenly feeling insecure. My arms began to shake. "Was I right?"

He paused. "I don't know. I wish you'd told me sooner before I became so involved with you. I don't think I could handle another break-up."

"I don't want to break up," I said, holding my elbows to stop the shaking. "My marriage is over. I want this to work. I think we have something good going here."

"I thought that, too," he said. He looked away again. "But that was before I knew you were married. I have to think about this. I'm sorry. I'll see you later."

"Please, Colton," I said. "I didn't mean to hurt you. I want to be with you."

"Yeah," he said.

He turned and walked out the door. I stepped out after him and watched him walk down the hall. He didn't look back.

"Be careful," I said, pulling my sweater more closely around me to ward off a chill as I watched him walk down the stairs and disappear from view. I didn't know where the chill was coming from this time. As far as I knew, all the ghosts were gone for the night. And now it looked like Colton was, too.

I swallowed hard as I stepped back into the room and closed the door behind me, wondering what this meant for our future together.

CHAPTER 14

The beach was quiet in the early morning when I took my camera and trudged barefoot down the bluff to go for a walk. Waves lapped softly against the cool, wet sand, and a light mist steamed off the surface of the lake. I hadn't slept well. Colton's devastated expression when he found out I was still married haunted my dreams. I hadn't meant to hurt him, and I was mortified to think that I had. But there was nothing I could do about it now except wait and see if time softened the blow. I hadn't seen him all day yesterday after our ghostly encounters the night before that, and Martha hadn't seen him either. He must have left the inn and returned to town, and I desperately wished that he would call me.

A loon hooted mournfully from the brume, and an elegant tern soared gracefully overhead. I captured the nebulous scene for a possible calendar page and continued down the beach. I hadn't realized how much I cared for Colton until I was faced with the prospect of losing him. Starting my life over suddenly seemed momentous and lonely. The exhilaration I felt in gaining freedom from my old life waned at the possibility that I wouldn't have him to share it with.

I snapped a photo of a spotted sandpiper pecking and bobbing in the sand, and when I looked up, Susie and Bobby were running down the beach toward me, probably on their way back to the inn. Melanie was farther back, strolling behind them. We had not spoken since the dive, even though I'd seen her at the ghost sighting at the inn a few nights ago, and I wasn't sure what to say to her. I could pretend to be thoroughly engrossed in my work and let her pass by, but she might have information about Damon and Leif, for that matter, that could be interesting. I waved instead, but she didn't wave back.

"What are you doing?" Bobby asked as he stopped next to me.

"Taking pictures," I answered. "What are you doing?"

"Nothing," he said.

"We went to see Leif at the lighthouse, but he wasn't there," Susie said, putting her arm around Bobby. "It was locked."

"Really? That's strange. I wonder who's taking care of the light."

"Nobody. It's automated. Don't you know anything?" Susie asked.

"Oh. That's good," I said. "I wonder what happened to him."

"Mom does, too. I bet I know," Susie said, lifting her chin. "It's the same thing that happened in my detective story."

"What?" I asked.

"You and my mom are so dumb," Susie said, "Come on, Bobby. Let's go."

"See you later," I said, unsure whether to grin or not.

They ran toward the inn, and I turned to see Melanie approaching. I'd kept my distance, not only because she scowled at me whenever I saw her and because of the way she acted during the ghost sighting, but because I couldn't help but wonder if she was involved in Colton's near-death experience on the dive. She didn't seem capable of violence, but maybe she would be if someone put her up to it. Damon could have been that someone.

If he treated her the same way he had treated me and was jealous of her interactions with other men, he could have told her to hurt Colton. And she could have done it. Susie said her mother did whatever Damon told her to do. I didn't trust Melanie anymore if I ever did.

"Nice morning," I said, when she reached me, hoping I appeared amiable.

She gave me a cool glance and seemed about to walk on by, but then she paused and turned to look at me.

"I heard you found a bag of gold coins in the coroner's car. I want you to know that it wasn't from the shipwreck or, the prison or, the cabin, or anywhere else you've been looking. The sheriff told me you'd been snooping around when he came by to ask questions about Leif and the coroner's disappearance. Dr. Pearson must have found it somewhere and gotten himself killed for it. You might want to be careful what you say or where you look from now on," she said, appearing to grit her teeth.

"Is that a threat?" I asked, shocked that she was so aggressive.

Her normally placid face was scrunched and shadowed, and she looked more like a witch than the angel she had first appeared to be when I met her at the inn.

"Only if you think it is," she growled, stalking past me. "Oh, and one more thing," she said, looking back over her shoulder. "People who believe in ghosts and stolen gold ought to be careful what they say around here. Someone might come after them and make them leave."

"Another threat?" I asked, trying not to look dumbfounded. I didn't know why she was so angry.

"Just saying," she said.

She turned and stomped away toward the inn, and I felt my heart thump an extra beat. I put my hand to my chest to steady my breathing. Now, more than ever, I was convinced that

Melanie was involved in the theft of the gold and maybe knew who the night stalker was, as well. She was too emotional for it to mean anything else. And I wondered how much Damon had to do with it, too, given that they were involved with each other. It seemed probable that he at least knew about it. But I didn't know how. And one more thing she said had bothered me. It was curious that she had mentioned the prison. I hadn't looked for the gold there. Yet.

I took a deep breath and continued down the beach, trying to put Melanie out of my mind and searching for photo opportunities. A purple finch flitted through trees nearby, and as I headed toward it, a man stepped out of the woods, startling me. It was Stan holding a camera, with a black-and-white husky by his side. I wasn't sure whether to say 'hi' or not.

"Hello, Layla," he said, saving me from my dilemma.

The dog ran up to me and back to Stan after I petted him.

"Hello," I replied, deciding the best course of action would be to make small talk. "Are you taking photos to sell in your shop?"

"Yes. It's a beautiful spot. I don't usually see anyone else out here. You surprised me," he said, smiling.

"You surprised me, too," I said, trying to relax. I wondered if it was just a coincidence that he was out here, too. It seemed odd that I ran into him.

"How's Colton doing? I haven't seen him in a while," he asked.

"Oh, he'll be fine. He's almost as good as new," I said, smiling to cover up the trepidation I felt.

He seemed genial and not at all like someone who would stand by and exchange furtive glances with people after his friend almost drowned. But I had seen it with my own eyes during the dive on the shipwreck. I didn't trust him any more than I trusted Melanie. But then he mentioned something that made me wonder if I was wrong to feel that way.

"By the way," he said. "After you visited my shop when you first came to town, a man came in asking about you."

I shivered inadvertently.

"A man? Who was it?" I asked.

"He didn't give his name, and I didn't tell him anything. I thought you should know."

"Thank you. I'm glad you told me. Was he tall with dark hair and dark eyes?" I asked, thinking of Damon.

"No. He was blond with a medium build." He paused for a moment. "You don't have a private investigator following you or anything, do you? He had that stealthy look about him."

"Really? I don't know. I hadn't thought about that," I said, suddenly wondering if that could have been who called the inn about me. I remembered wondering about the possibility at the time. Maybe Damon had had a private investigator follow me at home when he was gone. He could have followed me to the island and told Damon where I was, and Damon could have followed me here. It seemed like something he would do and would explain why he showed up. It could also explain why someone, possibly Leif, tried to run me off the road when I got to the island. Damon could have told someone who didn't want me here the make of my car, or he could have told someone to do it. He was capable of that.

"I hope not," I said.

I didn't want to discuss it anymore with him. I wasn't sure I liked the fact that I ran into him. He could be following me, too, for all I knew, and I didn't care for that idea.

"I took some nice shots of a sandpiper if you want to get some for yourself," I said. "It's down the beach there."

"I think I'll just head back," he said. "Nice to see you. Say 'hi' to Colton for me and tell him I hope he's feeling better. I know Bob and Larry wish him the best, too."

THE COPPER ISLE GHOSTSLAYER

It seemed strange that he hadn't talked to Colton himself yet, but I didn't say anything.

"I'll tell him," I said, not sure if I would.

I watched him head back toward the inn with the husky, not knowing what to think about him anymore. He'd told me about the possible private investigator, which he didn't have to do, and I didn't know why. Maybe he was just curious about who he was, or perhaps it was something else. I wasn't sure what. He could have been protecting himself or someone else from having something about them uncovered by a P.I. But what? I shook my head and turned back toward the woods to look for the finch. My phone buzzed suddenly, and I nearly dropped it in my haste to answer it, not bothering to check the number.

"Colton?" I asked, desperately trying to think of the proper words to say to make things right with him.

"This is an automated call from Averytown Prison," a metallic voice hummed. "The following message is for Layla Devereaux. Tyler Lawrence has been transferred. For further information, contact prison social services."

The call ended abruptly, and I stood staring at the phone, unable to comprehend what I'd heard. Tyler was gone and had been transferred to the prison down south? I thought I had more time to get him out and keep that from happening. What was I going to do now? I'd probably never see him again, or at least not very often. I dropped to my knees and put my head in my hands. Everything was falling apart. If I didn't have Tyler in my life, what was the point of anything anymore?

I sat down in the sand and hugged my knees, gazing at the glassy lake and taking in the serene pinks and pale blues of the muted sky. It was so beautiful and so peaceful. I wished I had that peace for myself.

My phone rang again, and I rushed to answer it, hoping it was another call to tell me it was all a mistake. This time, it was

Colton.

"Layla, I'm glad you answered," he said.

"Colton?" I asked breathlessly, trying to control the tremor in my voice. I didn't want to cry with relief or hopelessness.

"Yes. It's me. I'm at the sheriff's office near the harbor in town. Can you meet me here right away? Something's happened that I think you should know about."

"What is it? Are you okay?"

"Yes, I'm fine. But I need to talk to you. Can you make it?"

"I'll be right there," I said, hanging up and heading for the inn.

I wondered if the Ghostslayer had claimed another victim in the form of a missing person or something, and someone had made a report. It occurred to me that people on the island could blame the Ghostslayer instead of Leif for the coroner's disappearance, but I didn't think the sheriff would go along with a theory like that. It could also be that people at the inn had been terrorized again by the night stalker, and Colton was getting the sheriff involved this time. Whatever it was, I needed to get there now. Colton sounded serious.

I ran to my room, grabbed my purse, and slipped on a pair of sandals before heading back downstairs. I would have mentioned where I was going to Martha, but I didn't see her. I wasn't surprised. The events a few nights ago had affected her deeply, and she had been spending a lot of time in her room. I hurried to my car and put my camera in the trunk before driving into town as fast as possible and locating the sheriff's office. When I walked in, Colton was talking to him at his desk.

"What is it? What's wrong?" I asked.

Colton's hair was messed up, and his shirt was wrinkled. He wiped the sweat from his forehead with the back of his hand as he turned toward me. He looked like he hadn't slept in days.

The sheriff stood when I walked over.

"Miss Deveraux, I'm glad you came. Your interest in the coroner's whereabouts led to a formal investigation into his disappearance and the whereabouts of more possible gold. Because of that, I wanted you to know that, after further leads, deputies spoke a few days ago with Leif Drendahl, the tour guide at the lighthouse."

"Was he involved?" I asked, hoping my deductions were correct and had been confirmed.

The sheriff looked at Colton and then back at me.

"I can't confirm or deny that at the moment. Unfortunately, Leif was found dead at the lighthouse by my deputies when they returned to speak with him yesterday evening."

"Leif's dead?" I gasped, feeling a strange sense of unreality.

It couldn't be true. If he was dead, we would never find out who killed the coroner. All the clues had led to Leif, and now there was no way to confront him and insist that he lead us to the gold. And there was no way to find out if he killed Pappy, either. That meant Tyler would remain in prison as a convicted murderer. My knees buckled, and Colton rushed over to catch me.

"Thank you," I said, grasping at the protection of his strong arms.

"I'm afraid he is," the sheriff said.

"What happened?" I asked, recovering myself but still leaning against Colton.

"It appears he was murdered. His neck was broken."

"No," I said, shaking my head. "That's the same thing that happened to the previous tour guide."

"You know about that?" he asked, tilting his head and staring at me.

"Well, only that it supposedly happened that way. The woman at the coroner's office told me that," I replied, feeling suddenly on edge.

"Hmm," the sheriff said. "Is there a reason you asked her about the previous tour guide's death?"

I wasn't sure what to say. I didn't want to tell him I was Tyler's sister, but I didn't like the suspicious way he was looking at me. After glancing up at Colton, who nodded at me, I decided to be honest.

"Tyler Lawrence is my brother. I came to the island to clear his name, and I've been asking around to try to find out what happened last summer," I said.

"I see," the sheriff said, holding my gaze. "He was already tried and convicted for Pappy's murder. I'm not sure there's much you can do."

"I have to try," I said. "He's my brother. And he's innocent."

The sheriff rubbed his chin.

"Well, your theories so far led us to the gold. I suppose it's okay for you to ask around about things. But you'd do well to be careful, especially now, after we found Leif dead. We don't know what we're up against."

"Yes, of course, I'll be careful. Thank you," I said, regaining my balance and standing on my own.

"One other thing," the sheriff said, looking at Colton, who looked at me with an unreadable expression on his face.

"What? What is it?" I asked, not sure what to make of the sheriff's gruff tone of voice.

"Colton was seen on the beach last evening near the lighthouse soon after Leif was found dead. He was brought in by my deputies, questioned, and released this afternoon, which is when he called you."

"I gasped and looked up at Colton. He was looking at the floor."

"What are you saying? What does that mean?" I asked.

"It means that he is a potential suspect in Leif's murder," the sheriff said.

"No. That's impossible. Colton would never do such a thing."

"That's what I told them," Colton said. "I got a call from Leif asking me to meet him at the lighthouse yesterday, and I was on my way over to see him. I don't know why he called or what he wanted. But that's what happened, and that's why I was there."

"Oh, well, you believe him, don't you?" I asked the sheriff.

"For now," he said. "But we're continuing with our investigation. Neither one of you would be wise to leave the island at this time."

"Why? I'm not planning to, but why shouldn't I leave?"

"In your case, Miss Devereaux, it's because, in my estimation, you would be better protected on the island than on the mainland from whatever is going on. In Colton's case, it's because he hasn't yet been cleared as a suspect."

"Oh my goodness," I said.

"Yes, well, you can both leave now."

Colton nodded at the sheriff and took my arm, and we walked together out to the street. It had turned out to be a beautiful day, and the contrast between the bright sunshine and the dim interior of the sheriff's office was hard to adjust to. I felt as though I'd had a brush with losing my freedom, and I wondered if Colton felt the same way about himself.

"This is awful," I said. "How could anyone think you're capable of murder? We have to clear your name now, too, along with Tyler's."

"Yeah," Colton said. "It was a rough night. I'm glad you came when I called. Let's go back to the inn now. I need to get some sleep."

"Sure," I said, walking with him toward my car. He looked so exhausted and devastated, and my heart went out to him. I planned to stand by him no matter what happened, and I hoped he would do the same for me.

When we arrived at the car, I unlocked the door for him, and while he was getting in, I walked around to get in on the driver's side. I had parallel parked down the street near the harbor. As I stepped off the curb, I glanced toward the sheriff's office and gasped. Damon had just pulled into a space in front of the office and was getting out of his car. I couldn't imagine what he was doing there. I watched with my mouth open as he opened the door and disappeared inside. Why would Damon be talking to the sheriff? I wondered how far he would go in his attempts to get me to return home. He may have known that I just talked to the sheriff and wondered if I'd told him who he really was. Would he make things up about me in his alternate persona as Gregory Wellington to try to get the sheriff to make me leave? What could he be saying to him? Unless he wasn't talking to him about me. Maybe Damon knew something about Leif's murder, and the sheriff wanted to find out what it was. I shook my head to clear it. My mind was racing, and now was no time for that. I needed to take Colton home so he could take a hot shower and climb into a warm bed to rest. I opened the car door and sat down behind the wheel.

"Is everything okay?" Colton asked. "You were standing out there a long time."

"Yes, everything's fine," I said. "I just needed some air."

I didn't want to mention seeing Damon at the moment and my fears about him and upset Colton in his current state.

I put the car in drive and drove down the main street to the harbor road to head back to the inn. I hoped Colton would recover from his ordeal soon and that he had forgiven me by now for not telling him I was still married. Everything I had deduced had fallen apart, and everything I had worked for and come to the island for had been shattered. He was the only person who could help me put things back together again. And I desperately hoped that he would.

CHAPTER 15

I walked through the backyard of Colton's house in town with a tray of lemonade and cookies and set it on the patio table in the gazebo. We had spent the morning and most of the afternoon moving things from the inn to the house, which was more of a generous lakeside cottage, and finding places for them. It was hard work, and we decided it was time for a break. The closing date for the inn wasn't finalized, but we wanted to be prepared when it was. Colton seemed to have accepted the fact that I was legally, if not emotionally, married and had come to terms with it, considering that he still wanted me to move into his house. But I wasn't sure exactly how he felt about me now, and I was afraid to ask. I set the tray on the patio table and turned to see him sauntering toward me. He looked much better than he had when I picked him up at the sheriff's office a few days ago, and I hoped he was recovering from his ordeal. We needed to make a plan to clear his name of the murder, and we needed to do it fast. I wasn't going to wait around and have another person I loved convicted of something they didn't do.

"I just got off the phone with Bob," he said, walking up the steps to the table. "The sheriff's deputies brought Leif's dog over to him. Since he already owns a husky, he agreed to take in another one when they asked. The dogs were in a sled race together, along with Stan and Larry's, last winter, so he knows they get along."

"They were in a dogsled race?" I asked.

"Yes. Gregory Wellington ran the island race in the winter and used the huskies. I think he ran it with the four dogs owned by Stan, Bob, Larry, and Leif. Why?"

My heart skipped a beat. I hadn't known Damon had been on the island even then, pretending to be Gregory Wellington. Something about the time frame clicked with me, though. He and the dogs had something to do with what happened last summer. I felt it, but I didn't know what it was. And then I thought of something.

"Did Gregory ever rent the cabin on the lake?" I asked.

"The one we checked for clues in?" Colton asked.

"Yes."

"I don't know. He may have rented it in February when he came back for the race. I remember hearing something about that. The dogs were all dropped off at his rental cabin the week of the race for him to practice running with them. It's possible it was the same one. Is that significant?"

"I'm not sure, but I think we need to find out," I said, pausing to think for a moment. "It seems like more than a coincidence that there was a dogsled at that cabin when we went there."

"You're right," Colton said. "I'll check with the real estate office.

"I'm glad you're going to look into it," I said. "It's important that we know. I'm not sure why I feel that way, but I do."

"Okay," he said, nodding.

We sat in the patio chairs, and I poured lemonade for us both. The breeze off the harbor was pleasant and cool, and I leaned back and crossed my legs as I smoothed my fluttering sundress, smiling when I saw Colton take notice. He seemed to appreciate the casual island look I'd adopted since coming here, which was so different from the sophisticated, coiffed look that Damon preferred. Something about the atmosphere and the slow pace of the islanders made me relax and feel more casual, and I liked that. I felt more like my real self than I ever had before in my life, even though there were also a lot of frightening things going on.

"Anyway," Colton continued, "Bob said the deputies told him everyone in town is on alert about there being another murder at the lighthouse of another person no one knew much about. They also told him I was a suspect. He said no one's going to take that seriously, but I wonder."

"We'll have to find out what really happened as soon as possible," I said. "We can't have your good name sullied like this."

"Thanks. I'm glad you and your perceptive, analytical skills are on my side."

"Always," I said, thinking, even as he said it, that he needed me to watch out for him with his friends as well as other people.

He seemed to have forgotten about what had happened on the dive and treated them as though nothing had changed. To me, everything about his relationships with his friends changed on that day. But he didn't seem to feel that way, although he could just be unwilling to accept the possibility that his friends might not be his friends, which was understandable. Something else bothered me. I hesitated to bring it up because Stan and Melanie were Colton's friends, but I thought it needed to be discussed.

"By the way, I was out on the beach near the inn when you called me the other morning from the sheriff's office. I was taking photos, and I ran into Melanie and her children and Stan, as well," I said. "I can't help but wonder if it was more than a coincidence that they were there the morning after the murder.

I'm not saying they had anything to do with it, but it doesn't seem out of the realm of possibility. I think we should keep that in mind."

"Stan and Melanie?"

"Well, they weren't together, but they were both out there. It's just something to consider. I don't trust either one of them, even though they're your friends, and I think someone is trying to frame you for Leif's murder. I don't know who killed Leif, and I don't know who's trying to frame you. But I think we need to be open to all the possibilities if we're going to get you out of this."

"Hmm." Colton rubbed his chin and nodded. "You could be right. I wouldn't have said that before I was arrested for Leif's murder, but now, I don't know who to trust anymore. But I trust you, Layla. I trust your instincts."

"Thank you," I said, relieved that he took what I said into account and didn't dismiss it as idle ramblings like Damon would have. More and more, I was beginning to trust Colton and confide my thoughts to him. It was a good feeling.

Colton picked up his drink and leaned back in his chair.

"Tourism will definitely suffer because of this, and I'm more convinced than ever that I'm doing the right thing in closing the inn," he said. "Bob is concerned about his business prospects on the island diminishing, too."

"I can imagine," I said.

He paused and took a sip of lemonade before continuing. "It's strange, though. He didn't seem as upset as I thought he would be. I don't know why I feel that way, but it's almost as though he was expecting a downturn and had a plan to deal with it."

"Well, you did," I said. "You made plans to close the inn."

"That's true," Colton said.

"But you think it's more than economic foresight?"

"I don't know. Maybe."

I thought for a moment. "I know Bob's your friend, but have you considered the possibility that he has the gold or knows of its whereabouts, and that's why he isn't so concerned about losing money?"

"What?"

"Consider this. If he and your other friends know where the gold is, they don't have to worry about the island going under financially. They can wait for the fervor over the murders and the stalking to drive people off the island and have it to themselves along with the gold. They could then become power brokers on the island and make even more money."

"They?" Colton asked, grimacing and rubbing his forehead.

"The scope of this could easily encompass more than one person. I mean, I thought Leif stole the gold and murdered Pappy, but now we know he didn't, at least not by himself."

Colton looked at me, and slowly, his eyes widened. I wasn't sure what his response would be. My statement could easily be taken by him as an islander who had lived here all his life and led the Chamber of Commerce to be a preposterous deduction. On the other hand, he was now a suspect in a murder, and that could lead him to consider more possibilities as to what was going on. I let out a breath when he nodded.

"You could be onto something," he said. "This is all too much for one person to do, or even two people. It's hard to imagine that Bob and Larry and Stan could be involved in something like that, but gold and power can corrupt, and it could be too much to resist."

"Don't forget about Melanie," I said.

His face shadowed. "I suppose it's possible she's involved," he said, "much as I'd like not to think so."

"Try not to let it bother you too much," I said. "I'm sure it's hard to think that someone you loved may not have your best interests at heart. But I've been there with Damon, and I know what it's like. I'm here for you now, and whatever went on between you and Melanie is in the past. I'll watch out for you. I won't hurt you like she did. I promise."

"Thanks," Colton said, furrowing his brow. "I believe you. I think you do have my best interests at heart, especially after you came and picked me up at the sheriff's office. Maybe they did all join forces to abscond with the gold. I'm only considering the possibility because I got hit on the head on the dive, and it made me reconsider things. If you're right, you know what this means, don't you?"

"What?"

"We must be dealing with a crime ring."

The words hung in the air like a ghoul. I had considered that before but had been convinced that Leif was the leader. There could still be a crime ring, but one that was led by a different person. To hear it said out loud was chilling. Colton had validated my feelings and given them reality, and I sat for a moment, realizing that he and I both knew something that could very easily cost us our lives. We needed to stick together now more than ever.

"I agree," I said, holding his gaze. "I do think we could be dealing with a crime ring. We need to make a new plan. We need to find out what's really going on and who's in charge of things. If it wasn't Leif, it had to be someone else from on or off the island. It's possible that they joined forces with a larger operation, and if they did, the scope of this could encompass more than just the island."

Colton shook his head. "I'm with you," he said after a moment. "Hard as it may be for me to accept."

"I'm glad," I said. "I know it's been a harrowing few days. I wanted you to know that I'm glad we're back together. We are, aren't we?"

Colton looked away and gazed out over the harbor. The afternoon sun shimmered on the clear blue water where sailboats and jet skis left slow wakes in the waves. I held my breath, waiting for him to answer.

He looked back at me.

"I've never met anyone like you," he said. "You make me feel good about myself, and you help me to see things that I wouldn't otherwise see. And you're beautiful, intelligent, and caring. I don't want to be without you now that I've met you. In answer to your question, yes, we're back together. We'll find a way to make it work. If that's what you want."

"It is," I said, leaning forward. "I know you're still dealing with your feelings about Melanie, and I'm still dealing with the loss of my marriage. But time heals. I truly believe that. And I think we can recover and move on. I think we could have something good."

"Me, too," Colton said. "We already do."

I smiled, and he smiled back.

"Well," I said, standing and picking up the tray. "The first thing we have to do is take this back into the house. Then we have to go out to the lighthouse again."

"The lighthouse? Why?" Colton asked, following me through the yard.

"Something Susie said resonated with me, and I want to look into it. She told me she overheard someone threaten her mother. He told her she would end up at the lighthouse like the doctor if she didn't do as she was told, and I want to find out what that means."

"What doctor?" Colton asked, holding the screen door open for me. "As far as I know, there was never a doctor out there."

"I know, but I can't help but wonder if it was a reference to the coroner. It makes me think we should check there for his body."

"Wow. Okay. Who threatened Melanie?" he asked.

We walked into the house, and I set the tray by the sink before turning to Colton.

"I'll tell you, but you have to promise not to mention this to anyone. I'm only telling you because I trust you, and I think our relationship can handle this now. I hope so, anyway."

Colton gazed at me for a moment before walking over and taking my hand.

"Tell me. Who was it?"

"It was my husband."

"Your husband? What do you mean? I thought you weren't with him anymore," he said.

"I'm not. I'm with you now. Let me explain. Susie overheard her mother talking to Gregory Wellington, who is really my husband, Damon Devereaux. I didn't know he had another life here on the island until I got here. He threatened Melanie, Colton. And he's threatening me. He's not the type of person that lets someone leave him. I don't know what he's up to, but I'm sure it's something bad."

"Oh, man," Colton said, dropping my hand and pacing through the kitchen. "This is worse than I thought. We have a true menace to society living and working on the island in plain sight, and none of us knew it. At least, I didn't." Colton rubbed his chin. "Maybe the others did. Maybe they know who he is."

"I don't think so," I said. "Or maybe they do, but they don't know he has a different name. I don't think Melanie knows he has another name, either. She's in love with him, and, according to Susie, she does whatever he tells her to do."

"Susie sure keeps on top of things," Colton said.

"She's a good person to talk to," I said. "Listening at doors and eavesdropping could get her into trouble, but it could help us out in our investigation if she tells us what she knows."

"I'll keep that in mind," Colton said. "But I'm worried about you now. I think you should tell the sheriff that Gregory is really Damon. You need to be protected."

"Not yet. I want to find out what's going on first. Otherwise, Damon could find out someone's on to him besides me and leave the island, and we'll never find out what he's doing here. He could be involved in the crime ring. Besides, you're not the best person to tell the sheriff anything right now while you're a murder suspect."

"Hmm," Colton said. "You're right. Okay, we won't tell the sheriff yet. But keep me informed about Damon, and be careful."

"Okay."

We unloaded a few more things from Colton's truck and put them away before hopping in the cab to drive out to the lighthouse. On the way there, we passed through town, and I saw Damon's car parked in front of the hotel.

"Damon's still on the island. That's his car," I said, pointing it out to Colton. "Melanie thought he was leaving days ago. He must be up to something. Did I tell you I saw him there with the woman from the coroner's office? They were having a heated conversation in the hotel restaurant."

"The clerk, you mean? The one who told you Pappy's date of death was different from the one at the records office?"

"Yes, and it looked like they knew each other pretty well from the way she was gesturing at him."

"I'll keep that in mind," Colton said. "That adds credence to the possibility that he knows what happened to Pappy and maybe what happened to Dr. Pearson."

We drove in silence as we headed down the harbor road. White-tipped waves rolled leisurely to shore, and I glimpsed the lighthouse on the bluff far in the distance through the trees lining the road. It looked so majestic, standing tall against the wind under an azure sky. It was hard to imagine that two murders had happened there in less than a year.

When we pulled up the gravel driveway to the lighthouse, the first thing I noticed was that Leif's car was gone. The sheriff's deputies must have taken it. There was no other car in its place, and I assumed that meant the lighthouse was abandoned. It reminded me of the lighthouse Leif had told me he'd abandoned on the mainland to come to work here on the island. I was glad Susie had told me the lights were automated and didn't need a person around to keep them shining for the sailors. Colton got out and knocked on the door and tried the latch, but it was locked. He stepped away and looked around. Something in the woods caught my eye as I was getting out of the truck. I looked more closely and saw the slow movement of low branches as though someone had been there and left. I felt a chill even as the sun warmed my shoulders. I looked back toward Colton, who was looking up at the lighthouse balcony and shielding his eyes.

"Hello," he called.

There was no answer.

"Yeah, no one's here," he said, turning toward me. "I didn't think there would be."

He stepped back for a minute and kicked his shoe against the cement step before scraping it back and forth on the scraggly grass.

"What the heck is this?" he asked, scrunching up his face. "There's some sort of black mold or goo on my shoe."

I walked over to take a look.

"I know what that is," I said. "I saw it at the prison. It's all over the walls and outside grounds around there. It must be some sort of creeping mold, but what's it doing on the step here? It's too hot at the lighthouse for mold like that to grow. It only likes dark, dank places."

"I don't know, but it mucked up my shoes."

I looked around and saw a few dark spots in the sand. They looked like footprints with bits of mold in them. I thought for a moment. "These must have been left here by someone who was also at the prison," I said. "And it must have been recently, or the rain last night would have washed them away. I think someone's still out here." I shivered and looked around. "It must be someone who's doing the same thing we are, looking for clues. Or it could be the murderer revisiting the scene of the crime."

I looked at Colton, and we locked gazes. I felt a chill.

"Maybe we should get out here," he said.

"Maybe that's a good idea," I said, turning and heading quickly back to the truck. "And maybe we should check the prison to see if there are footprints in the mold there," I called over my shoulder. "It could be related to the murder here. We can come back out sometime with the sheriff if we can convince him to look for the coroner's body. Right now, we better go."

"I'm right behind you," Colton said.

We ran through the sand and jumped into the truck, and Colton crunched through the gravel and headed for the harbor road. The branches in the woods moved again, and I caught a glimpse of what looked to be a sallow-faced, gray-haired man peering out at us, but he was obscured by the brush. He looked a little bit like Leif, but it couldn't be. Leif was dead. Unless it was his ghost. I shivered again as the figure disappeared into the trees.

"Let's go home," I said. "Now."

Colton nodded as he floored the accelerator, and we screeched through the gravel and down the driveway and headed for the inn.

CHAPTER 16

We moved more things from the inn to Colton's house over the next few days with Martha's help. I didn't have much to move for myself because I was keeping my clothes and cameras at the inn until the last minute. I helped them and picked out a bedroom at the house to stay in. It was charming, with pink rosebud wallpaper and a bay window that looked out over the harbor. I could picture myself being very happy here.

We decided after our last trip one afternoon, when most of the things had been put away, to take Martha back to the inn and head out to the prison with Andy. He had agreed to bring his equipment and search for ghosts again after we told him we were going to the prison to look for the gold. He agreed with me that it could be convenient for someone that the rumors of ghosts kept people away from the prison and that it was possible there was illegal activity going on there. And he wanted to record any paranormal activity that might show up.

We pulled up next to the prison in the late afternoon and headed for the boarded-up windows. This time, Colton had brought a crowbar, and he pried away a few boards so that we could climb through into the prison. The black mold was pervasive, and I stepped gingerly inside behind Andy, letting my eyes adjust to the dark interior.

"So you think the gold is here somewhere?" Colton asked, following me in.

"Could be," I said, moving aside to let him in. "That's why I wanted to come out here again with you and Andy and check the paranormal readings. Everyone is afraid of the ghosts here, and no one ever comes out here. It seems like it would be the perfect place for someone to hide stolen treasure. I wonder if there are really ghosts or if someone made it up."

"That's a good point," Colton said.

"Yes, it is," Andy said. " But, there could be a good reason people are afraid. I've gotten an EMF 5 reading here, which is evidence of a dangerous ghost. And it was probably the Ghostslayer. No one wants to run into him. But I haven't gotten readings on any other ghosts. I'll be right back. I want to check the reading in the corner." He walked toward the boarded-up windows on the far wall.

I glanced around at the crumbled ruins of a wall and at the rusted bars on a far window, and the hairs on the backs of my arms stood up.

"This is a terrible place. I can feel it. It's a good thing it closed down," I said.

"Yes," Colton said. "Pappy was released when it did more than thirty years ago. It was in an old newspaper article I found in the archives at the library."

"So he was here," I said, looking around some more.

"Yes, but the article also said the prison was closed down due to improper management and human rights violations."

"How awful. I wonder what that means," I said.

"Yeah. I can only guess. Given what happened to the Ghostslayer, the possibilities seem unspeakable. What was even more disturbing was that the article said that many of those kept here were wrongly imprisoned and held against their will."

"How is that possible?" I asked.

"I don't know," Colton said, rubbing his chin. "But, if, as we were saying, there's a crime ring on the island, it could be that it was operating even back then and had something to do with it."

"You mean it could have been operating for thirty years?" I asked.

"Yes, or even before that in a covert fashion. Then, when the gold was found last summer, they could have sprung into operation to steal it."

"I hadn't thought of that," I said, putting my finger to my lips and thinking. "That's a good deduction."

"Thanks. I have to try to keep up with you," Colton said, grinning.

Andy came back, and we stood huddled together in the cavernous room. I imagined the suffering of the people trapped here years ago inside the dank, gray walls and rusted bars of the prison. I remembered when Mrs. Pinley at the funeral home had said that the Ghostslayer had come from here, brought to a terrible end by his captors, and turned into a demon by his underground torment. It was a horrifying thought.

"I think we should branch out and see what we can find," Colton said. "It's a huge place, and there could be any number of hiding spots."

I glanced around again at the crumbling ruins.

"I'm not going anywhere here by myself," I said. "I think we need to stick together. I'll follow you."

"All right," Colton said.

He stepped through a scraped-up door jam into a hallway where there was another, smaller room that looked as though it could have been a jail cell. I followed him, and Andy followed me. More openings down the hall signaled more cells. This one had black iron bars on a small window that looked out over a seemingly impossibly beautiful view of the lake from the dark, hidden cell. I wondered what it must have been like to see such beauty and be trapped in the darkness, away from it all. An old, stained mattress leaned on top of rusted springs on a bunk. A messy pile of jeans and flannel shirts lay in the corner next to a crumpled sleeping bag stuffed with a brownish pillow.

"What's this?" I asked. "It looks as though someone lives here. How could that be?"

Colton walked over and kicked the pile. "It does look that way," he said. "Look at this. There's a black cape and gloves and what looks like a black ski mask."

"The night stalker," I said. "That's something he would wear, given Martha's and others' descriptions of him. He must be living here. We've found him."

"Let's not jump to conclusions," Colton said. "You could be right, but we don't know that for sure. Let's look around some more."

I shivered. I didn't want to look around anymore. I'd seen enough. The night stalker was no one to mess with. But I didn't want to leave so soon after we arrived and let Colton and Andy down. We were all there to solve the mystery.

Colton picked up a satchel near the mattress, turned it upside down, and shook it. Nothing fell out.

"I don't know who or why someone would live here, but there's a bucket of water by the wall and a few cups. And there are coals surrounded by rocks and a shovel in the corner."

"A shovel?" I asked.

"Yes, he must use it to stoke the coals," Andy said.

"It looks like someone cooks here, too," I said. "It looks like there are crusts of blackened bread in the fire."

Colton walked over and pushed coals around with his foot. "It's hard to say what it is or what they used the coals for. Boiling water, maybe, or grilling. What's this?"

He leaned over and brushed soot away from his shoe.

Something clinked against a rock.

"It's a coin," Colton said gruffly, picking it up and standing to show me. "It's a gold coin."

"Andy, we found something," I said, hurrying over to Colton.

Andy stopped what he was doing and ran over to join us.

"It's from the 1800s. It must be from the shipwreck. You're right, Layla. The gold is here somewhere. I don't know where it is or how it got here, but I think we've found the stash. And I think someone lives here and guards it. And you're right. It could be the night stalker hiding out."

I gasped. "Really?"

"Yes, really," Colton said.

"If there's gold here from the shipwreck, there could be ghosts from the shipwreck here, too," Andy said. "But as far as I know, the ghosts from the shipwreck are a pretty amiable group. I don't know why anyone would be afraid of them. Unless the Ghostslayer is here a lot, there doesn't seem to be much to be afraid of. And he only comes around during storms. I wonder if whoever lives here purposely frightens people away."

"That's possible," I said. "It could be the same person that frightens Martha and others on the island and tries to get them to leave. It must be the night stalker."

"Or the murderer," Colton said.

A hush fell over the jail cell.

"The murderer of Pappy and the coroner and Leif could be hiding out here with the gold," Colton said.

Andy and I remained silent, and we all stood looking at each other. I didn't know what to say. A breeze rattled the boards on the windows in the other room, and I glanced out the barred jail cell window to see gray storm clouds gathering in the distance. A tall, black thunderhead puffed into the sky behind them.

"You're right," I said after a moment. "And he could also be the night stalker."

Colton nodded as the boards rattled more loudly.

"What's all the racket?" Andy said. "It doesn't seem like a breeze would make this much noise. Is there a storm coming?"

"Could be," I said. "Look."

I pointed out the window at the thunderhead, and Andy paled.

"I don't want to be out here when a storm comes in," he said. "There's too much possibility that the Ghostslayer could show up again. And I don't want laypersons exposed to him. It's too traumatic."

"We'd better go," Colton said, turning to leave the jail.

A scurrying sound like a pack of rats scratching a wood floor sounded from the other room, followed by footsteps and a loud thump. Colton ran out of the jail cell with Andy and me close behind him.

"What was that?" I asked.

"Someone was here," Colton said. "The person who lives here must have returned and seen us before running away."

"Did you get a look at him?" Andy asked.

"No, but one of the boards on the window is at an angle. He must have come in and left through there."

"We're lucky we weren't killed," I said, hearing my voice quiver.

"I think we scared him away," Colton said. "He wasn't expecting us to be here, and there are three of us. We had the element of surprise in our favor."

"It's a good thing," Andy said.

Suddenly, a sheet of rain hit the iron bars on the jail cell we'd just left and splashed through the window.

"Maybe that's how the mold gets in," Andy said. "It's too late to beat the storm. I guess we'll just have to ride it out until it lets up enough to make a run for the truck. Unless you want to make a run for it anyway."

Just then, a crash of thunder hit, and lightning cracked across the sky.

"Maybe we'll wait for a bit," Colton said. "Storms come up fast on the lake, but they can end just as quickly. And whoever was here could still be right outside. We'll give it a little while before we run for the truck."

We stood in the cavernous room, away from the windows, listening to the rumbles and spits of the storm. Colton put his arm around me, and I leaned into his comforting warmth, hoping we'd be able to escape this terrible place soon. Andy walked away from us and scuffed his shoes on the prison floor, back and forth, back and forth, pacing in rhythm with the rain. The blue light from his EMF meter glowed dimly in his hands. Suddenly, the meter emitted a loud shriek.

Andy stopped short and turned to us. "We have to get out of here," he said. His voice was raspy. "We have to get out of here now."

"What is it? What's wrong?" I asked, hearing the fear in my trembling voice. Andy looked scared, and if he was frightened, I was, too.

"It's that sound. Do you hear it? The whooshing, moaning sound of the wind in the trees."

"Yes," I said, listening.

"I do, too," Colton said.

"It's not the wind," he said. "It's the Ghostslayer. He's come back again."

"I thought you'd never heard him or seen him," I said.

"I have. I just told you I hadn't. Be quiet, and duck down. It's too late to leave."

I swallowed hard and pressed my lips together to do as he asked. Colton and I crouched together as Andy peered through the hole in the boards on the window. The moaning grew louder until it turned into a deafening howl as though a wounded wolf was dying of agony.

I buried my head in Colton's shoulder and put my hands over my ears.

"Who's he after?" I whispered after a while, moving my hand off of one ear to listen for an answer.

"Shh," Andy said.

I barely heard him over the moaning and howling. A dim red glow passed by the window and washed Andy's face with its bloody hue. He suddenly appeared a ghoul himself, and it was all I could do to keep from screaming. A board shook and rattled, and for a moment, it seemed as though the Ghostslayer was coming in the window. I sucked in a breath and buried my face in Colton's shoulder again. When would this end? And how? Who was he after? I pressed my hands more tightly against my ears, taking them on and off occasionally to listen to the sounds. Eventually, the noise diminished, and I peeked out but stayed in Colton's grasp. When the moaning finally ended, and the glow disappeared, Andy turned to us and motioned that we could relax.

"Is he gone?" Colton asked.

"Yes," Andy said.

"Well, thank goodness for that," I said. "That was terrifying. I don't want to experience anything like that ever again. What does he look like?"

"You never want to see him," Andy whispered. "The image would haunt you for the rest of your life as it does mine. It's his eyes. They shoot the fire-red glow of a demon. He has the hollow, gaunt face of a ghoul and the wide, foaming mouth of a rabid dog. Long strands of sopping, white hair hang from his skull, and skeins of rotted flesh drip from his bones. He moans in agony, the agony of a lost soul, and he haunts to find others to share his pain. He's horrible."

I shivered again, contemplating the dreadful description.

"What could have brought him back this time?" Colton asked.

"Leif, maybe, now that he's dead. He could be after his ghost. We know nothing about Leif other than to suspect him of stealing the gold. If he's the one who murdered Pappy and the coroner, he could be another lost soul that the Ghostslayer is after. I wouldn't wish it on anyone, but it's possible. Or, the Ghostslayer could be hovering like a vulture, waiting for someone he wants to die. He could know that imminent death is in someone's future and come back during storms to see if they're dead."

"That's a terrible thought," I said. "But if he's after Leif's ghost because Leif murdered Pappy and the coroner, then who murdered Leif?"

"Well, it wouldn't have been the Ghostslayer. He only takes evil spirits that are already dead or people who had something to do with his death years ago. And most of those people probably left the island a long time ago to get away from him," Andy said.

"That means that if a crime ring is still operating on the island, it could be based on the mainland and managed by people who are afraid to be here themselves because they fear the Ghostslayer's wrath," Colton said. "They could have other people working for them here."

"Maybe Leif had something to do with the Ghostslayer's death," I said.

"I doubt it. He'd only been around the island recently, and the Ghostslayer's macabre death happened a long time ago. It seems more likely that someone else killed Leif, and whoever it was probably killed Pappy and the coroner, too, or at least knows who did," Colton said.

"Maybe that's the person the Ghostslayer is after. He could be hovering and waiting for him to die. Maybe he knows he lives here," I said.

"Maybe," Andy said. "But we still don't know for sure who that is."

"You're right," Colton said.

The rain let up, and Andy peeked through the boards again.

"He's gone. We should go," he said.

"Maybe," Colton said, "but don't you want to stay and look around for the gold?"

"Not now. I'm not sure the storm's over, and if it isn't, the Ghostslayer could be coming back. We need to leave while we still can."

"All right. Maybe Layla and I can come out here another time."

"We could, but I'm pretty sure I already know where the gold is," I said.

"Really, where?"

"Did you see the shovel in the corner of the jail cell?"

"Yes."

"It didn't have ash or coals on it. It was covered with dirt and mold. Someone used that shovel to bury something. I think the gold is buried on the grounds somewhere, and that could be anywhere. It would take us a long time to find it if we ever did."

Colton rubbed his chin. "That's an interesting observation. You're probably right. We may have found out as much as we're going to for the moment. We need to go home and concentrate on finding out who took the gold. Then we can find out from him where it's buried, and we would probably have our murderer, as well."

Andy nodded. "I agree. Can we get out of here now?"

"Yes, let's go," Colton said.

We stepped back through the window onto the muddy ground below, and Colton nailed the boards back into place behind us. I peered around for the Ghostslayer, but all I saw were dripping trees and matted brush. But then, for a moment, I thought I saw something. I stopped and called out to Colton and Andy to wait for me.

The dripping leaves of the brush shook with an otherworldly motion. No one seemed to be there, but they moved as though someone was. I splashed forward through the puddled mud and wet grass of the glen until I reached the outskirts of the woods. I peered through the dark trees, and after a moment, I saw what I was looking for. A man, or what looked like a man, was tripping through the deadwood of the forest. His back was to me, but something about him looked familiar. I gasped. It was the same figure I'd seen at the lighthouse several days before. Leif's ghost. Or was it? I looked more closely. The gray hair was the same, and the clothes looked like those he wore. But it couldn't be him, could it? He was dead. The figure disappeared into the deep darkness of the woods.

As I moved away from the brush to head back to the truck, a hawk soared over the trees and called loudly as it swooped for its prey. It was like the Ghostslayer in that way, making itself known to its victim. I wished I had its perspective and could see far and wide around the prison from the sky. I would know, then, where those who harmed others were, and I could use that knowledge to find them and stop them. But that wasn't to be. I would never soar overhead and have the gift of piercing, distance sight. But I would use the enhanced sight of my own to the best of my abilities to do so anyway. I turned and sloshed back to the truck where Colton and Andy were waiting for me.

"What is it? What did you see?" Colton asked.

"I'm not sure," I said, returning my thoughts to the present. "Someone was there. It looked like Leif, even though it couldn't be him. It must have been the person who lives in the prison and found us there. He must have been watching us."

Colton looked toward the woods. "You're probably right," he said. "We should tell the sheriff about this."

"What? And risk your being arrested again? I don't think so," I said. "Let's wait and see what happens. Maybe we can find out who it is on our own eventually."

"Maybe you're right," Colton said.

"Let's get out of here before the storm picks up again," Andy said. "I've had enough of this for one day."

I nodded and climbed into the truck. Andy took the seat behind me. Colton got in and drove the truck off the grounds, and I breathed a sigh of relief as the prison receded from view in the dark glen behind us.

CHAPTER 17

I drove through town the next day on my way to the bird observatory at the elementary school on the harbor, relieved to have a beautiful, relaxing day to myself to recover from visiting the prison the day before. I didn't sleep well the night before because I kept reliving the experience in my dreams. Coming that close to the Ghostslayer was the most terrifying thing that had ever happened to me, and I hoped it would never happen again. I still felt shaky. Now that I knew what the signs of his appearance were, I would be on the lookout for him and hopefully escape before he showed up. Even so, I was glad Colton and Andy were around to protect me.

I'd found out from Susie that the science teachers kept a running log of banded birds and photos of endangered species that were protected on the island, and I wanted to see what they were. The school hosted a bird observation camp through the summer, and I hoped they would allow me to take photos. If I was going to remain on the island, I had to create a steady source of income, and making calendars still seemed like the best way to do that. Susie hadn't been very forthcoming when I saw her at the inn before I left. She had been playing checkers with Bobby on the deck, and they both looked like they'd rather be somewhere else when they saw me. I replayed the conversation in my head as I rounded a curve.

"If you keep coming over to talk to me, my mom's going to get really mad at you," Susie said. "She doesn't like you very much."

"Yeah," Bobby added.

"I only wanted to know how your detective story was going," I said.

"I told you, they found out who the murderer was."

"Well, who was it?"

Susie looked around before leaning toward me conspiratorially. "One of the mom's boyfriends," she whispered. "But no one knew who it was except me until the last minute."

"Hmm. That's interesting," I said. "Why didn't anyone else know?"

"Because," she said, "he was hiding in plain sight."

"But how did he hide?" I asked.

"He pretended to be somebody he wasn't and made people love him so that way they wouldn't be on to him," she said.

I immediately thought of Damon, but then I realized Susie would have no way of knowing that Damon was Gregory or the other way around. She could have written the story about him anyway, but I didn't think so. It didn't make sense that Damon, who had been my husband for years, could be the murderer. The only other person she could have been talking about was Colton, and I knew he didn't do it. Only the sheriff thought that, and I didn't think much of anything he thought. Maybe she had written the story with Tyler in mind before he was convicted and thought she had been right about thinking it was him when he was arrested. I decided to discreetly ask if that was the case.

"Did the murderer pretend to be a waiter in a restaurant?" I asked.

Susie laughed. "You'll have to read my story to find out," she said.

"I'd like to. Will you show it to me?"

"Nope. I told you. I don't let anybody read my stories except Bobby."

"Hmm." I turned to Bobby. "Well, did he?" I asked. "Pretend to be a waiter, I mean."

Susie shook her head. "Don't answer, Bobby. You and I are the only ones that know, and we're going to keep it that way."

"Yeah," Bobby said, scrunching up his face and glaring at me.

"Okay," I said. "Maybe I'll talk to you guys later. By the way, I hope you get kinged," I said to Susie.

"It doesn't matter. I'm going to win anyway."

"How do you know?"

"I just do."

"Yeah," Bobby said. "She always wins."

I thought about that now as I neared the school. Susie could know things other girls her age didn't know, given that her mother was a teacher and considering how well she did in school. I couldn't help but wonder if she had solved the mystery on the island and had written it down in her detective novel. Maybe one of her mother's boyfriends was the murderer, and I needed to follow the clues to find out who it was. She might not have written the story about Tyler. It could have been about someone else. Melanie could have another boyfriend that I didn't know about.

I pulled up next to the school and saw a large deck with viewing telescopes overlooking the harbor, and more pointed toward the woods out back. Kids and teachers were taking turns looking through them and writing things down in notebooks. Another group was gathered down by the water and appeared to be taking notes on shorebirds and gulls inhabiting the area. I walked over to talk to a young man, who didn't look much older than a teenager, typing on a computer that was set up on a picnic table on the deck. He was wearing a plastic lanyard with a nametag on it that said, 'Staff.'

"Excuse me, are you one of the teachers here? I was hoping to find out more about the observatory for an article I'm doing about Copper Isle," I said, holding out my hand. "I'm Layla Devereaux."

He stood and shook my hand.

"Nice to meet you. I'm Bryce Miller. I teach science here and study bird migration habits. Are you interested in the birds we track or in something more specific?"

"Yes, I'd love to know about that, and I was hoping to take photos, as well, especially of exceptionally interesting birds for a calendar I'm doing."

"Oh. Now that you mention it, we have been tracking some migratory birds, a few of which we haven't seen before. Follow me, and I'll point them out to you if I can find them. It would be very helpful if we could have professional photos of the birds we've been looking at."

"I'd love to take some," I said. " I have the perfect camera for detailed, avian photos."

"Great."

I followed Bryce toward the woods and snapped photos, using my camera and my cellphone, of red-winged blackbirds perched in ash trees and flying overhead. A goldfinch flew by as a woodpecker tapped a staccato cadence in the background.

"What a beautiful place," I said.

"It is. It's my favorite place to be," Bryce answered. "See the pond over there? I've seen eight white egrets and a Great Blue Heron all standing in it at the same time."

"Wow, that's amazing. What's that?" I asked, pointing to an extremely tall, thin bird I'd never seen before.

"That's a sandhill crane. There is a trio of them that run around together. Here, let me show the birds I was talking about," he said, walking toward the pond. "See the brown ones with the rust-colored wings. They're new to the island. I think they may have migrated from down south."

"Yes. I think I've seen them before flying over the harbor," I said. "I lifted my camera and took several photos of them. I snapped a few with my cellphone, too. "Yes, they're very interesting," I said when I was through.

Bryce nodded. "We're going to put bands on their legs and track them. But, if we can't determine what they are or where they came from, we may need to name them ourselves. That's where the photos you're taking could help us out. We can use them to register a new species," he said.

"Great. I'll make sure to get them to you," I said.

Bryce showed me around some more. We walked to a garden near the back of the schoolyard, where a tiny, iridescent hummingbird flitted through a sprinkling of white lilies. I was humbled by its fragile beauty and innocent flight, grateful to be witness to such an unusual sighting. Hummingbirds were like ghosts in that way. They kept out of sight if they could, and seeing them was a rare gift.

I followed Bryce down the path past the garden and took more photos of the observatory, the students, and the teachers.

"I'll send these to you," I said as we walked back to the deck. "It might help in advertising this place and bring in more donations."

"Great idea. Thanks," Bryce said, handing me brochures and information about the observatory I'd asked for earlier to use in my article. "Donations have dropped off over the past few summers, and we could really use the money to keep us running. The kids love coming to the camp here in the summer, even though they're officially on break from school. Something about taking care of the birds appeals to all of them, and it's really rewarding to see how it brings out the best in them. It's extremely educational, too."

"I'm sure it is," I said.

"Would you like to look through a telescope before you go?" he asked, leading me around to the front.

"Sure," I said, following him over to one that overlooked the harbor.

I scanned the harbor and got a fantastic, close-up view of a pair of ring-necked ducks springing off the water into flight. I was effusive in my praise of the observatory when I finished looking and turned to go. Bryce thanked me and walked me to my car. He waved as I drove away.

"Come back soon," he called.

"I will," I said, waving as I drove away.

I stopped before I turned onto the harbor road and called Colton to ask him to meet me at the Schooner Bar and Restaurant. I wanted to show him my new bird photographs. He said he'd meet me there, and he arrived not long after I did and joined me at an outdoor table.

"Are you doing okay?" he asked, taking my hands in his when he saw me.

"Yes," I answered. Visiting the bird observatory was just what I needed to get my mind off of visiting the prison. How about you?"

"Yes, I'm fine. I feel like the visit to the prison was worth it for the information we uncovered. I think we're closer to finding out who the night stalker is and maybe closer to finding out who really murdered Pappy," he said.

"I hope so," I said. "I'd like to think we didn't go through all that for nothing."

"Oh, we got something," Colton said. "We got a lead on where the night stalker is. And that's huge."

"I'm glad you think so," I said.

"So you got some good photos, huh?" he asked, sitting

down across from me.

"Yes. Would you like to see them?" I asked.

"Sure."

"I took some with my professional camera that I haven't transferred yet, but I took some other ones with my cell phone that you can see in the photo library on my iPad," I said.

I opened my iPad and accessed the photos before turning it around to show them to him.

"These are sandhill cranes," I said, pointing to a photo. "And this one is of a red-winged blackbird in a tree near the pond. Its Latin name is 'Agelaius phoeniceus'. I looked it up just now. I plan to add Latin names to my calendar pages in the future. I'm hoping to turn into an online business."

"That's a good idea," he said. "Those are nice pictures. If you're serious about having an online business, I could give you some tips and help you create a website."

"That would be great," I said. "With your help, I'm sure I could get a business going."

"I'm sure you can, too," he said. "You take some great photos."

"Here's another one I took of a particularly interesting bird with fascinating markings that I can't wait to crop and turn into a calendar page."

"Can I see it?" Colton asked.

"Sure." I pulled it up and showed it to him.

"Wow. That is unusual," he said.

"Yes, isn't it? It has rust-colored wings. They say they saw it last year and again this year, and they're checking into what it could be."

"Cool. What are these other photos of?" he asked.

"Oh, those are photos I took of the lighthouse and sailboats on the island when I first arrived here. I transferred them to my iPad from my camera."

"Colton leaned over the table and peered at them closely. "Can I see that?" he asked, taking the iPad from me and looking intently at a photo. "When exactly did you take this?" he asked after a moment.

"The day after I arrived on the island. Why? Is something wrong?" I asked.

"I'm not sure. Can you make it larger?" he asked.

"Yes," I said, putting it on full screen.

"There," he said, pointing at the sailboat. "Can you make that larger?"

"I might have a bigger photo of it that I took with a zoom lens," I said. I scrolled through my library. "How's this?"

He leaned in to look at it and sucked in a breath before sitting back and looking at me. "That's Pappy at the rudder," he said.

"What? Pappy Johnson? It can't be. He's dead," I said.

I sat, stunned, for a moment before looking more closely at the picture. The man resembled the figure I'd seen in the woods at the lighthouse the day Colton and I had gone out there after Leif's murder. I'd thought it was Leif's disparate ghost, but now I didn't know what to think. "Are you sure?"

"Yeah. That's him. I don't know how it's possible, but it is," he said.

I thought for a moment. If Pappy was alive, and we could prove that he was never murdered, we could get Tyler out of prison. But where was Pappy? And why would he pretend to be dead?

"If Pappy's alive, he must be involved in the crime ring," I said. "There's no other reason he would pretend to be dead and let someone else go to prison for his murder. That also means that other people know he's alive and that they set my brother up to take the fall for a murder he didn't commit." I put my head in my hands and stifled a sob. The thought was overwhelming, but I felt more angry than sad. "Why would people do such a thing?" I asked.

Colton put his hand on my shoulder and patted it. "Greed and gold have a lot to do with it. You never know what the possibility of owning that kind of fortune could do to people."

I nodded my head. "You're right," I said. "I have to look at things as they really are and not as I wish they would be. Sometimes, it's hard to face reality."

"I know," Colton said. "I agree."

If Pappy was still alive, something else seemed possible.

"I wonder if Pappy killed the coroner and Leif. Maybe he pretended to be dead so he could find a way to keep the gold for himself and ended up murdering them when they found out."

"I hadn't thought of that," Colton said.

"If he did kill the coroner, he would have been in the perfect position as a tour guide at the lighthouse to bury him there before Leif arrived to take over. He could have hidden it in a place no one would think to look for it."

"You're right," Colton said. "I'll call the sheriff and ask him to search the lighthouse for the body."

"Good," I said.

I waited while Colton made the call. His face paled as he talked, and he grimaced when he hung up and turned to me.

"That didn't go very well," Colton said. "I don't get the feeling they think much of me anymore."

"Really?" I said. "After you've lived on the island all this time?"

"I think they're still suspicious of me," he said.

"That's just wrong," I said, wondering again how anyone could suspect Colton of murder.

I hadn't known him long, but I knew he was a good person. The sheriff was heading in the wrong direction, and I didn't know why. Did he think he knew something that I didn't know? My phone rang, and I checked the number. It was the sheriff's office.

"Yes?" I said. "Yes. He's here with me right now. I agree that it would be a good idea to check the lighthouse for the coroner's body. Okay. I'll wait to hear from you," I said, hanging up.

"The sheriff's office said they're going to check and get back to me. I wonder why they wouldn't get back to you," I said.

"Something's strange," Colton said. "We'll have to wait and see what they find."

I nodded. "I'm sorry they're treating you this way. It isn't right."

"Me, too. We'll have to keep trying to solve the mystery anyway," he said.

"I'm glad you feel that way," I said, "because something else occurs to me, although it could be a stretch."

"What is it?"

"I didn't know Pappy, but is it possible that Melanie could have been seeing him?"

"Seeing Pappy? In a romantic way?" Colton shook his head. "I suppose stranger things have happened, but I knew Pappy, and that's not something I would think. Why?"

"No reason. Just something Susie said," I said, recalling her reference to the mom's boyfriend being the murderer in her detective novel.

I wasn't ready yet to give up on the possibility that she was writing about one of her mom's boyfriends in real life, and I wondered if Pappy was one of them. I had to find out if Melanie had more boyfriends besides Tyler, Colton, and Damon and add them to my list along with Pappy.

"Well, anyway," I said. "Now we have to find Pappy along with everything else. We'd better get to work. I'm not sure how much longer my brother can hold on, especially since I found out he was recently transferred away from me to a prison down south. We have to get to the bottom of this and save Tyler from a future of wrongful imprisonment and you from being wrongfully jailed."

"I'm with you," Colton said. "We're getting closer to clearing this thing up and finding out what really happened last summer. We have to trust ourselves, and we have to follow your instincts. They'll lead us to the truth. I'm sure of it."

"I hope so," I said.

"There's one other thing I think I should tell you," Colton said. "I checked with the real estate office. Gregory Wellington is listed as having rented the cabin on the lake through the fall and winter of last year. It seems your husband started renting it the week after Dr. Pearson, the coroner, did. It's interesting that Dr. Pearson disappeared soon after that. Your instincts about something being wrong in that regard could be right again."

I sucked in a breath. There was definitely something nefarious going on, and I was afraid that Damon, as well as Pappy, could have something to do with it. It seemed possible that he, too, could have been the cause of Dr. Pearson's disappearance, but I wasn't sure yet exactly how. He could have helped Pappy cover things up. I hoped the sheriff would get back to me soon about whether they found his body at the lighthouse, along with any clues as to how he died. That could go a long way in determining who the likely suspects were.

"That's interesting," I said. "I think that means something. Thanks for telling me, and thanks for believing in me and my hunches."

"I do," Colton said. "You have a much clearer view of reality than anyone I've ever known."

"Thank you," I said, relieved to hear him say that and amazed that I had finally found someone who listened to me, no matter what. If we worked together, we could solve this. At least,

I hoped so. Tyler's freedom, and maybe even his life, depended on it.

"So Damon was renting the cabin at the time of the dogsled race this winter?" I asked.

"It appears so," Colton said. "But he may not have been there in the fall, even though he was listed as renting it then. There's a note that Portland's Plumbing was sent over to turn off the outside water spigots in November in preparation for the cold weather, so no one was there then anyway."

"Portland's Plumbing? Larry Portland, your friend?"

"Yes. Why?"

"No reason. It just seems like he must have known Damon wasn't on the island then. Maybe he knew where Damon was and who he was if he knew him well enough to let him borrow his dog in February. I wonder if Larry is more involved with the theft of the gold and with using the cabin as a drop-off location than I thought."

"That's an interesting observation," Colton said.

A waitress came over and asked if we'd like to order, which we did.

"Why don't we quit talking about this for a while," Colton said when she left.

"Okay," I said, smiling. "Let's do that." I was happy to have a respite from my thoughts.

We talked about other things until the waitress came back with our meals. We had a nice dinner and stayed talking and sipping wine in the warm night air well after most of the other diners had left. Something about the way the light breeze ruffled Colton's wavy, brown hair made me want to lean over and run my fingers through it. I was about to do that when his phone rang.

"What? Just now? I'll be right there," he said, hanging up the phone and jumping up.

"That was my mom. She just chased the night stalker into the woods with a broom. He was hiding on the deck steps when she stepped out of the kitchen to sweep the back stairs. She hit him with the broom and ran after him before the kitchen staff heard her yells for help and came out to help her. He disappeared into the woods, but she was pretty shaken up. I think we should get back."

"Of course. I'll follow you home," I said.

We paid the check and hurried out to the parking lot.

"It was nice having dinner with you tonight," Colton said over his shoulder as he jumped into his truck. "Let's come here again soon."

"Okay," I said. "I had a good time, too."

I got in my car and followed Colton back to the inn.

CHAPTER 18

Martha left the inn the next day and went to stay at the house in town.

"It's too much," she said when I helped her carry her suitcases out to the car. "I can't stay here another night. Not with the night stalker around. It's sad, but in a way, I'm glad the inn is closing. My health couldn't take much more."

"I'm so sorry it came to this," I said. "You deserve so much more. The inn is lovely and charming, and it's a shame it has to close down. It will be a real loss for the island."

"I agree," Martha said. "Maybe at some point, things will settle down, and we can return, but for now, I'm glad I have another place to stay. You have no idea what it was like to find that man hiding under the stairway when I went to shake out the rugs last night. He told me he was going to kidnap me if I didn't promise to leave today. I whacked him with the broom and chased him into the woods, but I didn't want to take the chance he'd come back. I just don't know why the sheriff won't believe me. He doesn't believe in ghosts or the night stalker, and I guess he thinks I don't know what I'm talking about because I do believe in them. He doesn't believe anything I say, so now I have no choice but to leave my beloved inn."

She choked on her last words, and tears welled up in her

eyes. I bent over and hugged her, hoping to give her some solace. She looked so devastated. Her usually perfectly made-up face was bare and pallid, and her hair was loose and flyaway instead of in its usual pulled-back style. I hoped she would be okay.

"Try not to worry too much. I have to think things will work out eventually," I said. "I'll join you with Colton before too long, and the three of us can live peacefully together in the house, away from the tumult of the inn."

"I hope so. That would be nice," Martha said, sniffling and hugging me back.

I helped her load her bags in the trunk. She closed the trunk and walked around to get in the car.

"There is one other thing that bothers me, though," she said, pausing to talk to me. "I know most of the staff have found other positions on the mainland, but I'm worried about the good ghosts that live in the inn. Now that I know that the night stalker is a real person who was being malicious and not one of the ghosts, I hope they'll be okay when it closes down. It's never been vacant as long as the ghosts have been around. I don't know how they'll deal with that. I don't know if they'll even be here when we open back up again."

I smiled. "They'll be here. They've been here since the shipwreck, and they're not going anywhere, not when they've found a warm place to stay. And it still will be, even after we leave. It will be warm enough, anyway, to keep the ghosts happy. They tend to be a pretty cold group if the digital thermometers Andy uses are correct, and being inside anywhere is probably better than nothing."

"I hope so. Believe it or not, I've become quite attached to them, and I think I'll miss them," she said. "I know Andy and Kirsten will, too. They went back to the mainland, but they told me to let them know if the inn reopened, and they'd come right back here."

"That's good to know," I said.

She nodded. "Yes, it is," she said. "Well, goodbye for now. I'll see you soon."

She sat down behind the wheel and gave a slight wave before closing the door and driving away. I waved back before shoving my hands into my skirt pockets and shuffling back to the inn. It was another beautiful morning, but it was hard to enjoy it, knowing that Martha had left the inn and that the inn was closing. A sorrowful mourning dove cooed from the slow-moving branches of an evergreen tree, mirroring my feelings of loss, and a goldfinch flitted in the leaves of a nearby ash. I would miss this lovely place. I ran into Colton in the hallway on my way to the back stairs.

"I'm glad I saw you," Colton said. "My mom just left, and I called the sheriff about the night stalker again. The security service isn't working, and I complained about last night's incident and insisted that they do something. It backfired. They seem convinced that I have something to do with the stalking and with Leif's murder. They called back after I hung up and told me they're going to take me into custody in a few days for Leif's murder."

"What? That's awful. How could they do that?" I asked.

"I don't know. I don't know what's going on anymore," he said.

I thought for a moment. "We need to prove that Pappy's alive," I said. "If he killed Leif, and we can prove it, we can keep you out of jail."

"How will we do that?" Colton asked. "We don't know where he is."

"I think we need to talk to Mrs. Pinley at the funeral home again. She must know that he's still alive because she knows they didn't bury his body in the graveyard. She may know where he is."

"Good point. Let's go," Colton said, taking my arm and not bothering to go back to his room.

I had my purse with me, so I followed him to his truck and got in. My phone rang as I jumped in the cab. I talked as Colton drove down to the harbor road before hanging up and turning to him. I nipped my lip before telling him what they said.

"The deputies checked the lighthouse for the coroner's body, and they didn't find anything. They said they were very thorough. But they also said they want me to stay away from you."

"What? Why?"

"They think you're dangerous, and they think you had something to do with Leif's death," I said.

"I knew it," Colton said, banging the steering wheel. "What good is a sheriff that blames the wrong people when bad things happen? This has got to stop."

I nodded, not knowing what to say. It must be an awful feeling to be accused of something you didn't do. I was sad that two people I cared about, both Colton and Tyler, were dealing with that. We drove out to the funeral home in silence and parked in front of the decrepit steps. Colton got out and went up and knocked on the door. I followed slowly behind him.

After a short pause, the curtain at the window moved to the side, and Mrs. Pinley peered out. A moment later, she opened the door.

"What brings you out here again?" she asked. "I thought after the last time, you'd be too frightened to visit me again."

"We'd like to ask you a few questions if you don't mind," Colton said. "We need to find out more about Pappy. He's not dead, and we think you know that."

She stepped back, and her face paled. "What makes you say that?" she asked. "Of course, he's dead."

"He's not. We have a photo to prove it. Now, why don't

you tell us what's really going on," Colton said firmly, pressing his hand on the door.

"A photo?" she asked.

"Yes. It proves Pappy is still alive. Now, will you let us in or not?" Colton asked. "It might be a good idea if you did."

She pondered for a moment. "Yes. All right," she said, holding the door open.

We followed her into the dim living room again but didn't sit down.

"Would you like some refreshments?" she asked.

"Not this time," Colton said. "What are you hiding, Mrs. Pinley? Or are you in the habit of pretending to bury people who aren't dead?"

"Now, Colton, you know that's not true," she said.

"There's a tombstone over a grave with no one in it. Now, what's going on?"

Mrs. Pinley sat down heavily on the sofa. Her cats jumped on the sofa and sat on either side of her, staring at me in their intense way.

"Well, I guess it had to come out sometime," she said. "Things haven't been working out the way I thought they would."

"What hasn't been working out?" Colton asked.

I stood next to Colton and listened carefully to what she was saying, trying not to look at the cats. I had a terrible feeling of unease.

"You're right. Pappy's alive. He told me he'd give me money from the sale of some gold he found on a shipwreck if I helped him pretend to be dead, but I haven't seen it yet. I don't know what it's all about, but I need the money. The funeral home hasn't made much income lately, and I need it to stay in the house. I'm an old woman. I have nowhere else to go. So I told Pappy I'd go along with it."

"But where is he?" I asked, impatiently.

One of the cats hissed at me.

"Somewhere on the island, I guess," she said, "keeping out of sight until he can sell the gold. I'm waiting for him to do that so I can get the money."

"How did you do it? Pretend that he was dead, I mean?" I asked.

"It wasn't hard. Like I said, he didn't have any friends, and no one planned a funeral or inquired about attending one. I just told anyone who asked that respects were paid, and he was interred. No one questioned me much after that, especially after the tombstone was erected."

I shook my head. "This is wrong. It reminds me of the same kind of thing that happened here long ago. Only that time, this funeral home really buried someone who wasn't dead instead of just pretending to."

"That's not fair. I didn't have anything to do with what happened to the Ghostslayer back then," she said.

"Maybe not, but it's still wrong." I paused for a moment. "Why is he called the Ghostslayer anyway? Why not the ghost murderer or the ghost destroyer or something?" I asked.

Mrs. Pinley sat still for a moment before answering.

"Because he didn't just kill the family. He slayed them," she said in a low whisper. "That's what the islanders say."

"But how?" I asked, moving closer to Colton.

The cats were both glaring at me now.

She stood and walked over to loosen a drape from the bronze hook that pulled it back, and it fell across the window, darkening the room. She did the same with the one on the other side until the entire living room was dark and quiet. She sat down again and smoothed her wrinkled, print house dress, motioning to us to sit on the sofa opposite her. Colton sat down, but I stood, keeping my distance from the cats. There was something wrong with them. They both hissed at me.

"I'll tell you, but then you will know what few people know. You must keep it to yourselves in honor of the dead," she said, staring at us.

"Of course," I said, clenching my hands to control the trembling in my arms.

Mrs. Pinley looked like a ghost herself with her pale, drawn face and hollow eyes that glowed in the dim, amber light of the table lamp. She paused briefly and took a deep breath before continuing.

"He killed them with a spade," she said quietly

"A what?" I asked.

"A shovel. The same one that was used to bury him alive in his coffin prison and dig him up again after his terrible torment. He bludgeoned them to death with a spade in the most horrific way possible, a slaying, leaving permanent bloodstains on the wood floors upstairs that are covered up with rugs. That's why they call him the Ghostslayer."

I clutched Colton's arm, and he put his hand over mine to steady me. I could feel the evil in the room. It seemed to emanate mostly from the cats. They must be evil spirits. I had to get away from them, but I wanted to hear the story.

"Do you want me to continue?" Mrs. Pinley asked.

I swallowed and nodded.

"The prison closed down, and the prisoners were released soon after the murders," she said. "Some people said it was because those that operated the prison were afraid that the Ghostslayer would return to slay them and that most of them left the island and went into some sort of operation together on the mainland. The ones that didn't had good reason to be afraid. Many of them disappeared, and their bodies or their souls were never found. The islanders say they were taken down into the darkness of permanent torment by the Ghostslayer."

I shivered at Mrs. Pinley's words. I wondered if the crime

ring that we suspected operated on the island now was the same one that operated back then and ran the prison. They could still be in operation on the mainland, according to what Mrs. Pinley said.

"You need to be careful," I said. "Colton and I think Pappy may be involved in a crime ring operating on the island, and it could be the same one that operated the prison years ago. It's very important that you don't tell anyone that you know, and we know that Pappy is still alive."

Mrs. Pinley's eyes widened. "A crime ring? Pappy? That's hard to believe. He was just helping me out of a tough spot. He said we would share the money from the gold he found."

"No, it's much more involved than that," I said. "You could be in danger."

She looked at Colton, who nodded, and then back at me. "All right. I won't tell anyone he's alive or that you know that he is. But I do hope Pappy will be okay," she said. Her lip trembled.

I was startled for a moment. I wondered if she cared for Pappy. It made sense that she would have gone along with a scheme like that if she had feelings for him.

"I think Pappy can take care of himself," I said.

The cats jumped off the sofa when she stood, and I jumped behind Colton. They each emitted a low growl.

"We need to go," I said, as they slunk toward me. The fur on their backs was standing up. One arched its back and hopped sideways toward me.

I stifled a shriek. "We need to go now," I said, grasping Colton by the arms and running for the door.

We left the funeral home without saying goodbye and ran out to the truck. I couldn't wait to get out of there. There was definitely evil in that house. The way the cats acted when Mrs. Pinley spoke of the Ghostslayer confirmed to me that something unspeakable had happened there. After we drove down the driveway to the road, Colton said he needed time to think before driving back to the inn. He drove to an overlook on the side of the road, and we got out of the truck together and walked toward the lake.

"There's something wrong with those cats," I said, trembling.

"There's something wrong with the whole island," he replied, shaking his head. "How could Mrs. Pinley pretend that the funeral home buried someone who wasn't dead? It's unthinkable. It's hard to imagine all this happening in my small town. And on the rest of the island, as well. It always seemed so idyllic to me as a child. I guess when you grow up, you find out things people keep from you when you're young. I'm still trying to accept that my friends could be involved in this."

I touched his arm and nodded.

"You're right. It's a terrible thing that she did. And others are obviously involved as well. But we'll get through this," I said. "We'll get through this together, and then maybe the world will look a little more idyllic again."

Colton slowed as we neared the overlook.

"I hope so," he said, walking out onto the wooden deck.

I followed him. A Great Blue Heron soared above the harbor and out over the trees beyond before disappearing into the deep green woods. Something about its majestic flight reminded me of Colton striving to overcome adversity and save the island he loved and called home from financial ruin. He would never give up. I could see that. And he would never give up trying to protect his mother from harm, either, no matter what it took. I admired him for that.

"Do you see the heron?" I asked.

"Yes. He's amazing. He comes back every year. I love to watch him fly with such freedom and joy. He loves the island as much as I do. You can tell."

I nodded. "I think you're right."

Colton put his arm around me, and we stood together, watching the peaceful scene.

"Could we make one more stop before we go home?" I asked, after a while.

"I suppose. Where do you want to go?" he asked.

"I'd like to visit the dog breeding operation on the harbor road. I first saw it the day after I arrived on the island, and we pass it all the time. I think something there could help solve the mystery of the murder. I need to find out what it is that makes me feel that way."

"All right. Let's go," he said.

We drove up the road a bit, and Colton pulled into the gravel parking lot behind the large, old farmhouse advertising Siberian husky puppies for sale. We walked up the cement steps onto a porch surrounded by a white railing, and Colton knocked on the door. A pleasant young woman holding a puppy answered and asked us to come in.

"Are you interested in adopting a husky puppy?" she asked after we introduced ourselves. She told us her name was Katherine.

"No, although they're really cute," I said. "I just wanted to ask a few questions about the dogs, if that's okay?"

"Sure. Won't you sit down?" she asked, gesturing to the wood chairs with red-checked cushions that surrounded a wooden kitchen table.

"Thank you."

We sat down, and I continued.

"Are there a lot of huskies on the island?" I asked.

"Oh my, yes. We've been breeding them for quite a while, and they're very popular. They're wonderful, friendly dogs," she said.

"Yes, they are. I wonder how old they need to be to pull a

dogsled. I mean, is it quite strenuous for the dogs?"

"The huskies usually need to be at least 18 months old to pull a sled. It depends on how much they're pulling and how fast they go and a number of other conditions, such as weather, as to how stressful it is on them."

"I suppose that's true. Can they pull a lot of weight?" I asked.

"They can pull quite a bit. At least the dog sled runner and a few other supplies that may be needed. It usually takes at least two huskies or more to pull one person. They're pretty strong dogs, and with the right owners, they can pull the sleds quite well with no adverse effects. People are careful not to overload them, though, and, of course, with running on the ice, the weight has to be reasonable, although the lake freezes pretty solid in the winter.

"That makes sense."

I was glad she told me the huskies could pull the dog sled driver and more weight, as well. Something about that seemed important.

And do they usually run with four or six huskies?" I asked.

"It depends on the driver. They can run with even more than that. Of course, if more dogs are pulling a sled, they can pull more weight," she said.

"That's what I wanted to know. Do you keep track of them after you sell them?" I asked.

"Not really. We make sure they're going to a good home in the first place. We sold a litter a few summers ago to mostly islanders. I remember Larry came in here with Melanie from the inn and picked out Peko. He was a beautiful black-and-tan husky with a banded, agouti coat. I remember because he was such a striking-looking dog."

"Larry, the plumber?" I asked.

"Yes. Do you know him?"

"Not really. I just know who he is," I said, glancing at Colton. I wondered how finding out that Larry had been here with Melanie made him feel. It gave me a strange feeling to think that Larry could have been involved with Melanie. Was he the boyfriend of Melanie that Susie had been writing about? Was he the murderer hiding in plain sight in her story? Did he have something to do with the coroner's disappearance? I shook my head to clear it. That could be stretching things a bit, but something about the dogs seemed important. Maybe that's what made the hairs on the back of my arms stand up.

"I know, Larry," Colton said quietly, looking down. "I didn't realize Melanie did, too."

I felt bad for him when I saw how sad he looked. It seemed like there were a lot of things Colton didn't know about Melanie.

"Well, he really got the pick of the litter. I hope he knows how lucky he was. I hope Peko is doing well," she said.

"He is," Colton said, looking up again. "Peko ran in the dogsled race last winter."

"Oh, yes. Now that you mention it, I think I remember seeing him," she said. "Did they come in second or third?"

"Third," Colton said. "They ran a good race."

"It must be fun to watch the dogs race," I said.

"Oh yes. It's a lot of fun for the town and the island," Katherine said. "Almost everyone turns out for it. We look forward to it every year. I think I've seen Colton there before."

"You probably did. I go every year," he said, turning to me. "It's a big event."

"That's nice," I said.

I laughed when more puppies rolled and tumbled into the kitchen to join the one she leaned over to put on the floor.

"Well, thank you for your time. We won't keep you. It looks like they keep you pretty busy," I said.

"They do. Thanks for stopping by. Come again, and let me

know if you're interested in getting a puppy," she said, walking us to the door and waving as we left.

On our way out to the truck, Colton's phone rang, and he said a few things before frowning and hanging up. He turned to me and shook his head.

"What is it? What's wrong?" I asked.

"That was the sheriff," Colton said. "They're taking me into custody for Leif's murder by the end of the week. I guess we'd better be prepared for it."

"No. This is so wrong," I said. "They can't, especially not when we're so close to solving the mystery."

"Are we?" Colton asked. "Or are we just kidding ourselves? I keep waiting for it all to come together, but it keeps falling apart at the last minute like it is now with the sheriff planning to arrest me."

"We're not kidding ourselves," I said. "The information we found out here today about the huskies is pertinent to the investigation. I feel it. I just need to figure out what it means. We'll make this work. I know we can if we stick together."

"If you say so," Colton said half-heartedly.

"I do," I said, hoping to make him feel better. It didn't look like it did. His face was ashen. "Come on, let's go home," I said.

He nodded, and we got in the truck and headed back to the inn.

CHAPTER 19

I began to worry about Colton by the next evening when I hadn't seen him all day and went to his room to check on him. Something about how empty the inn seemed after most of the staff had packed up and left made me uneasy, even more uneasy than I had been when it was occupied and the night stalker was around. I hoped he would stay away now that everyone had left and leave us in peace.

Rosie had said she was staying on the island and working at the hotel in town, but most of the others seemed to have left the island altogether. It was strange to be at the inn with almost no one around. Melanie had moved to a rental property in town with her children and had told Martha she was going to take the summer off and teach school in the fall while looking for another place to live. I was going to miss talking to Susie even though I didn't think she would miss talking to me. She was a bright girl, and her insights fascinated me. I walked down the deserted hallway to Colton's room. He answered after I knocked a few times, with his cell phone pressed to his ear, and motioned for me to come in.

"It's the sheriff," Colton said after putting his hand over the phone and grimacing. He talked for a while before hanging up and turning to me. "The deputies are on their way over to take me in. I have to get ready," he said. "I'm sorry. There's nothing more I can do."

I followed him as he walked toward the closet.

"We have to do something," I said. "We can't just wait around here for the sheriff to come and arrest you."

Colton looked down and shook his head. "There isn't anything," he said.

I scrunched my eyelids together, trying desperately to think of a solution. It couldn't be over. There must be something more we could do. Tyler wasn't free yet, and Colton could be arrested at any minute and tried for murder. I had to think of something. I sat down on the bed, keeping my eyes closed. Pictures floated through my consciousness as I took deep breaths and concentrated. There were scenes of the harbor and the inn and lighthouses. Suddenly, an idea came to me. I opened my eyes and looked at him.

"There is something we can do," I said. "We can go to the mainland and find out what Susie was talking about when she said she overheard Damon threatening her mother about ending up like the doctor at the lighthouse," I said. "If Dr. Pearson's body isn't at the lighthouse on the island, maybe it's at the one Leif abandoned on the mainland. There's nowhere else to look. It's our last and only hope to prove that the coroner is dead and that Pappy probably killed him.

"It wouldn't have been Leif that murdered the coroner because Leif was murdered himself. If the sheriff agrees and searches the island for Pappy, he could find out that he's still alive. The sheriff would have to find Pappy himself because he doesn't believe you anymore and probably wouldn't take my grainy photo of him in the sailboat as proof that he's not dead. And Mrs. Pinley would probably renege on her story about Pappy being alive and promising her money from the sale of the gold if the sheriff asked her about him. If he found Pappy in person, though, it would prove that Tyler didn't murder him, and Tyler would be freed."

Colton rubbed his eyes with his hands as he turned away from the closet and walked toward the middle of the room. I'd never seen him look so defeated, and I desperately hoped we could turn things around and keep him out of jail. After a moment, he turned and looked at me. I gave him what I hoped was an encouraging nod.

"All right," he said. "We'll try it. Let's head downstairs and hop in the truck. We'll take the ferry to the mainland. The next ride out is in half an hour. Maybe we can make it before the deputies find out where we are. I'll call Bob and tell him to pick up Larry and Stan and meet us at the ferry. And I'll tell him to step on it. They've been waiting to hear from me about the sheriff's decision, and when I tell him they're coming to take me in, I'm sure they'll want to help out. They know I'm not a murderer."

"Are you sure you want them to come with us?" I asked, grabbing my purse and following him to the door. "What if they tell the sheriff you're on the run?"

"They won't," Colton said, pausing. "They want to keep things quiet as much as I do. And if Dr. Pearson's body is at the lighthouse, I want to see how everybody reacts. I want to know who killed him."

"Okay. Let's go," I said. "Do you know where the lighthouse on the mainland is?"

"Yes, I've seen it from a distance, and I'm sure whoever's running the ferry can tell us what road it's on. They know where the lighthouses are."

We hurried down the stairs together as Colton dialed his cell phone to call Bob and ran to get in the truck. Evening was descending, and the waning sun stained the clouds purple and blue over the dark, rippling waves of the harbor.

We made it to the ferry just before it pulled out. Stan, Larry, and Bob were in Bob's car in front of us, and Larry waved to us out the window when we pulled up behind them. We followed them through the preliminary boarding preparations and onto the ferry. The evening turned to twilight, and a few stars twinkled in the pale indigo sky. We drove below deck, parked, and walked upstairs to the main deck. The air was crisp and clear, and a cool breeze blew in across the harbor. Colton and I stood with the others, leaning against the railing and watching as the ferry skimmed its way through the lightly rolling waves. I couldn't believe I was on the ferry again with Colton. So many things had changed since I first met him there on my initial trip to the island. And now, here we were, not knowing what we would find on the mainland and desperately trying to preserve his freedom. As we neared shore, I saw the lighthouse in the distance flashing its bright light across the dark harbor and pointed to it.

"That's it," Colton said. "All we have to do is get there. I'll be right back. I need to get directions from the ferryman."

He left, and I stood away from the others. I didn't feel like talking to them and let myself get lost in my own thoughts. I didn't know what we would find at the lighthouse, and I wasn't thrilled about going there with Colton's supposed friends. And I was especially wary of Stan after running into him on the beach the morning after Leif was killed. But I didn't see any other options if we were going to keep Colton out of jail. Colton returned just as the ferry pulled into the harbor on the mainland.

"Passengers prepare to disembark," a voice said over the loudspeaker.

"Okay, we're here," Colton said. "Follow me. I have the directions."

We went below deck to retrieve our cars, and the others followed Colton and me off the ferry. We drove through the town to an isolated dirt road and headed down the road near the water until the headlights shined on the lighthouse on a hill before us. Colton pulled up next to it, and Stan, Bob, and Larry pulled in behind him. I was surprised to see another car parked there because I thought we would be the only ones there.

"I have a crowbar in the bed of the truck," Colton said. "In a situation like this, I'm going to use it. The worst thing they can do is take me into custody for vandalism, and they're going to arrest me already. I have nothing to lose."

The lighthouse stood on an isolated bluff looking out over the lake with a copse of trees on either side. The woods were dark and impenetrable, and I shivered as I wondered what they could be hiding.

We walked up to the lighthouse, and I peered in the window, wondering if the car that was parked there belonged to anyone already there.

"There's someone inside. There's a light on," I whispered to Colton, who lowered his crowbar and walked up next to me.

He pushed the door lightly, and it swung open, creaking.

"Who's here?" he called out.

"Who are you?" someone called back.

"This is Colton Harding. I'm here to check on the lighthouse."

A man stepped out from behind the door. It was Pappy.

"Hey, Colton. Nice to see you," he said.

"Pappy," Colton said, stepping back and taking a quick breath. "What are you doing here? Why were you pretending to be dead all this time?"

I stepped back, afraid of Pappy since I thought he was probably the murderer of Leif and Dr. Pearson. Colton appeared to be keeping a close eye on him, as well.

Pappy grinned. "Sorry, buddy. It's just the way things worked out. Bob called and said to meet you here. What's up?"

Colton turned to Bob. "So you knew he wasn't dead, too," Colton said. "What is this all about? What did you call him for?"

Bob shrugged. "I had to. Gregory wanted us all to be here."

"Gregory?" Colton said.

Damon abruptly stepped out from behind Pappy. "Yeah, me. Surprised? Don't be. I've been keeping tabs on you, and I knew you were coming here. I'm calling the sheriff to take you back to be tried for Leif's murder."

I sucked in a breath when I saw Damon and the deferential attitude the others in the room had for him, as evidenced by them looking at the ground and not at him.

"What's going on?" I asked.

No one answered.

"Not happening," Colton said to Damon. "These guys are with me now, and we're looking around."

"You won't find anything," Damon said.

"Wanna bet?" Colton said, pushing past him.

Damon pushed back and curled his hand into a fist before pausing and looking over Colton's shoulder at me. "What are you doing here?" he asked, scowling.

"Same as you," I said. "I followed Colton here to make sure he does the right thing and turns himself in instead of running away." I looked away, hoping he would believe me.

He paused, and for a moment, I thought he was going to come after me, but Colton reared back suddenly and punched him in the face. He fell to the floor, and Colton, Larry, and Bob ran past him and headed down the lighthouse stairwell. Stan stood with me, away from Pappy and Damon. After a while, the stairwell rattled.

"Oh, my God, the body's here," Larry yelled, running up from the basement. "We found a crawl space underneath the stairs filled with loose dirt, and Bob dug up the body with a shovel left there. It's in a plastic freezer bag. Come and see."

Stan and Pappy rushed downstairs while I stood awkwardly next to Damon, who had stood and was holding a hand to his bruised and swelling face. I wondered what to do next. He seemed to be the only person who wasn't surprised by the announcement. And it hit me that it was probably because he, rather than Pappy, had something to do with the body being there. I moved away from him, closer to the stairwell. After several minutes, they ran back up.

"You killed him, Wellington, and buried him here. You hoodwinked us all," Pappy yelled from the top of the basement stairs before running toward Damon. "When Bob called me on the mainland and told me to meet him at the lighthouse, and I called you, you told me it was too dangerous to come out here by myself. You said that they were all waiting for me because Bob knew I'd disguised myself to leave the island on the ferry for the day and thought I was up to something. You told me that since you were on the mainland yourself, you'd come with me to protect me. But that's not true. You came here to stop them from finding Dr. Pearson's body."

A tremor crashed through me, and I struggled to remain standing. Suddenly, everything became clear. They were all involved in what happened to Tyler.

"This isn't Gregory Wellington," I said, hearing my voice tremble. "This is Damon Devereaux. My husband."

"Your husband?" A chorus of voices responded.

"Yes. My husband, although hopefully not for much longer. I'm divorcing him as soon as possible."

"Not happening, Layla," Damon said, turning to me with a threatening look in his eyes.

I couldn't believe he was still so obstinate even in the precarious situation we were both now in.

"You're coming home with me," he continued.

"I'm not," I said, standing my ground and fighting through the fear I felt at doing so, especially in front of a group of probable criminals who could be on his side.

"Save it for another time," Pappy shouted. "We want justice."

"Yeah, justice. We want justice," the others shouted.

"You did it. You did it all," Pappy yelled, turning to Damon. "You were never going to give us the money from the sale of the gold. You were going to keep it all for yourself. After everything we did for you and everything you put us through. You killed Leif when he told you the sheriff said you double-crossed us, didn't you? The sheriff told us you arranged with a crooked gold dealer on the mainland to ship it off the island disguised as a container of copper from your mine on a freighter coming into port next week." Pappy's face turned purple as he spat out the words. "What do you say to that?"

Damon didn't answer.

I pressed my hand in a stop gesture toward Pappy and turned to Damon. I swallowed hard before speaking. I had to tell everyone what I knew, whether they believed me or not. I wasn't going to keep it in anymore and pretend I didn't know what my intuition told me was true.

"And you killed the coroner last summer because he knew that Pappy wasn't dead and pulled out of putting his career on the line to sign the death certificate. You'd convinced him to do that as part of the scam after he went on the dive with all of you and brought up the gold, didn't you?" I said. "Then you had the clerks in his office and the records office cover up the fact that he didn't sign, by telling them Dr. Pearson made a mistake on the date of death and needed to be protected by them from prosecution by the sheriff. And they believed you. That's why they were afraid of me and my questions and wouldn't tell anybody anything or produce the certificate. And the fact that it didn't exist at the time got lost in the confusion that there were two different dates of death listed on the computers, which you probably had something to do with, as well."

"What are you talking about?" Damon asked.

"Then you had everyone else set Tyler up to take the fall for Pappy's faked murder. You framed my brother, Damon. Why? He never did anything to you. Was it to get back at me? He didn't even know you were here."

"No, Layla," Colton said, moving toward me. "He did it because he found out from Pappy that Tyler knew about the gold being found. You told me Tyler had told Pappy that the gold belonged to the island and not to him because it was found within the boundary waters. Pappy told Damon that, and Damon knew that Tyler wouldn't go along with the scheme, so he framed him to get rid of him. And, as an added bonus for getting him sent away, he got Melanie for himself. Right, Damon?"

"Damon, how could you?" I yelled.

I threw myself toward him, but Colton caught me and held me back. I struggled in his arms to free myself and get to Damon, but he held me tight. I turned back toward Damon when I thought of something else.

"And when your private investigator told you I arrived on the island, you were afraid that Tyler had somehow figured out that you were involved with framing him and told me something that would ruin your cover-up. So you told Leif to run me off the road to scare me into leaving and keep me from finding anything out. But it didn't work, did it? I'm still here."

"Where do you get all this from?" Damon asked, smirking.

"Listen to her," Colton said, holding his hand up and addressing the group. "She knows what she's talking about."

I continued. "And, since you didn't know that Dr. Pearson had obviously stolen gold coins from the cabin and stashed them in his trunk, you parked his car in the ferry parking lot after you killed him and started a rumor that he had left the island. That way, no one could object to his murder, and you could continue with the scam," I said, clenching my jaw and feeling my face get hot.

"You crazy bitch," he said.

Colton released me and moved toward Damon, telling me to stay where I was. I grabbed his arm, but he pulled it from my grasp and kept walking until he stood in front of him.

"You're going to hear what she has to say," he said loudly, pointing at him. "Go on, Layla."

I continued. "Borrowing the huskies from everyone and keeping them at the cabin the week of the dogsled race last winter makes sense now, too," I said. "That gave you time to harness the dogs to the sled and take the coroner's body from the cabin over the ice road to the mainland. You'd hidden the body in the fish freezer after you killed him last summer and waited for the lake to freeze over. Then you brought it to the lighthouse because you knew it was abandoned after Leif transferred to the one on the island, and no one would ever look for it here. It effectively disappeared and exonerated you. No body, no murder. Then you ran the race like nothing ever happened."

"Shut up," Damon said. "You don't know what you're talking about."

"And you tried to do the same thing with Colton you did with Tyler," I said, walking up to stand next to Colton, gathering strength from his solid support and the deferential silence of the rest of the group.

"You tried to frame him for a murder, didn't you? It was you that we saw chasing Leif around the restaurant the night before he was killed. You found out from Leif that the sheriff's deputies were coming back out to talk to him about the gold we found in the coroner's trunk, and you thought he was going to turn you in for the scam or be found out himself. So you held him at gunpoint and made him call Colton the next day and ask him to meet him for some reason. That way, after you killed Leif, Colton would be discovered near the lighthouse by the deputies when they found Leif dead and think he had something to do with his murder. And it would throw them off the trail of the gold, too."

I glanced over at the quiet men who were watching Damon, seemingly waiting for his reaction.

"Who do you all think you are?" Damon yelled, moving away from Colton and me and looking around at everyone. "I'm the boss here. My organization owns the copper and the copper mine. It's a mainstay of the island's economy. Now you better listen to me unless you want things on the island to get real bad real fast."

There was a short pause before Pappy stepped forward.

"Forget it. It's over, Devereaux. We believe Layla and Colton, and the sheriff. You're done using people. We're cutting you out and keeping the gold," he yelled.

"Ain't happening, boys," Damon growled. "Leif got what he deserved. So did Pearson. Same as any of you will if you mess with me. I know what I'm doing, and you'll get your share of the money from the sale of the gold if you do as you're told. Got that? You work for me and my organization."

"Not anymore," Pappy shouted. "I've had it with you. You're a liar and a cheat, and a killer. I went along with the scam, but murder is where I draw the line."

"Me, too," Bob said, "even if Melanie doesn't. She hit Colton on the head with a rock on the dive. I saw it."

"We all did," Larry said. "We were too scared of Melanie and Leif, who was in charge at the time, to do anything about it. We thought he was the one that put her up to it, but now I think it was you, Wellington. And, I think everyone here draws the line at murder."

"Yeah," Stan agreed.

"We're keeping the gold and giving it back to the island," Pappy said. "You're not getting any of it. We're digging it up from the grounds of the prison where we buried it and where you all know I've been looking after it. And we're taking you in, Devereaux, or whatever your name is." He reached into his jacket and pulled out a gun.

"No one crosses me," Damon yelled, yanking a gun out of his pocket.

"Drop it," someone shouted.

I turned and screamed when I heard a shot. The last thing I remember before darkness overtook me was seeing Damon fall to the floor.

CHAPTER 20

When I awoke in a sheriff's cruiser later, the deputies told me that I had fainted and had been carried out to the car. The shock of seeing Damon killed by a deputy in front of me had obviously been too great. They said the sheriff on the island had called the sheriff on the mainland after finding out from the ferryman that Colton had taken the ferry and asked for directions to the lighthouse. The sheriff on the mainland and his deputies had shown up just in time to hear everything.

The seat was cold and hard, and the night was dark. My head pounded, and I rubbed it as I leaned against the car door, but the aching only got worse. How could this have happened? How could any of this have happened? It was so surreal and unbelievable. But it did happen. This was reality, and all the times that Damon had told me my feelings were wrong, they had been right. I had seen who he really was and what he was capable of with my own eyes. And I had seen him die for it. I swallowed hard to try to control my emotions, whatever they were. I was too upset to know. Colton stepped out of the lighthouse and walked to the car. The sheriff's deputy opened it from the outside, and Colton leaned in to talk to me.

"Are you okay?" he asked.

"I've been better," I said. "But yes, I'll be okay. Give me a little while," I said, taking a deep breath.

"Sure," he said, leaning back. "I only came out to tell you that Pappy admitted to being the night stalker, and they took him into custody."

"Thank goodness for that," I said, pressing my hand to my forehead. "The inn and the island will finally be safe from him now."

Colton nodded.

"He also said to tell you he's sorry that he tried to scare you away on the first night you came to the island and stayed at the inn. He said he was threatening you outside the door to your room, and he wouldn't have done that if he'd known what you were like."

"Was that him? I'm glad you told me. At least I know now that it wasn't a ghost. I'm still upset that he did that, though. He had no right to terrorize the island and the inn in that way."

"Of course. I understand. It's unforgivable what he did to you and my mother and so many others, it appears, in his fearsome run as the night stalker. I'm sure he'll be held accountable," Colton said.

I nodded and sat for a moment, trying to gather some strength. "I think I'm feeling better," I said as I gingerly stepped out of the car and struggled to stand next to Colton.

The brisk night air revived me, and I eventually stood, talking to him as we watched people go in and out of the lighthouse. Waves lapped to shore in the distance, and a few boat horns sounded. The night seemed so ordinary, and yet it wasn't. It was far from that. It was the kind of night that would change our lives forever. We made plans to stay overnight at a motel on the mainland after the sheriff finished sorting things out and to take the ferry back to the island in the morning. It didn't look like any of the others were coming out to join us, and I wondered what happened to them. It seemed probable that they were in trouble with the sheriff after revealing everything that had been going on. Maybe they had been arrested.

When they rolled Damon's body away on a stretcher, I stared at the black vehicle they loaded it into and squeezed my eyes shut. I couldn't believe he was really gone after all this time. He had been my husband but my tormentor, as well, and I wasn't sure whether I felt relief or sadness or some combination of both. I had loved him once, and the memories of that love flooded back in a torrent of grief over its loss. But the death of our love had happened a long time ago, and I was just now coming to terms with it. Colton held me close as I sobbed.

Colton told the sheriff he wasn't going to press charges against Melanie for hitting him on the head underwater with a rock, but the sheriff said she would be required to leave the island anyway, with her children. I hoped that Susie and Bobby would be okay and that Melanie would find employment elsewhere. They were good kids, and Susie was smart. I could see her being an excellent detective someday and writing amazing detective stories. She had been right about the way the story ended. The murderer was one of the mother's boyfriends, but only she, and others who weren't involved with him were able to deduce that. Sometimes, people who are too close to other people can't see their faults and can't imagine their capabilities. I knew that for a fact about me in regards to Damon, and I imagined it was true of Melanie with Damon, as well. Susie was smarter than both of us, and she had written it down to prove it. But she was smart enough not to show anyone her stories and risk being criticized for being wrong. She, and she alone, knew that she was right. And she had kept it that way.

After the sheriff made notes and walked away, Colton stood staring at the ground.

"Are you all right?" I asked.

"Yeah. It's just that it's hard to accept that Melanie did that to me, hit me on the head, I mean," he said.

"I know you cared for her," I said, pausing and trying to think of something more to say. "If it's any consolation, I think Damon put her up to it. I'm not excusing her behavior, but sometimes people who get caught up and trapped in dangerous circumstances do dangerous things."

Colton nodded. "I'll try to think of that," he said. "And I'm sorry you had to see Damon shot in front of you. I'm sure that's very traumatic."

"Yes, it is. Thanks for being here for me," I said.

"No problem. Thanks for being here for me, too," he said.

"Sure," I said.

Two of the deputies stepped out of the lighthouse and walked over to the car. When I asked where the other men were, they shook their heads and declined to answer. The sheriff came back over and told Colton he was free to go and that he was no longer a suspect in Leif's murder because Damon had confessed to being the killer of Leif and the coroner before he was shot. He told me that Tyler was being released from prison since Pappy was still alive and there was never a murder in the first place, and that he would have a bus ticket home within a few days. I couldn't remember the last time I'd felt so happy.

After the sheriff walked away, we got in Colton's truck and headed for the motel he knew about. The night was dark, and the road was desolate. I shivered at the isolation, realizing we were only two people, all alone on a dark road in the middle of the night. It reminded me of my first night on the island and how frightened I'd been, although I'd really been alone then, dealing with imminent danger. At least, this time, I had Colton to share things with and to keep me safe. I shook my head to clear it.

We found the motel on the outskirts of town, nestled in a woods near the road. To my relief, the yellow neon sign blinked 'vacancy,' and Colton pulled up next to what looked like the office and went in after telling me to wait in the truck. He came back shortly with a key, and we drove to a green door at the far end of the single-story, whitewashed motel and went in.

"What a relief," I said, plopping down on one of the duvet-covered double beds in the sparsely decorated room. "It looks like this is finally over, and we can get our lives back."

"I hope so," Colton replied. "I'll feel better when we're back on the island, and I can reopen the inn and get things moving at the Chamber of Commerce again. Now that this is over, we have a lot to do to boost tourism and get the island's economy moving again. It may take a while for people to recover from everything that's happened, but I'm confident that now that the law is on our side, things will turn around."

"I hope so," I said.

"And a lot of that was due to you," he said. "If you hadn't come to the island and discovered what was going on, we'd still be in a never-ending cycle of crime. Now that the sheriff knows what's going on, if any more people from the crime ring or Damon's organization show up, they'll have him to deal with, and he'll kick them off the island. So now that the crime ring has been stopped, we can all get back to normal, and the islanders can live in peace."

"Except for the Ghostslayer," I said.

"That's true. But if the people in the crime ring from years ago that he was after are gone, and the evil ghosts that remained on the island have left, he probably won't come around much anymore. The islanders can live and thrive with the good ghosts that the tourists come to see."

"I hadn't thought of that. You're probably right," I said. "I hope all the evil ghosts are gone."

"I hope so, too," Colton said. "We'd better get some sleep."

"Okay. I'll talk to you in the morning," I said, climbing under the covers with my clothes still on. I was too exhausted and overcome with the events of the evening to get ready for bed.

Colton climbed into the bed next to me and turned off the light.

"Sleep well, Layla," he said. "You've done a wonderful thing solving the mystery and getting your brother out of prison. You're an extraordinary person."

"Thank you," I said, yawning and giving in to the waves of exhaustion that washed over me. I closed my eyes and sighed. Nobody but Colton had ever said anything like that to me. "See you in the morning."

"You, too. Good night," he said.

We stayed overnight and headed back to the island on the ferry in the morning after eating granola bars for breakfast that we procured from a vending machine at the motel. I stood on deck, lost in my own thoughts, as I watched the mainland recede from view. So much had happened, and so much had changed in one night. We sailed to the island in silence. When we got back to the inn, we talked as we walked through the parking lot and decided to stay overnight at the inn before heading to the house in town the next morning.

Colton said the sheriff had called him after I went to sleep last night and told him that Pappy admitted he tried to scare Martha and the others on the island into leaving so that the crime ring could have the gold all to themselves. He had been placed under strict observation by the sheriff and would have to wear an ankle bracelet that relayed his whereabouts to the office when he was released from jail. But he would still probably face charges of some sort in the future.

"Finally," Colton said. "The sheriff believes us, and we got rid of the night stalker. He's going to apologize to Martha for not believing her and blaming her for calling him all the time."

"Well, that's good. It's about time," I said, walking up the stairs to the door.

"I agree. I'm going to call her and tell her the inn is safe now, and we can come back. I'm sure she'll be thrilled. I'm going to wait to tell her Pappy was the night stalker, though, because when she finds out it was him and that he's still alive, she'll probably want to go after him with the broom again, or worse. I noticed he has quite a lump on his head that was probably due to that. This has all been very hard on her," Colton said.

"Yes. It's been awful. I'm glad it's finally resolved," I said. "Maybe she should go after the sheriff with a broom for not believing her."

"I don't think she'll do that," Colton said, grinning, "but regardless, I think she's going to start feeling a lot better."

"I hope so. She put up with a lot for a long time," I said. "And that's too bad. It took someone from off the island to finally determine the true scope of what was going on. The sheriff on the mainland saw the big picture that the sheriff on the island was apparently unable or unwilling to see."

"I know what that's like," Colton said. "When you're on the inside of a group, like on an island, it's hard to see what someone from the outside can see."

"I think that's true," I said. "And, he might not have suspected Damon of being involved in a crime ring if he knew him as Gregory Wellington and thought he was the owner of the copper mine. That would have given him credibility as an upstanding citizen of the community."

"You're right," Colton said. "That could be why he didn't look into the suspicious things Damon was involved with sooner."

I nodded.

"But I think the main reason he took another look at what was going on was because he met you when you picked me up at his office and saw how determined you were to free your brother from prison. You came all the way to the island to find out what was happening, and I think that held some sway with him. I think that made him rethink how he was handling things around here. I told you that if you believed in yourself, other people would too, and I was right."

"Do you really think that? I'm so glad. But it doesn't matter why he changed his attitude. It only matters that he did," I said.

"I thought you'd feel that way," he said. "You're very humble about the things you do. There are a few more things I think you should know. The sheriff on the island recovered the gold last night after Pappy told the sheriff on the mainland where it was buried on the prison grounds. It's evidently quite a stash. And it legally belongs to the island because it was found within its boundary waters, as you know. The money brought in from its sale could help restore the island's economy and get tourism up and running again. I'm hoping for that. There may even be enough to contribute to the bird sanctuary fund and the bird observatory at the school."

"That's wonderful," I said.

"Yes, but there's something else that's not so wonderful," Colton said, looking down. When he looked back up, his eyes were glistening.

"Stan, Larry, and Bob were all arrested for stealing the gold and placed on probation. They'll still be working on the island, but not as my friends anymore. I consider them distant business associates now."

"Oh, I feel so bad for you, but I think that's wise," I said softly. "It's sad it came to this, but they can't be trusted."

"I know," Colton said. "I finally realized that. It's going to take some getting used to, but I will."

"Give yourself time to adjust," I said, touching his arm. "Finding out your friends aren't your friends isn't something you get over quickly."

"Yeah," he said.

We walked in silence up the ramp to the inn. Just as I

opened the door, my phone rang, and I answered it as I stepped into the reception area."

"Layla?" I heard a thin voice say on the other end.

"Tyler?" I asked, feeling suddenly shaky.

"Yes. It's me. They let me make a phone call before they start to process me out of here. I'm coming home, Layla. They're releasing me."

"Tyler, is it really you?" I dropped into the chair behind the desk and leaned my forehead on my hand. "Are you really coming home?"

"As soon as I can. They told me Pappy was still alive, and I'm free to go. You did it. It was you, wasn't it? You found out he wasn't dead?"

"Yes," I said. "I found out a lot of things with my friend, Colton's help, and I'm glad it got you out."

"Colton Harding? Martha's son?"

"Yes. Just a second." I put my hand over my phone and turned to talk to Colton. "It's Tyler. They let him out. Can he come back to the island and work at the inn?" I asked.

Colton nodded. "If he still wants to," he said. "He can have his old room back."

My cheeks felt wet, and I removed my hand from the phone and brushed my fingers under my eyes. The phone blurred in front of me. "Colton says you can have your job back at the inn if you want," I said, swallowing hard. I couldn't believe this was really happening after all this time. Tyler was coming back to me.

"I do," he said. "I'll take the bus and the ferry and be there in a few days."

"I'm so glad," I said.

"Love you, sis. I better go. I can't wait to get out of here."

"I love you, too, Tyler. See you soon," I said.

When the phone went silent, I sat for a moment, wishing Tyler was still on the other end but relieved that I would see him soon.

"My brother's coming home," I said to Colton. "He'll be here in a few days."

"That's wonderful, Layla. I know how much this means to you. You really did it. You got him out."

"We got him out," I said. "I couldn't have done it without you. I'll always be grateful for your help and support and for your belief in me."

"I do believe in you, and you'll always have my support," he said. "I hope you'll still stay in the room at the house that you picked out. I don't want you to move back to the inn. Would you like to do that?"

I nodded. "If you want me to. I'd love to stay there. I don't want my own house on the mainland anymore, and I plan to sell it. I want to start a new life on the island."

"With me?" Colton asked.

"If you want me to," I said.

He smiled and nodded.

"I do," he said.

I was glad to see him looking so confident and self-assured. He seemed to finally trust me enough not to hurt him like Melanie had and to want to move forward with our relationship.

"Here. I want to show you something before we go back to our rooms," I said, pulling some papers out of my purse.

"What's this?" he asked when I placed the papers and a photo in front of him.

"It's a Harding Copperwing," I said. "Soon to be duly registered and named and published in a scientific journal. It's the first of its kind to be banded on the island."

"They named a bird after me?" Colton asked.

"Yes," I said, smiling. "They did. They appreciate the generous donations from the Chamber of Commerce, and I helped come up with the idea. We identified a new species at the bird observatory, and this will be its common name. You're going to be immortal now."

"Wow," Colton said. "I don't know what to say."

"You don't have to say anything," I said.

"That's amazing," he said, smiling.

He walked me to my room, and we continued our conversation while I unlocked the door. I looked up at him, feeling a deep connection to him after all that we had been through and all that we had shared. He was the first person who had ever seen me for who I really was and accepted me, and I would always be grateful for that. But there was more to it than that. He touched my soul with his humble ways and quiet fortitude. And I admired the fact that his intrinsic intelligence and dogged determination to do what was right had saved his mother from harm and the island from financial ruin. But most of all, I wanted to be with him because he had helped me solve the mystery and free Tyler from prison.

"So, do you think it's possible for someone who doesn't see ghosts to love someone who does?" I asked, pulling the scarf out of my ponytail and combing my fingers through my loosened hair.

Colton paused for a moment before gently pulling me to him. "Oh yeah," he said, gazing deep into my eyes. "More than possible. Let me show you."

He leaned over and kissed me, and the ordinary world changed forever for me in an instant. I trembled, but in a good way, because it wasn't because of a ghost this time. It was because of a real person.

CHAPTER 21

The banging that night at the inn scared me even worse than it had before when I'd first come to the island. I sat straight up in bed and tried to get my bearings as I peered through the inky blackness of the room. The banging crescendoed, incessant and desperate.

"Who is it?" I yelled, scooting my feet out from under the crumpled sheets and struggling to stand on my shaky legs. "What do you want?"

No answer. The pounding continued. It sounded like it was outside this time and not at the window. I stepped into the hallway and wondered where Colton was as I padded through the darkness to the bottom of the staircase. Was I the only one that heard this? I tiptoed halfway down the hall and peeked into the reception area. Lightning flashed suddenly, and a shadow hung outlined in the curtained pane of the door window. It looked like a person. What else could it be?

The racket stopped, and I stood, stunned, in the sudden silence, which was broken only by the light patter of rain.

"Colton?" I asked, softly.

"Let me in. He's after me," a strangled voice rasped through the door.

It didn't sound like Colton. It sounded like somebody else.

"Who are you? Who's after you? I called, shivering, as I inched closer. It was his voice. But it couldn't be. I had watched him die.

"You know who I am. You put me here with the dead. I'm a ghost now. The Ghostslayer is after me. He's real. He's evil. Let me in."

A cold rivulet of sweat ran down my back as I realized who he was or who he had been. "Damon, go away," I screamed.

"No. He's here. Open the door. Now."

And then the moaning started, as though from a distance, and the howling soon after that.

"Go away," I screamed again.

A red glow lit the window behind the curtain.

"Help me!" the shadow shrieked.

Lightning split through the thick darkness of the ghoulish night amidst a deafening crack of thunder, and the shadow disappeared.

Terri Greening is a creative writer in the Great Lakes region. She enjoys yoga, gardening, nature parks, walking, and biking. She has a B.A. in journalism from Central Michigan University and an M.B.A. from Grand Valley State University.